SPORT...

I made her stand there while I caressed her hips and buttocks through the fine gauze of her harem pants. I stroked the insides of her thighs through the gap those pants so obligingly offered. Gently I pulled her an inch or so toward me, slipping my knees between hers while I continued to fondle and stroke her hips and bottom. She caught on quickly and continued to inch her way toward me while I went on enjoying those oh-so-feminine curves and the promises they offered.

Sporting Girls

Faye Rossignol

HEADLINE
DELTA

First published in 1997
by HEADLINE BOOK PUBLISHING

A HEADLINE DELTA paperback

10 9 8 7 6 5 4 3 2 1

ISBN 0 7472 5430 3

Printed and bound in Great Britain by
Cox & Wyman Ltd, Reading, Berkshire

HEADLINE BOOK PUBLISHING
A division of Hodder Headline PLC
338 Euston Road
London NW1 3BH

Sporting Girls

The girls of the Mustang, Nevada

I adore American hookers. If I had to pick my own six houris to spend eternity with me in paradise, they'd all be American hookers. They are lively, frank, open, unabashed, healthy, corn-fed, luscious, and quite unashamed in parading themselves, their charms, and their skills for a man. They've got this little sign that lights up behind their eyes: SHOW HIM I'M THE BEST!

Actually, that sign is behind their left eye; behind the right eye there's another that says: TAKE HIM FOR ALL HE'S GOT! But then, it's a fair trade when they're giving you all *they've* got.

Before I get to the episode with Estelle, I'll give you an example of what I mean.

I was driving up from Sacramento, California, one night, making for Reno, Nevada, where I'd been asked to advise on a big humidifier and air-conditioner plant for a ninety-checkout store. As the whole world must surely know, Nevada is the one state in America where the noblest profession is both legal and open. I'd read every article and book about it that came my way, and I decided that what I really wanted to do first was visit the Mustang Ranch near Reno and take the four-hundred-dollar special (which nowadays costs over a thousand, of course).

Somehow, around Truckee, I took a wrong turn and then got hopelessly lost among mountain lakes, small towns, and state highways whose numbers seemed to change every time I looked at them. Also, every sign saying Reno took me ever closer to Carson City. I ended up heading for Reno as if I were coming from upstate, which is how I accidentally came across the Mustang even before I hit the city. It was close on three in the morning by then and the building looked dark and deserted. But the Mustang neon and the glittering-girl cutouts were still lighted — as was the sign that said OPEN. So I thought, *Why not?*

"Yeah?" asked a sleepy voice on the gate intercom.

"The sign says you're open," I said. "So I just wondered ..."

A light went on and, no doubt, the madam scanned me through the CCTV.

"Only two girls at this hour, honey," she warned me.

"Okay, but don't wake them yet. I'll choose them from pictures. You got pictures of them or something?"

"Sure." She yawned again and the electric lock sprang open with a buzz. I walked up the path to the house itself, where lights were already going on.

You enter the meat market straight away — when it's all in full swing, I mean. There's a bar over to the right and a salon to the left. It's lined with pictures of naked dream girls with big breasts, bright smiles, wet lips, and pubic hair like cat's fur. Beneath their frames are red plush couches, normally filled with up to twenty girls, depending on how busy the place is. On that night, none, of course — just a tired Madame Cora waiting for me with a glassy smile. "English, huh?" she asked.

"Yes sirreee, ma'am, doggone it!"

She laughed as she led me to her office, which was right behind the salon. "There's a choice of Fern, a peachy blonde, and Ebony, who's ... well, guess!"

Fern was a very peachy blonde, with large, soft breasts, a trim waist, and long American legs; her lustrous, wavy hair reached down to the small of her back. Ebony was a black gamine with afro hair, an athletic body, a big, curvaceous bottom, and high, firm breasts with chocolate-button nipples. I hesitated so long that Cora prompted me with a suppressed yawn.

"Fern," I said.

What tipped the balance was an idea that had flitted across my mind as I walked up the path outside. "Would she be willing to act out a little fantasy with me?" I asked.

"At this time of night?" Cora replied.

"It's a perfect fantasy for this time of night," I said. "I'd like her to pretend to be asleep! Or ninety percent asleep, say. Pretend we went to bed together about ten last night and we've been sleeping together all this time and I've just woken feeling ready for a bit more." I had a rock-hard erection already at the thought of it. "Could she do that?" I concluded.

"Could she ever! Let's get this straight. You don't want to wake her up, talk to her, discuss your needs, *then* begin the fantasy — right? You want me to tell her, instead."

"Right."

"And you don't want her to wake up when you get into bed?"

"Just stir a little, maybe — yawn — open up enough to let me inside her — and then go back to sleep if she wants."

"She could go back to sleep for real!"

"I don't mind that. I presume I can pay you instead of her?"

"How long d'you need — an hour would be a hundred dollars."

"Forty minutes would do."

"Seventy-five, then."

I paid her, making sure she could see I was good for a lot more — just in case the fantasy took a different turn and I stayed longer.

"And I gotta string you," she added.

This kind of inspection was new to me. What they do is grip the base of your prick and pull toward the tip. This should yield a little blob of pale, straw-coloured fluid — the sign of an undiseased organ. Condoms were actually forbidden by law in Nevada whorehouses in those days!

"My!" she exclaimed admiringly when I took out my tackle. "She should give it you for free!" Now that I *had* heard before. She grabbed it and went through this stringing ritual. It yielded no straw-coloured harvest.

"You been drivin' a long time?" she asked.

"Most of the day," I admitted.

"That could explain it. You need to urinate?"

"No, I went about ten minutes ago, back in the desert. Why?"

She took out a little tube of something, pushed its nozzle gently into the end of my prick, and squeezed some of its contents out — enough for its coolness to tickle. Then she pulled what the doctor had left of my foreskin up and massaged the cream all the way down inside my sperm tube. "That'll take care of any doubts," she said. "Tincture of methiolate. It don't hurt none. Now you gotta wait five minutes. Don't you go off the boil, y'heah!"

"Come to think of it, I could do with a shower," I said as I tucked everything away again.

"There's one in Fern's bedroom, but I guess that would spoil the fantasy. You can use the one at the end of the corridor."

She gave me a towel and led me back to the salon, from which five passages led off into the five wings that contained the girls' bedrooms; she picked the third. "That's Fern's room," she said as we passed — just in case I couldn't read the name on the door. "One thing's not going to please her," she added. "Having to stay quiet and pretend to sleep while partying with an Englishman."

"Why? Are we such wonderful lovers?" I asked naively.

"No! It's the *accent* she adores." Her tone suggested that the idea of a 'wonderful lover' was the last thing that would occur to any of her girls.

While I was having my shower a girl came and used the lavatory next door. I knew it was a girl because she was *singing* — at that hour of the morning and after a hard day's grind, too! *It can't be Fern,* I thought.

My tool, which had fallen back to half stiff, began hardening again at the thought — and at the sound of a vigorous stream of urine hosing deep into the water. It's funny, I've never had the remotest desire for a woman to urinate on me — the famous 'golden shower' — but the sight of a woman urinating, or the picture conjured in my mind's eye by the sound of it, has always been profoundly erotic to me. I think I can trace it back to when I was about four and used to walk across the fields to and from school, sharing part of the journey with a girl of my own age. She would often squat down for a piss and I would squat down, too, and peep underneath her, fascinated to see she had nothing but a cut down there — pale and hairless at that age, of course — and that the piss came out of it in the wrong direction.

Anyway, if it was Fern pissing so mightily next door, I knew from her photograph what she must look like, sitting in there. And my fertile mind's eye could place itself inside the bowl and imagine what a splendid picture it made. I finished showering and started to dry myself. The girl stayed on next door, still humming prettily, occasionally running some water, and putting something hard down on glass shelves — by the sound of it. Jars of cream? Albolene to lubricate her pussy? The full wonder of our situation struck me just then.

There was I in one small cubicle, having driven several hundred miles to get here; and there, in the cubicle next door, just inches away perhaps, was a beautiful blonde whom I'd never even seen, preparing her pussy for my pleasure, and singing a happy little song while she was about it. In a few moments I'd slip into her bed and she'd open up and let me in, and let me take my pleasure, all without a word spoken. This was surely the best of all possible worlds!

I heard her leave. I waited until she must be almost back at her door — if, indeed, it was Fern — and then peeped out.

She knew I was going to do that. She was only halfway there, stark naked and walking with a sexy roll that almost had me coming just to watch it. I could hardly believe I would, within a couple of minutes, be privileged to enjoy that provocative and alluring body. I closed the door before she reached hers, in case she glanced back. Eye contact now would mar the fantasy. My hands were shaking and I was sweating almost enough to need a second shower. Not that I took it. I gathered up my clothes and rolled them loosely in my damp towel. By then, I reckoned, Fern would be back in bed, pretending to sleep. I trotted up the corridor, almost overbalanced by my erection, which lolloped around to a rhythm of its own, and I paused outside her door in a futile effort to catch my breath and calm my excited pulse. Talking of pulse — a doctor wouldn't have needed to hold my wrist to take mine, just one look at my tool, whanging the air in time with it, would tell him all he needed to know and more.

My heart was hammering in my throat as I opened her door and let myself in. A couple of those fake-flame neon 'candles' were flickering away on her dressing table, casting enough light for me to spread the towel and arrange my clothes. As I approached the bed I saw she had laid a pot of Albolene on the sheet on 'my' side of the bed. I took the hint and spread a fingerful over my knob before lifting the sheet and climbing in.

I can still feel the warmth of her, and the female smell of her body, despite the overlaying of factory perfumes. Still feel it, did I say? Hell, I still get erections just thinking about it! I certainly had the mother and father of all erections then; I was amazed it hadn't gone *s-s-s!* — like water on a red-hot iron bar — when I touched the Albolene to its tip.

I put a hand to her waist. She shivered and stirred, as if in sleep. But she'd obviously decided to play her own slight variant of my fantasy. "Darling?" she murmured.

There's something about the way American girls say that word which makes me tingle all over.

"Only me," I replied.

"You want some more pussy?" Her voice was salty and rough, as if she had only just awakened.

"D'you mind? I can't get enough of you."

"D'you mind if I go back to sleep while you carry right on? You took so much out of me before. I never knew I had that many orgasms in me!"

I kissed her neck tenderly. "You go right back to sleep," I said. "I'll be as soft and gentle as I can."

"Talk to me," she said. "That'll help me sleep. Talk about anything. Your voice is so soothing."

So that was it! I hadn't, of course, believed much that Cora had said — certainly not about my erection being so exciting that Fern should give it me for free. Nor about her just loving the English accent. But maybe that bit *was* true! Or it was one hell of a conspiracy they ran here at the Mustang. Tell all foreigners you love their accent and all Americans that you're tired of tourists — and all men that they should be getting it for nothing with a cock like that!

I kissed her on the neck again and, in doing so, brought my knob to the very gates of paradise down there in her cleft. She arched her tail toward me and in I slipped.

Every time is like the first time; that's the real bewitchment of sex. I've lost count of the number of vaginas I've entered like that. It must be many hundreds — getting on for a thousand, maybe. Yet all, without exception, have been magical. And I spend so much time thinking about it in between — so many happy hours remembering the last one or looking forward to the next — that you'd think I'd be conscious of its precise quality by now. But no! As the warmth of a new vagina opens around and yet clings tightly to my knob, as her juicy-smooth skin massages mine, the astonishment, the wonder, the marvel renews itself and I realize that, for all my obsession with it, I had forgotten all the most important things about it. Then I come alive again, remembering that *this* is what it's all about — and this is *all.*

Her breath shivered as I pushed in all the way, rammed to the very hilt of me, and relished the tight, succulent heat of her clench. And that was really all I did for the next half hour or so — just lay behind her, holding her round the waist and pushing myself gently, slowly, in and out of her. To start with I kept up an almost unbroken stream of endearments, telling her how superb she was and what an unbelievable privilege it was for me to be partying with her — all in a veddy veddy English accent. Then, as I ran out of simple, obvious things to say, I began a little embroidery — telling her of some of the girls I'd enjoyed in the past, even though not one of them had quite come up to her standard. She didn't respond but I knew she wasn't asleep.

Toward the end, invention and memory alike ran out, but by then I was having difficulty breathing and keeping my voice even. It was shaking all over the place. I was on that unstoppable roller-coaster ride to orgasm, which, by careful pacing, I managed to stretch to a glorious five minutes — not the orgasm but the long ride into it. It's the nearest a man can get to the multiple orgasm of the female — that long, luscious glide into the frenzy of detumescence — and I think I made more of it that night than I'd ever done before. It resulted in an unusual sort of orgasm, too. There was little of the usual rampage about it — the express-train rodding, the deep pelvic thrusts, the ecstatic shouts. Instead, as the first great gout of semen ignited and launched, I pulled her bottom tightly to me, stretched myself rigid from toe to scalp, and let out one long sigh of satisfaction.

The last faint twinge of pleasure came almost two minutes after the first mighty rush. She let me stay in her all that time — which is rare, even among American hookers, generally the most considerate of all the girls who, regardless of race, share a culture that is western. But when I withdrew at last and made to get up, she reached behind her, grabbed my wrist, and said, "Stay?"

"Eh?" I responded.

"Don't go just yet." She sat up and stuffed several Kleenex into her crotch. "You in a hurry to go on someplace?"

"Un-unh."

"Sleep out the night with me and we'll have another party in the morning. Wouldn't you like that? I would."

"For how much more?"

She pushed me flat on my back and half lay on top of me, pressing one of her gorgeous breasts to my chest and resting a long, slender thigh over where an erection would lift it if I were still capable of such a thing. She kissed me full on the lips, which is something you don't expect of a pro. "I really *would* like it — if you know what I mean," she said.

"How much?" I repeated faintly and in a tone that said if she kissed me again, I'd stop asking entirely.

She kissed me again. Then she picked up the house phone and told Cora I was staying on till morning.

We woke up around nine-thirty. I was piss-proud and she must have known it, but she pretended to think it was *all* on account of her. She wet a paper towel and gave my fellow a good wipe before she settled between my thighs and treated him to some of the most delicious frenching ever. It should be called 'americaning' because those girls over there are the best in the world at it. She only gave me a couple of minutes but I lay in paradise for every second of them. Then — all innocence — she smiled at me and said, "Is that true — no matter how hard you want to piss, you just can't while you've got an erection?"

"Well, now you mention it ..." I said.

When I returned from the lavatory I found her half dressed. "I have a better idea," she said. "Let's have breakfast, go out for a little stroll in the desert — let some air into this place — then come back all nice and refreshed and you can give me the best hour's sex I've had in a long time. Howsabout that?"

When I drew breath to ask the obvious question she said, "A hundred dollars. You'll have some pretty good sex, too — now that I think of it. Just thought you might like to know."

We ate alone because the other girls were all dragging themselves wearily out to compulsory gymnastics on the whorehouse's landing strip. Breakfast was pretty lavish — two eggs easy-over, french fries, and that curious American bacon which is more saltpetre than meat and which shatters at a touch. And a four-stack of waffles and maple syrup, plus, of course, cereal and fruit juices till it poured out of one's ears.

The aerobics were in full swing as we strolled past the end of the strip. The sight of twenty gorgeous young women touching their toes, bouncing their breasts (or, to be more accurate, doing various things that caused their adorable breasts to bounce in the most breath-stopping manner), swaying from side to side ... and all in the skimpiest costumes, designed for cooling off rather than covering up ... was stimulating beyond words. Certainly I couldn't find the words when Fern said to me, "What does that do for you?" with a nod toward the pulchritude.

"Only a cardiologist could answer that," I assured her. "If you were walking past a building site on a hot day — I mean a construction site — and you saw a couple of dozen slim, fit, bronzed young men half naked, what would it do for you?"

She gave a sarcastic laugh. "I'd remember all the gorgeous young men who have fucked me so hard it hurt — and who wouldn't stop when I told them. And it's mostly the young ones, too."

"Yeah, but you're rather special. What d'you think a woman who didn't have your particular memories would feel?"

She shivered as if something especially nice had just happened to her. "I lo-ove your English courtesy," she said, quoting me: " 'A woman who didn't have my particular memories'! That is just so ... so *neat!* An American would just say 'a whore'!" She made it sound like the first syllable of 'hor-rible.' "I guess she'd feel kind of interested," she conceded.

I was still gazing at the calisthenic beauties. "It's something we can't really comprehend," I murmured.

"We?"

"We, your customers. Each individual one of us experiences one individual encounter with you, so we know something of what you do. But we can't imagine our magnificent event as just one small, insignificant part of your day. I mean, each of those girls is going to be fucked by at least half a dozen men today. You, too — right? Maybe a dozen."

She made noncommittal noises, not yet sure where this was leading.

"And tomorrow and tomorrow and tomorrow … But even if I take my perception of our encounter and multiply it half a dozen times, all I do is take half a dozen giant strides *away from* the truth as you see it. Our perceptions, yours and mine, hardly touch at any single point. Making love with you last night — and I refuse to call it fucking or partying — making love last night was the nearest thing I've ever experienced to making love with a girlfriend. But for you, I *know* it was no more than …"

She reached out and touched my arm, forcing me to look at her. "You don't know," she said simply. "Any more than you know why I asked you to stay." She was very intense suddenly.

I licked my lips. "Tell me, then," I asked.

"It's just the way I am," she said uncomfortably. "From noonday onward I could party for hours and not feel a thing — except maybe sore! You could line up Burt Reynolds, Steve McQueen, David Soul, Paul Newman, Jack Kennedy … you get the picture? You could line them up and it'd be like they were wagging their dicks around inside the Hollywood Bowl as far as I was concerned. But sometime around three or four in the morning there's a little time switch throws itself in here" — she tapped her forehead — "and I flip. 'Course, it still has to be a man in the movie-star class, but if he …"

"Which lets me out," I said.

"Don't you believe it, man. You're even higher. But listen — what I'm telling you is … d'you know the best time of all for me?"

I checked my watch. "Ten-twenty-three in the morning?" I guessed.

She grinned. "You're close. Shall we go back?"

"It sounds as if we'd better."

I didn't believe her, by the way — I hope that goes without saying. But then we don't believe the actress on the stage is really Ophelia, do we! She can still make us cry, even in the depths of our unbelief. The real question is: How well does she carry the deception off?

"I've still got to charge for it, though," she went on.

"House rules," I said.

"Not just that. If I partied with every man I wanted to, what would that make me? A tramp, that's what. When you pay me, you buy me a hundred dollars' worth of respectability."

"And do I *lose* a hundred dollars' worth of respectability at the same time?" I asked.

"Of course not. Believe me. I've thought this whole thing out. You gain an equal amount, too, because you're asserting your economic power — which is, like, your birthright in the capitalist system — plus you're not turning me into a tramp. So you keep your conscience clean."

"Then it should also work the other way," I pointed out. "If you expressed *your* economic power by paying me, you couldn't possibly be a tramp, because tramps have no economic power." I knew that by 'tramp' she meant 'slut,' whereas I meant what she would call a 'hobo' but it didn't change the joke.

She laughed. "You're cute, Limey, but it doesn't work like that — not here."

"Well, I didn't imagine it would," I admitted.

"Tell me about England," she said. "Are you married at all?"

"No."

"Do you have any sort of ties there, or are you as free there as you are here?"

"I'm free everywhere." I felt we were getting somewhere — close to the *real* point of all this charming fakery.

"D'you see a lot of … what was it — 'girls who have my sort of memories'?"

"A lot — but frankly, Fern, I've known very few as warm as you."

She took my arm. It was a sign of some genuineness in her that she hadn't done so from the beginning. "The thing is, you see … have you met many girls who travel a lot?"

"Not many, strangely enough. If I were a woman, I think I'd be a hooker — though I guess a lot of men would say the same. Unlimited sex, take it or leave it, whenever you wanted it — *and* get paid! Whew — every man's dream! But if I *were* a hooker, I'd travel with my assets. I'd aim to see the whole world by the time I was thirty. Last time I was in London I had a woman in Soho who told me she'd been 'on the game,' as they say, in that one street — Old Compton Street, it was — for *forty* years. Since just before the Second World War. She started when she was thirteen. She'd been seventeen years in this one room. Eight by eight by eight it measured. Can you imagine it — something like thirty thousand fucks in that same tiny cell!"

"Jesus!" She closed her eyes and shook her head. "And I'm fit to scream after eight months in this one bedroom here. And that's after only … let me see …

only nine hundred, sixty-two fucks — give or take the odd show of impotence."

"You count?"

"Boy do I count!"

I did a quick calculation. If she averaged a hundred a time — because some of the services went up to $500 — and split fifty-fifty with the house, that was close on $50,000. If her keep and other expenses came to, say, $300 a week, that'd be ten grand. So she'd still have forty grand in the bank. "Why don't you jack it in and travel?" I asked.

We were back at the Mustang by now. Cora was going round the empty salon feeling for lost coins and packets of white powder in the upholstery. She paused long enough to palm the five twenties I gave her. "Have fun, kids!" she said as we left her.

"Why don't you just light out into the great blue yonder?" I asked again as we went down the passage.

She laughed. "It would be pretty blue in my case, huh! Listen, it's too big a subject. Let's talk about it after. Right now I want to" — she paused and used my words — "make love. Can you *believe* that? A ten-times-a-day whore feeling horny? Git your pants off!"

She went into the usual raptures over the size and stiffness of my fellow and then said, "For this I gotta snort. You want some?" She popped the lid liner of her Albolene jar and four lines fell out. Why it's called the *liner,* maybe!

I declined the offer, explaining that a girl called Chantal had once made me snort coke, in Mexico City, and that it had given me a night-long erection but had deprived me of the ability to come. But she took my warning the other way round, said, "Goody goody!"

and laid out a line for me, too. So we both snorted. In the three seconds while she waited for her rush she peeled off her clothes. I was so horny by then that I was shivering uncontrollably. My jaw would hardly stay closed and my stomach was falling forever. I expected to see lightning flickering round my knob, the way it felt down there.

She flung herself at me, arms round my neck, legs round my hips, and bore me back on the bed. There was no finesse about it and no pause to lubricate herself. But her professional experience had already done plenty in that way and she slipped herself on me as slick as oil. When she felt me all the way home she let out the breath she'd been holding and stretched herself on me from head to toe, shivering all over, too. Then she gripped me tight and rolled over, bringing me on top of her. "Fill the hour, Limey," she said. "And fill me, too."

It was probably the coke speaking but the rapport between us was amazing. She seemed to know exactly what to do to increase my pleasure in each new situation — without brimming me over to a premature conclusion. The coke definitely helped there, though I'd taken less than half the amount Chantal had given me in Mexico City that time. And I was on Fern's wavelength, too; I seemed to know how to keep her rolling on from one orgasmic wave to the next.

After forty minutes she cried, "Enough!" But when I stopped she said, "No — go on!"

Five minutes later she said stop, again, and this time meant it. I was back on top of her by now — having been in every position in the book meanwhile — and just lay there, stiff as ever, panting hard from my exertions and thinking I might be able to come in another ten minutes — if she could take any more.

"I had a ring in my clit once," she said out of the blue. "In my nipples, too. And I had eight here." She showed me her right ear. "Can you see the scars?"

I couldn't. "How about down there?" I asked.

She giggled. "Okay — see for yourself." She humped me off her with a strong pelvic thrust and spread her thighs wide.

Funnily enough, in all that time I had not looked at her pussy. It was one of the neatest, trimmest I ever saw, with slim, sinuous outer labia and swollen, excited inner ones that went up like a gothic arch, which parted just before meeting in order to form a protective cowl round her clitoris. "It's the prettiest pussy I've seen in a long time," I told her.

"Any scars?"

"Nothing visible. Maybe I could feel them with my tongue." I flattened it over the whole of her clitoral area.

"Oh, don't!" she gasped. "Please don't!"

But her hands gripped me by the hair and held me tight against her. And so she twitched and writhed beneath me once again, this time with clitoral orgasms. Wouldn't it be fantastic if men could have two kinds of orgasm, too! So that when you'd finished shooting your load into a sporting girl, you'd go on for the really *big* one — a head-to-toe orgasm like women have. Oh, man!

Anyway, the greater intimacy between my head and her sex turned me on so much that I came almost at once, and quite violently. And, in the end, quite painfully, too, since I'd already shot a fair whack of sticky into her just seven hours — seven very happy hours — earlier.

"I had to take the ring out of my clit," she said when I showed signs of reviving. "I was getting orgasms just walking down the street. One Christmas, just sitting watching TV with my dad, I was getting one every ten seconds. You can't live like that."

"Well, *I* sure couldn't," I said feelingly.

"Oh, I envy men." She laughed. "One mighty thrill and it's all over and done with. They're free to go play pool, fish, read a book ... With me ... I mean, I'm the same with a box of chocolates: While there's one left, I just gotta eat it — know what I mean? Chocolates, orgasms — orgasms, chocolates. I've no self-control once I start."

I rolled over on my back and linked arms behind my head. The pain had dwindled to an almost pleasant ballsache by now. "You were going to tell me about travelling?" I reminded her.

"Oh yeah." She swallowed heavily, took a deep breath, and rose on one elbow, laying her nearer arm tenderly over me so that her breasts just happened to flatten themselves seductively upon my chest. "The thing is, if I came to London, and you're not married and you're free like you say, and, well, you knowing the local scene and all ..."

"Could I help, you mean? Of course."

"Just like that!" She kissed me warmly and lay down in the crook of my arm. "I'm on my own time now. Would you like another go?"

I snored. "In London," I said.

"That's a date. Are there any good whorehouses there?"

"Several. And in Edinburgh. And Dublin — you might as well combine it with some real tourism. But I think you'd do best in the escort business."

She pulled a face — which I felt more than saw. "Heavy meals and heavy conversation with heavy men — and a heavy time of it upstairs afterward! I'd prefer ten half-hour encounters in a good whorehouse."

"Montelimar, nougat, cherry cream, coffee delight ... cherry cream's best, eh?"

"You're right!" She laughed as if I'd told her something she'd never realized before.

I remembered it when we met in London about six weeks later, and I fixed her up in a massage parlour I often use. It may not have paid the best but she could make contacts and move on any time she liked; also she met real people there in as many varieties as she could wish for.

Anyway, that was Fern, who stands out in my mind whenever I want to explain why American hookers are the best. I didn't believe a word she said about adoring Englishmen in general (and if she did, her time in our massage parlours would surely put an end to such nonsense!), nor about turning on to me in particular, though maybe she did let herself go a bit that morning. Helped by the coke, of course. But, whatever the reason, she made me feel I was the only man in her life while we were together and she did it quite effortlessly. Dutch girls are pretty good at that, too, but Americans are the best.

Which brings me to Estelle.

I hadn't forgotten my determination to go back to the Mustang and see if I'd been wise to choose Fern ahead of Ebony. The chance came about a week later, on a Friday, as it happened. Fern hadn't left the house but it was her regular week off, so I knew I wouldn't even see her. In fact, as it turned out, I almost didn't see the Mustang, either.

Driving by day, on the correct road out of Reno this time, was an altogether different experience. It's a dry landscape. A little maize; shallow rivers, few of which run all the year; and dusty white hills dotted with creosote bush. I listened to the interminable hillbilly music that passes for a radio station thereabouts, tapped my fingers to its rhythm, and thought of the twenty-odd beauties I'd seen doing their morning workout on the airstrip the previous week.

"Hi, I'm Beth."

"I'm Dorothy."

"I'm Aimee, hallo."

"I'm Holly. How are you doing?"

... twenty times, and all of them really saying, 'I'll open my legs and let you inside me for X-amount of dollars.' No quibble, no fuss, no coyness, no will-she-won't-she? I was so lost in pleasant reverie I almost missed the hitchhiker.

She could have stood in that line-up, except she looked so pure and country. "Hi, I'm Estelle," she said. "Where are you headed, mister?"

I said, "Oh, about twenty miles."

She said that was fine — but only after she threw in her rucksack and hopped nimbly over the door. She had long, lustrous auburn hair straight out of a conditioner ad, luxuriant with highlights. She was slim-waisted but had wide hips, unless it was discreet padding. I hoped not. And her breasts were worth the dropped heartbeats they caused me — two good handfuls, well separated and with nipples like thimbles. She sat cross-legged on the front seat, flipped her gum out into the sagebrush, and smoothed her prim white skirt down over her legs. "Hokay," she sighed. "Let's go. You're English, huh?"

That took up the first few minutes. She'd been in England last summer. Loved it. Wouldn't mind going back.

I thought, *Getting girls over to England could become habit-forming.* But that didn't seem to be any argument against it.

What was I doing here?

Oh, just ... seeing the sights, you know.

Cheeky little grin. "Not many sights down *this* highway, young man. Unless, that is ...?"

My smile accepted the accusation — just as hers prepared me for what came next: "So — I'm going all the way with you, it seems."

"Well, I certainly hope so, Estelle. It's been on my mind from the moment I saw you. You work there?"

"I hope to."

"You mean you're just applying now?"

"That's about the size of it. Would it help if I told them I've brought my first customer with me, d'you think?"

"It might at that. Where did you work before?"

"Nowhere. Is that bad?"

"You mean literally nowhere? Not on the streets? Not in hotels? Not from a phone? You mean you *never* worked before?"

She bridled at the implication. "Well, I'm sure as hell no virgin, mister. Listen — I've been giving it away for years. So last month I thought, fuck this, if my pussy's made this generous way, she might as well earn our keep as keep me from earning. Honest" — she gave that infectious laugh again — "I lost more jobs sleeping around than I could tell you. Why do we call it 'sleeping around'? The only place I got to sleep was on my keyboard in the office. Anyway, now maybe I'll get to keep my job, for the same reason."

"You have a licence, I take it?"

There was a prickly silence. "I gotta get it licensed?" She lifted her skirt for a moment and said, "Are you hearing this? I gotta license you."

"That's the law in the State of Nevada. You can get a short-time one for about fifty dollars I think — maybe a hundred — but the Mustang won't look at that. To work there, or any of the major houses, you need the annual licence."

She swallowed heavily. "And how much …"

"A thousand."

"Shit!" She was glum for about half a minute. I turned a little idea over in my mind. Then she was bright again. I liked the way she always came bouncing back. "Maybe they'll grubstake me." The maybe was in the statement but not in her tone.

"I'm sure they will," I told her. "A beautiful young girl like you — you are over twenty?"

"Just."

"I mean twenty-one, sorry."

"Yeah — I'm just over that, too," she drawled.

"No licence under twenty-one. But they'll surely grubstake you — a girl like you, fresh as a peach and twice as pretty, doesn't come knocking at their door every week. I'll just bet you."

"Gee, are you sure?"

"I'll tell you how sure I feel. If they turn *you* down, *I* won't go in. How about that! I'm going there intending to take the five-hundred-dollar special. You know? Two girls, the Throne of Love, the jaccuzzi, and as many orgasms as you can manage. The works. So that's what they'll be losing if they turn you down."

"You've got five hundred bucks?" she asked, awe-struck. "And you'll spend it just on …" She swallowed again. "Show me."

It was loose in my pocket, held in a rubber band. I took it out and casually threw it — a tube of money — into that cream-white lap. It landed where she could not help but make the connection.

"Listen," she said. "If you can make that up to a thousand for me to get my pussy her licence, she just had a great idea about how to repay you!" She laughed. "And all legal, too!"

I was already making the U-turn. That was illegal.

It took her over an hour to get the licence. I went with her as far as the lobby. While I waited I brought myself bang up to date on the very latest bulletins from the US Fisheries and Wildlife Service. I could also have read, *The Brothels of Nevada — Etiquette for Customers,* but I'd done that yesterday, cover to cover. Three times.

It was lunchtime when she emerged. She fanned her face, meaning, "What an experience!" I took her to an expensive Japanese restaurant where we ate an exqui-site meal while I told her my plan. It was crazy, of course, but also kind of exciting — to me, naturally, but also, I hoped, to her.

"You say you slept around a lot," I began.

"I'm no slut," she protested.

"Okay. How many?"

"Jesus! How do I know? Forty? Fifty?"

"You could easily party with that many in your first week at the Mustang."

Her jaw dropped.

"You didn't know that?"

"I thought it'd be only three or four a day."

"That's still twenty-eight in a week. You'll be working three weeks on without a break, then one week off. You can probably work out which week that is."

"Whooo!" She was still dazed with numbers. "Forty or fifty a *week!*"

"Well, in a fast-sex joint like Cyd's — which is just round the corner from here, by the way, he's got *sixty* girls working, and they do two men an hour over a twelve-hour day — ten till midnight with two one-hour breaks. That's over a hundred and fifty a week."

She just closed her eyes and shook her head.

"So, anyway, what I was going to say was, you've made it with three or four dozen men so far, but because you chose them, they won't be anything like the range of men you'd meet in a week at the Mustang. Or even in a *day*. I, on the other hand, have enjoyed the professional services of several hundred girls by now. I've been in sporting houses where I could watch other men doing it. I've had many conversations with girls about us clients. In short, I think I know as much about the sort of men you'll meet as you'll need to know to start off with. So, what I'd suggest is that we go back to my hotel room now and I'll try, to the best of my ability, to give you the equivalent of a regular day's work."

She gawped. "You can come twelve times?"

"No, no. But simulated orgasms go with the territory."

"Ha — not just with hookers, either, let me tell you. Okay — that sounds marvellous."

"Have you any coke?"

She frowned. "I gotta snort, too?"

"No. I do. It would help."

She said she'd see what she could do; she knew at least one dealer in Reno.

"First we must get you some working clothes," I said as we left the restaurant.

I hadn't actually witnessed a Mustang line-up; I'd only seen the pictures and read the guidebook. At night they were in underclothes with a flimsy negligée over; by day they wore one-piece bathing costumes, polka-dotted or floral. We got both. We also got several brassieres; one left her nipples naked; one covered the sloping tops of her breasts but let her nipples and the rest nose out through a fringe of golden tassels; and one just ringed her breasts in black lace. We got a heap of old-fashioned silk stockings in red, cream, and pale blue with suspender belts to match. Garter belts, they call them. We got open-crotch panties; panties with detachable, heart-shaped gussets that covered her three vital holes; french knickers; silk cami-knickers; baby-doll nighties; and a lurex leotard with strategically opened seams. Much to her annoyance we didn't get any perfumes, but we did stop by a pharmacy for some electrode-terminal jelly; which, in those days, made the best vaginal and anal lubricant precisely because it is unscented. It was very like KY-Gel is now.

"You giving me a lie-detector test, too?" she asked when we left the place.

"Every minute we're together. And if I catch you telling the truth just once, you're off the show."

She found me some coke, which I snorted in the 'bathroom' of one of the dress shops.

A few minutes later, as we rode the elevator up to my room, she said, "Can I ask you one thing? You don't know me at all. We only met this morning. Okay, we had lunch together, but so what? The thing is, you don't really know me. And yet you're fixing to do just about the most intimate and private things with me that any man can do to a woman. Now how can you *do* that with someone you don't even know?"

No sporting girl had ever asked me such a question before — surprise, surprise! "The same applies to you," I pointed out.

"Yeah, but I'm doing it for money."

"That doesn't really alter the question — which is: How do you *feel?*"

My hands were full of parcels but she had one free, which she plunged into my trouser pocket; she grabbed my best friend and felt his fine, upstanding anatomy; then, laughing, she said, "About the same as you, I guess. Any law against it?"

She wanted us to shower together. She wanted to try on all her new finery. But I pointed to the time and told her she was in the line-up. "You take a step forward, smiling all the way, and you say, 'Hi, I'm Estelle.' And you step back again."

"Hi." She smirked. "I'm Estelle."

"Now do it properly."

"Hi, I'm Estelle."

"Do it properly."

"Hi, I'm Estelle."

"Properly."

On the fifth time she got it right. She also saw I meant it. We weren't playing charades here.

Maybe this all sounds stupid? I don't know. I remember an art lesson at school where the art master suddenly went berserk, shouting, "The wall's falling down!" And he flew across the room and leaned against the wall with his hands flat against it and his feet braced about a yard out from the skirting. Then, very quietly, he looked down at himself and, grinning at us, said, "A flying buttress!" And nowadays I never see a flying buttress without knowing in my very bones what it *feels* like to be one and to prop up a wall. That teacher's idiotic moment of exaggeration was worth a whole chapter of words and engineering diagrams.

Sure, Estelle and I could have ploughed through the sex manuals and read whole books on the joys of sex, but I think what I did for her was the equivalent of what that teacher did for me that time.

Anyway, back to the imaginary Mustang, with Estelle introducing herself to this unknown punter. Or john, as they call us.

I looked up and down the imaginary line. "Lemme see Estelle and Donna," I said, beckoning her and the imaginary rival forward. "Now you really smile at me." She did. "Turn round." She ground her hips. "Don't do that too obviously. The other girls don't like it."

"Why not?"

"If one girl does it, she gets an unfair advantage. So they all have to do it — and remember, you stand in ten line-ups or more for every one where the guy says, 'Estelle'! So it gets to be hard work if you've got to keep on putting out and strutting your meat."

I picked her, of course.

"Now what?" She looked at the bed, meaning we had to walk some kind of imaginary corridor before we arrived beside it.

"Walk me to the door and back." I said. "Pretend that's the passage to your room. Take my hand and walk in front of me. Half turn and talk to me. Ask me my name ... ask what do I do for a living ... and stuff like that."

I was Harry Finkelman, an animal mortician. She laughed. "So, stuffing pussies is all in a day's work for both of us, Harry! I hope you'll just *love* stuffing mine for me."

I swear I hadn't seen that possibility. "I hope I can make you feel it's more than just work with me, Estelle. You really have a most beautiful body." In a different tone I asked her, "Where are my eyes while all this is going on?"

"On my ass?"

"Right. Also, with one hand reaching behind you like that, what else are you showing me — in superb profile, if I may say so."

Briefly she covered her breast with her free hand. "Okay," she said. Then, as we had by now drawn back level with the bed, she opened her imaginary door. I dropped my pants and showed her how to string me, the way Cora had done.

"He's a fine big fellow, isn't he," I said admiringly as she repeated the ritual.

"Er ... yes. Yes it's ..."

"He's a fine, big fellow, isn't he."

"Sure is. Definitely on the large side, Harry, but I'm sure I'll manage."

"Say you like them big."

"Definitely on the large side, Harry, but that's just the way I like them. Small ones always fall out at my most exciting moment."

"Good. Now take me to the bed, lay me down, lie beside me, and tell me what you offer." Lucky I'd read that book.

"I don't know what I offer."

"Full french — that's a blow job all ..."

"I know what full french is," she protested.

"Harry may not — remember? Half and half — that's oral followed by straight sex. Sixty-nines — that's you eat me, I eat you. And straight sex any way you like — sitting, standing, on the floor, on the bed, in the shower ... on top, underneath, from the side, from behind, standing, and doggie. Also hand jobs. Also in fancy french clothes. Also play-dead, but no SM, no dominance, no bondage. Blindfold only if there's another girl present — not blindfolded, nach. Also you can handle anal."

"I can?"

"You never did?"

She shook her head.

"You will by tomorrow."

She curled up and tightened her ass in half-fearful excitement.

"Now tell me what you offer."

She ran through the list and ended, "A hundred bucks gets you my best half-and-half, with fifteen minutes in the shower after."

I asked her why she said that.

"I might get you going again — charge another fifty at your weakest moment."

"You've been thinking about this."

She laughed. "For *years!*"

I gave her an imaginary hundred, which she took to the imaginary madam while I took off some real clothes. When she came back, I helped her to do the same.

At that point our cool, calm, and collected simulation became a little difficult to maintain. She had the sort of figure that would double the print run of the average girlie mag. I had no difficulty playing Harry Finkelman; but Teacher-me was drowning. We did our best. She lay back on the bed and spread wide those gorgeous thighs. I put a cushion under her to increase the availability of her offering, which was, indeed, as lovely a pussy as Fern's had been the week before (but then aren't they all when you're that close to them!). The taste of her was a hundred percent gentleman's relish.

After about twenty seconds she started simulating an orgasm. I told her it was far too early.

"Don't be a jerk," she explained. "Look, this isn't going to work, not this time round. Couldn't we just enjoy a good old-fashioned screw together to get it out of my system. I really am turned on by you."

I tried telling her she'd just have to control herself, but she said she hadn't had sex in nearly two weeks — which was like eternity for her. She could have had it last night and the night before but she thought she ought to save it so as to make a good start at the Mustang.

I told her I was a sucker for a woman in distress and went back to letting her prove it. We wasted a whole hour in that way. I didn't come, of course, but I didn't complain, either. She had one of the most erotically sensitive bodies I've ever encountered; I couldn't

touch her anywhere without starting waves of something surging through her. And as for her nipples, the
skin of her belly, her spine, the small of her back, her
lovely, compact little bottom, the slender inner sides
of her thighs, the backs of her knees, her rosebud
clitoris, her smooth, lean labia, the cleft down to her
buttocks, her bumhole itself, and, above all, her vagina
... she was one seething, shivering charge of sexual
electricity. Which it took a full hour for me to discharge.
And I do mean discharge.

Then we began once more. This time I was Frank
Delgado, driver of a mobile ear-piercing salon; also
lips, eyebrows, nipples, clitorises to order. Also tattoos
undertaken.

"You could tattoo 'Nebuchadnezzar' here, Frank,"
she said, running a finger along the top of her lovely
auburn bush.

"Why Nebuchadnezzar?"

"That guy in the Bible who *ate grass* — remember?"

You learn something new every day.

We went through the I-can-do rituals again. This
time, when she said, "I can do anal," she slipped in:
"That's my favourite." And at the end, "A half hour of
sixty-nine and anal will only cost you two hundred, and
I'd really adore that. Let me tell you — I've had some
da-awgs today and I'm jus' 'bout ready for some
sophisticated, adult fun — know what I mean, mister?"

I told her some customers would resent being led so
blatantly.

"Shoot, hon," she came back. "Ah wouldn't a opened
mah mouth ef'n ah hadn't seen them peepers jes' laht
up when ah said that 'bout anal fust time."

I gave her the imaginary two hundred. She came

back from the madam and we fell at once into about ten minutes of the most delicious *soixante-neuf*. Then I took the electrode jelly and started working it into and around her bumhole. She lay absolutely still — so still I began to get my suspicions. "Are you turning on again?" I asked sharply.

"No!" she said at once.

But there was a patch as red as strawberries in the small of her back.

Furious Teacher fought with turned-on Frank Delgado. Frank won, and enjoyed twenty minutes of pure, cream-on-cream pleasure, ending in a fine simulated orgasm. Estelle came apart all over again, shouting "Oh!" and moaning "Aaaah!" in one long multiple ecstasy that left her exhausted and bathed in sweat. No simulation there.

"Oh God but I'm going to make a good whore," she murmured happily.

I told her she'd shown no sign of it so far and took her to the shower, where we stood back to back and I tried not to touch her.

"Sorry," she said in a tiny, contrite voice. Then she added, "Can I soap you down there? You're not making a very good job of it."

Then, of course, I had to soap her down there, too, because she, seemingly, couldn't make a very good job of it either ... and the upshot was I paid her an extra fifty and she disgraced herself with me once again. I shiver a little with desire even now as I recall her lithe, soapy young body wriggling and squirming all over me.

I put her straight back in the line-up. This time she was picked out by Bob Crawford, teamster, owned his own rig, all the way from Maine, randy as hell. When she strung me, I said, "Kind of on the small side, ain't he!"

"I've seen them a whole lot smaller than this, Bob," she assured me — determined to be professional this time. "Some fellers come in here brandishing night sticks like they were my birthday and Christmas shower all in one — and all I'm thinking is no way does *that* monster get inside me. I tell you, Bob, this is *exactly* my favorite size."

"Keep it up," I said.

She chuckled. "Isn't that *your* problem, sir?"

This time full french all the way was her favourite — at sixty. A wise choice, I thought. It would be hard for her to orgasm with me on this one. I sat on the bed, legs wide, and let my fellow beg. Just after she'd started she looked up at me and said, "You're not really going to come again?"

It seemed my fake orgasms had fooled her! "Why not?" I asked.

"Well, you already did" — her eyes vanished inside her skull a moment — "six times."

"Yes, but each time I was a different person."

"What are you talking about?"

"I'm talking about taking this business seriously, Estelle. If I say I'm going to be twelve clients, then by God, I'm going to be twelve clients. And I'll do everything they would do. Now do I get blown here or what?"

"Wow!" She applied her lips to her work with new seriousness — which lasted about two minutes. I was just beginning to relax into it when she broke off again. "How can you do that, man?" she asked. "God, I think it's wonderful. It gives me orgasms just thinking about it!" She caught her breath. "There goes one now!"

"Jesus!" I swore.

But she was telling the truth. She did get them just thinking about it — all over again.

When I 'came,' I pulled a mean trick that mean men play on even meaner whores — the kind who stick a little hand towel beneath you before they start frenching, implying it's just their daintiness. But when you come they whip their mouth away and wrap the towel around your spermspouter. Okay, they squeeze like experts and, as Robbie Burns almost said, an orgasm's an orgasm for a' that. But it's not what was in the contract.

So the mean trick is to grab her hair as you feel the sap rising. That way she's got to keep you in deep throat. I grabbed Estelle's hair and held her there — even though she had no intention of cheating me. I did it just to show her what to expect, but it turned her on so much — once again — that she flipped on her back and begged me to ram her as hard as I could and brim her over for good and all.

When we lay side by side again, breathless and exhausted, I asked her why. She wouldn't explain.

Louis Pescatore, loss adjuster, just wanted straight sex in lots of fun positions. He got it — and finally exhausted Estelle's own erotic responses. That was when it became work for her, and, finally — six clients later — for me, too. Even so I didn't manage to come. I was so used to simulating orgasms by then that I wondered if I'd ever feel the real things again.

I was awakened at four by a swollen bladder, a minor thirst, and — as I stared down at her soft, warm, beautiful young body — by a powerful sense of duty, too. She simply had to learn what those late-night calls were like, I told myself. And myself agreed.

I made her dress and stand out there in the light. I took ages to make up my mind between her and 'Donna.' Finally I let her take me back to her room, where she went through all the ritual — three times, before she got it right. I said all I wanted was to lie on top of her and poke away nice and slow and gentle. She must have thought she was in for an easy ride.

The moment I was in her, I told her to have an orgasm.

"Unh unh," she yawned. "I'm plum outa them things."

"Then you'll have to fake one for me," I sang.

"Why?"

"Because you're American, and you believe in the work ethic, and the free-market economy. Because no matter what, honey, you *deliver!*"

"And if it's fake?"

"It still has an honoured place in the 'Murrikan Dream. Where does it say anything about genuine?"

She wasn't bad.

"Okay," I told her. "Now you count. And every fifteen pokes I make, you give me a good fake orgasm."

She groaned but she gave me ten good ones — so good I was getting out of control myself. The next one was suspiciously good. "Are you giving it me for real?" I asked sharply.

"No," she said indignantly. "Certainly not."

I turned her over and finished myself off nice and easy from behind. She was a superb poke, I have to say that — genuine or fake.

Somehow we missed a day. Not through dalliance, though. First we overslept — for some extraordinary reason. Then we walked around Reno, believing only about ten percent of what we saw. Then we had dinner and went back to bed — but this time we just lay side by side and talked. I told her some of my experiences with hookers; she told me the lousy time she'd been having, giving it away. It was clear that even if she had a bad trip at the Mustang, it couldn't be much worse than things that had already happened to her. But the one thing she had in plenty was resilience.

She told me that when she was ten she saw a man masturbating in a wood. He told her she was naughty to spy on him and he'd have to punish her. So he sat down on a fallen tree, took her over his knee, and smacked her bottom. Next week at the same time she went back, spied on him again, and again he smacked her — enough to sting but never so hard as to make her actually cry. That second time he took down her panties first, and she said it had given her a funny, tickly, thrilling sort of sensation.

After several months of that sort of spanking he would put his finger into her groove and move it around a little; that was even more tickly and thrilling. And that sort of thing — nothing worse — had gone on for four years, by which time he was spanking her and then masturbating her all the way to orgasm. Yet, for all his excitement, he never tried to screw her nor to get her to do anything to him. She didn't even know if it gave him an erection because he always pulled his trousers on and buttoned them up before he started. It surprised her that, in all the years she had been giving men freebies, she had never asked one of them to spank her. But I remembered that profound response of hers when I had grabbed her hair at the end of her blow job on me.

"So what *did* you give in all those freebies?" I asked. "And, more important, what did you get?"

"What I gave was sex, of course. And plenty. And what I got was plenty of sex back, too. But also ... I don't know. There's an additional satisfaction that is kinda sexy and kinda ... something else. Pleasure, but not sexual pleasure. I just get a shivery thrill when a man tells me what he's going to do to me. I may not want to do it, it may be something I dislike, but if he tells me firmly enough, then I get that thrill. And being ordered about. That's the same. When they tell me how I'm to lie, or stand up, or turn over ... things like that. And being manhandled, too. Not so it hurts, but firmly. When you grabbed my hips last night and turned me over and lifted me up to do it doggy fashion — and went on holding them, *firm,* while you rammed your dick into me, hard as you could — phew! That was good. But it's not orgasm-good, you know? It's a different good."

Sunday afternoon I took her out to the Mustang. The closer we got, the more nervous she became. By the time that long, low cluster of trailers hove into view I thought she wasn't going to be able to go through with it. I reached across, fished her hooker's licence out of the glove locker, and placed it firmly in her grasp. She stared at it like she'd never seen it before, smiled gratefully at me, and pressed it to her adorable bosom. "Yes!" she murmured.

Finally, as we pulled into the parking lot, Fate stepped in and took over. An army jeep passed us in a cloud of dust and skidded to a halt at the gate, where an officer and a sergeant got out. The jeep, driven by one remaining sergeant, pulled round the back of the whorehouse; they didn't want to be spotted from the highway by any passing MP, of course. We were approaching the gate ourselves — Estelle clutching her hooker's licence and me, masquerading as gentleman, toting her backpack — when the driver-sergeant returned. He took one look at her; she took one look at him; and something happened between them. She stood a little taller, thrust her breasts out a little more pertly, swung her hips a touch more sexily. He leaned forward a little and adjusted something in his pants pocket. "I've got him," she murmured to me. I didn't disagree. Their eyes never left each other's until they stood, a mere yard apart, before the gate.

"Well hallo, lady," he said. "Do you work here I hope?"

"I hope so, too." She grinned saucily and flashed her licence for him to see. "Or it's a thousand dollars down the drain."

He eyed her up and down, taking no care to disguise his lust. "You mean you're just starting here? Right now?"

"Hoping to, like I say."

"You'll have no problem, doll. Where'd you work before? How have I missed you? I thought I knew every ..."

"Nowhere," she put in.

"You mean you worked private? You pulled johns off magazine ads?"

"No. Nowhere. I was never a hooker before. I'm hoping to start here."

All the while she spoke her body was never still. I'm not sure she was even aware of it — all those subtle, sexy movements she was making. But he certainly was. His hardon must have been straining up under his belt by now. It gave him slight difficulty in walking upright as he grabbed her by the wrist, banged the button, and yelled into the intercom: "Come on, Cora — I know you're watching all this. Let us in." Keeping his finger 'accidentally' on the talk button he added, "She'll take you on, doll. If she don't, I'll never bring another squad here on passing out."

She snuggled up to him as the latch buzzed and sprang open. He looked back over his shoulder and said to me, "Okay, buddy, I'll take her pack."

I told him I was going in, too.

He looked slightly nonplussed. "You ain't her driver?"

"No. She just hitched a ride with me, about ten miles back."

"Oh." Now he was embarrassed that he'd maybe muscled in.

"I have a date with a girl called Ebony," I added, much to his relief.

"Great," he said. "She's great."

Still, I could see he thought me odd for passing up the chance that had now fallen his way — to be a hooker's first client. "English, huh?" he asked.

"Right."

That satisfied him. We are beyond fathoming, much less explanation.

The last of the girls were still assembling into line as we entered. The smiles snapped on at the click of the door behind us.

"Hi! I'm Jodie."

"Hi! Ah'm Mary-Beth?" Her rising tone made it sound like a question — probably justified.

"Hallo. My name's Fern." She winked at me.

"I'll take Ebony," I said, looking straight at the young black girl — slightly to her surprise. I recognized her from her pictures in Madame Cora's album, of course. That slim, lithe body with the firm, provocative breasts and cute little ass was not easily forgettable.

She stepped forward, reaching out her hand for mine; the others all stayed roughly in line instead of flopping back into the sofas, for the gate had already buzzed again. Madame Cora was busy with Estelle and the sergeant, so Mary-Beth went forward and scrutinized the john before letting him in. The smiles were snapped on again as the door closed behind him — a small, nervous man who licked his lips every couple of seconds and had eyes, ravenous eyes, only for the girls.

Ebony, meanwhile, led me toward the bar, saying, "You wanna drink before we party? What's your name, by the way?"

"Riley. I'll have a Coke, thanks, Ebony. It's thirst-making driving an open tourer over the desert."

"You a limey?" She recalled Fern's wink at me and understanding dawned. "You're *that* limey. Hey! Whaddya know — you came back for little ol' me!"

The Coke was five dollars. I presume she got a cut; otherwise she'd not have suggested the delay. Her eyes looked tired. Not today-tired but long-time-tired.

"Not even an earthquake would have stopped me coming back, Ebony," I said. "When I saw your picture at three o'clock that morning, or whatever ghastly hour it was, I said to myself, 'I want to be good and rested before I party with *that* young beauty.' How old are you, by the way?"

"Twenny-one." She winked as she gave the legal minimum age for a prostitute under state law. "Though what became of *three* of those years, Lord alone knows."

So she was eighteen. I wondered at what age she'd started.

"That was some line she fed you, huh, that Fern? Did you swallow it?"

"I didn't think the johns did the swallowing in this House," I replied.

She laughed and punched me playfully. "That chick you came in with," she went on. "You her main man?"

I explained, telling her the full story, not the truncated version I'd given the sergeant. While I was speaking, Madame Cora, Estelle, and the sergeant come out of her office and walked off up the corridor. Estelle glanced back over her shoulder, saw me, grinned, waved, and then, waggling her hips shamelessly, led the sergeant up to the end and round the corner.

Ebony, following my eyes, saw them, too, and said, "Well, she's on trial, anyway. That's the first hurdle she's cleared. She may be lucky, too. Fern's leaving tomorrow."

"Uh huh. Do many girls turn up here looking for work?"

"At least one a day. Sometimes three or four. We take on one in a hundred I guess."

"And the rest — the other ninety-nine?"

"Oh, they'll find work somewhere. This is the first place they all try — because it's clean and safe and comfortable."

"And the pay is so high."

She chuckled. "Yeah." She eyed me speculatively. "So you parted with one grand for a weekend with … whatsername? Estelle?"

"Desirée, she wants to call herself professionally."

"That's cool. We don't have one of them right now. Does that mean you're broke?"

"Men who are broke don't come to the Mustang."

"Oh, I wish! I had a fight with a trucker last night. Wanted to pay me twenny for twenny minutes half-and-half! Said he could get fresh fourteen-year-olds in Reno for that. I tole the mothahfukka — go gettem!" She swelled out her chest in case I hadn't noticed her assets. "Me! For twenny!" Then she grinned saucily. "Well, ef'n you aint broke, Limey, half a cool grand'll get ya all the time you want and mo' lovin' 'n you can *imagine* in the VIP suite with me." She did not crudely swell out her chest, nor flagrantly grind her hips, yet subtle undulations of her body left me in no doubt as to the delights she was offering. "That's with the jacuzzi?" she added, using that question-tone which makes you respond with an instinctive yes. "And the love chair? You ever party with the love chair?" A genuine question at last.

I shrugged. "Things like it, I suppose. But not this actual one here, no."

"You ain't lived. You ain't even drawn breath yet."

It was tempting. But … half a cool grand! "How about one hour, no jacuzzi, no massage, but a bit of time on the love chair? Or *in* it — whatever one says?"

She showed no disappointment; trading at the Mustang always started at the top end and worked down toward the affordable — which usually meant to a forty-buck straight-sex deal. "Two hundred bucks," she said. "You'll still be very happy."

I finished my Coke and I paid the $200 to Madame Cora on the way. She only half remembered me until she heard my accent; then it all came back. "Right!" she said, looking at Ebony. "Unfinished business, right? Did you bring that Estelle girl here?"

"She hitched a lift with me, why?"

"I just hope she's as good as she *thinks* she is."

"She's got the equipment," I said.

"I noticed," she replied as she walked away.

Ebony winked at me and then sashayed her ass provocatively as we continued on our way to her room. "She looks about twenny-three?" she said as she opened the door to let me through.

Somehow her breasts got in the way as I squeezed past. She went, "Mmmm!" in an appreciative manner; you'd almost swear she'd never done that before.

"Twenty, I'd have said," I replied.

"Yeah, but you got trick eyes, man. Some forty-five-year-old whore tells you she's thirty, you'd say to yo'se'f, thirty-five and think how smart yo was. No, she's twenny-three, betchennything. You think she's really never sold ass before?"

She was undoing my buttons and zips as she spoke. "No'mally," she said, grinning naughtily up at me, "ah leaves the tricks to do this fo' thesselves, while ah takes the money to Madame Cora and tells her what's on the menu."

"I'm honoured," I said.

"Y'all are, b'leeve me." She jerked my pants down over my erection, which sprang out at her, hot, lusty, and throbbing. "My-oh-my! Jess lookit that!" she exclaimed in admiration that seemed as genuine as it comes. Her eyes gleamed.

"Don't you believe Estelle never turned pro before today?" I asked with some difficulty.

"Now that ah *do* b'lieve," she replied. "Else she'd'a knowed 'bout the thousan' dollahs an' she'da come heah wid it and wouldn' hitch no ride. An' she would'na given you no three-day weekend fo' a measly one grand." She shook her head in amazement. "Twenny-three and jes' startin' in the Life — Jeezes! Y'all gonna peel me, too, honey?" She turned her back to me and lifted her hair to let me unzip her blouse.

"A bit different from *your* experience, eh?" I said as I eased the flimsy cotton off her shoulders.

She wore no bra. Her breasts were high and firm, with sweet, conical nipples that just begged to be stroked.

"Ah'll say!" She settled back against me with an encouraging sigh and, reaching for my hands, brought them round to cover her breasts. "Oh, that is so *good!*" she murmured. Then, almost in the same breath, "Ah began when I was ten, ef'n y'all wanna know. Not screwin' o'course — though they tried. Man, did they all try!"

I was torn now between head and heart — or head and prick, actually. To fondle those gorgeous breasts and to feel her cute little ass wiggling against my working parts was the most stunning pleasure I'd felt in over twenty-four hours; I was loath to curtail it. But if not screwin' then what?

"If not screwing, then what?" I asked.

She flashed her pearly-white teeth up at me. "Lie on the bed an' ah'll show y'all," she said.

I lay on the bed and watched her as, with a grin that promised seven heavens all rolled into one, she smeared her hands with lubricating Albolene; the sticky noises it made were an erotic symphony in themselves. And then, stretching herself luxuriously between my parted legs, she took my erection in both hands — with a confidence born of all those years — and began to massage it with a skill that even my own hands had never approached.

I began to swoon from the pleasure of her touch but, when she saw the effect on me, she stopped and said, "Then, when ah wiz 'bout fo'teen, I graddyated to *this!*" And she popped her wide-open mouth over my old man and swallowed the crown of him right down into her throat.

I think I did pass out then.

She, seeing how close I was to a crisis, gave me only a token gobble or two before she lifted her head off me and said, "An' now, *Mistah* Riley, ef'n you'd jes tweak these little strings heah" — she swung one hip toward me where the cord that supported her g-string was tied in a cute little bow — "ya'll gonna see where ah done put this man-meat when ah turned sweet sixteen!"

She untied it herself and waddled up to straddle my chest, swaying her wide-open fork only inches from my 'trick eyes,' as she had called them. The only trick they were performing at that moment was the rather desperate one of staying inside their sockets.

"Ain't that jes' the pinkest, purdiest one o' them thangs y'ever seed?" she asked proudly.

It was, too — neat, sweet, flaming pink, and showing no sign of those years of heavy traffic she must have endured. An outrageous idea came to me then and, the more I thought it over (which I did for the best part of two seconds), the more determined I became to carry it through.

"Listen," I said. "How about this — forget the jacuzzi and all the gourmet sex we planned for tonight ... no! Not forget it. Postpone it until ... what's today?"

"Still Monday."

"Okay. Postpone it till Wednesday or Thursday. Tonight, you just do to me what you did to men when you first began, okay? The hand job. Even in the little sample you gave me I knew I was in the *hands* of a supreme expert. A fricatrice of world class ..."

"Fricasee ... what's that? Man, ah jes' lurve the way y'all can talk!"

"Fri-ca-trice. Latin. The same word that we get *friction* from — except I know where *I* want to get *my* friction from tonight! And then tomorrow night I'll come back again and you can french me like you did just now — but all the way to paradise, okay? Then I'll rest up two days and come back Thursday for the jacuzzi and the hour of gourmet sex we'd planned on tonight."

"But a hand job is nothing like two-hundred dollahs, man," she objected. "Mo' like forty."

And a blow job, it turned out, was 'mo' like fifty.' So I had a hundred and ten banked against gourmet night. We agreed on that but she had to go and tell Madame Cora about the change in plan.

"Make yo'se'f re-eal comf'table," she said archly as she slipped on a light cotton dressing gown and left me for a minute or so.

I lay on the bed with my legs spread wide and tried to imagine what it must be like for Ebony to lie in that same position anything up to a dozen times a day with too many men to remember. It was impossible, of course. Also, it was threatening the strength of my erection.

Fortunately she returned soon after, and the mere sight of her was enough to put the steel back where it belonged.

"Ah'm mighty glad yo didn' start wivout meh," she said, slipping out of her gown and settling once more between my legs.

There was more play with the Albolene. The little smacking noises it made as she soaped her hands in the cream were especially thrilling, suggesting as they did an almost supernatural degree of lubrication. Then, cradling my bone in her left hand, she started doing things I couldn't see — but could certainly feel! — with the fingers of her right.

I've had hand jobs on five continents, mostly with girls who have no intuitive feel for male anatomy. They sit beside you and grasp the top of your knob between all five fingertips and wank the foreskin up and down and try not to glance at the clock. Some make a ring of thumb and middle finger and go at you with the same mechanical enthusiasm until — in self-defence more than anything — you shoot your wad.

Well, Ebony wasn't from the same *planet* as those amateurs. I couldn't even guess what she was doing with her fingers but it was never the same thing twice, it was voluptuously, tantalizingly slow, it used the most subtle blend of movement, pressure, and variations in speed, or slowness … and the mind that directed all this stupendous activity was, I'll swear, in mystic communion with my most primitive nerves. For she seemed to know *exactly* how I responded — inside me, I mean, deep inside — to each new move she made.

And it *never* got faster. Instead of speeding up she applied both harder and softer variations in pressure, all up and down the most sensitive part of my hardon — the sperm duct all down its underside and the myriad nerves around the frenulum, that little fold of skin that runs up into the upside-down vee of the glans. And, of course, the glans itself. Man! If every nerve ending down there had gleamed out like a firefly on a tropic night, she couldn't have pinpointed them better.

She kept it going for a full twenty minutes, which made it the longest hand job I ever had, certainly at that intensity of pleasure. At the end, when even a blind girl would have known I was near to erupting, she turned her fingernails lightly against my erection and scratched from side to side, sometimes moving only a fraction of an inch, sometimes around a hundred and eighty degrees of feverish, steel-hard, quivering gristle.

And when at last I came — which was actually when she felt she'd given full value and so *permitted* me to come — she placed her face a few inches above my gusher and squeezed-relaxed, squeezed-relaxed in perfect timing with my ejaculations. In that way she milked me for every last drop. I watched in fascination as, with eyes closed and a seraphic smile playing around her lips, she turned her face this way and that, causing each new jet of my juice to fall on virgin skin. At the end her beautiful dark face was mottled with pearly beads and you'd think I'd done her the greatest favour in spurting each one there.

When there was nothing left to shoot she felt me still three-quarters stiff. She lay back beside me, still with that seraphic smile, still with her eyes closed, and let out a great sigh of apparent satisfaction. "Rub it in, honeh?" she said. "Didn'tch know it's better fo' a gal's complexion than evra cream that evah done come outa Paree, France? Chanel an' all them perfume houses. No, *not* wiv yo' fingah!"

She opened one eye, giving her the appearance of winking, and giggled.

Well, there was only one other part of me firm enough and handy enough to fulfil her request, so I used that instead.

After a few minutes' rest she rose and washed it all off in the handbasin, bending over and showing me the menu for Thursday.

"Now y'all go 'way," she said, caressing my balls as gently as only she knew how, "an' set these-heah two fahn fellahs to makin' mo' o' that cream for me to *eat* tomorra, huh?"

I said it would be impossible to stop those two fine fellows from doing just that.

On the way out I looked for Estelle — or Desirée, as she now was — and found her sitting at the bar, staring critically at herself in the long mirror behind it. She saw my reflection approaching and winked at it. "It's okay," she said. "Cool."

I ordered another glass of those exorbitant sodas. "You're in, then?"

"Well, Madame Cora won't say for sure till we close up tonight. But Harry, that sergeant, told her I was the new sensation."

"You did a good job on him, then?"

She sniffed and looked cautiously about her. "He did a pretty good job on me, too, if you must know. I forgot myself and came right along with him." She licked her lips and gave a litle laugh. "Hell, I was nervous as a kitten — and he was a gorgeous hunk of man, don't you think?"

"I'd certainly want him on my side in any fight."

"Right. Still it's over now. It won't happen again."

The buzzer sounded then and she went to join the line. I stayed to watch. Three guys came in, laughing, back-slapping, lip-licking, shivery with nerves and lust. Their bright eyes would have chosen all twenty in the line. One of them chose Desirée. She took his hand, smiled like she'd waited all week for someone like him to turn up, and waggled her tail enticingly before his goggling eyes — showing that curvy profile of breast, the way I'd taught her. And I watched her with pride all the way.

Ebony came back to the salon at that moment, having finished tidying up her room and herself. "Shoot!" she exclaimed sarcastically. "Ah done gone miss the line-up!" She must have passed Desirée on the way. "Your star pupil," she said with a jerk of her head over her shoulder.

I watched her thick, fleshy lips in fascination, thinking, *Tomorrow! Tomorrow!*

"She looks like a pro," she said. "An' she acts like a pro." She grinned. "Mebbe that's jess what she *is.*"

All the following day I could not get the image of those big, soft lips out of my mind. What Ebony had managed to do with her hands and fingers was more stupendous than most girls can achieve with the full kit, so I hardly dared think what her hot, wet mouth and deep, husky throat would add in the way of thrills. The image of her lips was tantalizing enough.

Of course, I knew the dangers of anticipating a thing too keenly — how disappointing the reality often turns out to be. So I, too, was 'nervous as a kitten' as I parked my car and buzzed at the gate.

"Well, hallo!" Madame Cora's voice was chummily ironic. "Long time no see!" It was a new phrase then.

"I believe I'm expected," I replied in my plummiest British best.

She chuckled as she buzzed the lock to let me pass. *"All* men are expected here, honey."

She didn't call a line-up, of course, so only Ebony was waiting for me, just inside the door — looking fresh as a black narcissus, too, though she must already have done half a dozen customers by then. Over her shoulder I saw Desirée looking up from a copy of *Cosmopolitan* and staring at me in amazement.

"Y'all wanna take a shower fusst?" Ebony asked as she closed the door behind us.

Those lips! They mesmerized me. *Please make it last,* I prayed to every erotic god on Olympus. I managed to stammer that I'd had a good long bath immediately before I set out.

"Okay. We'll jess give th'ole man a quick wash, huh?" She peeled off my clothes with expert speed and, grabbing me gently by the most obvious handle, led me over to the washbasin, keeping up a constant prattle as she worked.

"My-oh-my! Ain't he the b-i-g fella tonight! I guess we jess didn' take 'nuff starch outa him las' night, huh? Gotta see ef'n we cain't do bettah tonight. Down, boy! Ah decleah! He's *hot* fo' a touch and taste of cute li'l pussy — hot fit to burn mah mouf ..." and so forth.

And all the while her deft little fingers were soaping and cleansing every nook and fold of my fellow's surface, while her eyes watched my face closely, trying to guage how far or near I might be to a disastrously premature climax. She was only nineteen but nine of those years were filled with experience of this particular drama, so she didn't put a foot wrong — or a finger in this case.

When she'd washed off the last of the suds, she dried me with the same tender loving care and then — a surprise this, but a most delightful one — finished off with a hair dryer. It left my skin feeling all silky and cosseted.

"Theah now!" she said proudly as she led me back to the bed in the same amiable way.

I assumed I'd be lying on my back again, as on the previous day, and started to take up that position; but she said, "No, honeh, that comes later." And she made me kneel on all fours with my thighs spread quite wide.

Then *she* lay on her back, between my calves, and wriggled up the bed until her head was immediately below my fork. Except for her shoes, by the way, she was fully dressed still — if the skimpy dresses they wore at the Mustang would allow any girl to be called *fully* dressed. Peeping down past my dangling tackle I could see her breasts and, when she raised and parted her thighs, her bush and a little glimmer of the 'pinkest and purdiest.'

But I soon lost interest in even those charms as I watched her prepare for tonight's pleasuring, licking her lips and sucking them into her mouth and rubbing them over each other until they were as thick and moist and inviting as the labia of a much-trafficked pussy. She knew precisely what effect these preparations were having on me. And if she doubted it, she needed only to watch the throbbing pulse of my hardon as it responded with eager spasms to the pounding of my heart to be reassured.

While she tantalized me thus her hands stole up the backs of my thighs, caressing and scratching me lightly as they approached the big, soft bull-bag of my balls. At least, it was as big and soft and pendulous as a bull's when she started but, in response to her fondling, my balls shot up like clock weights at winding-up time and my scrotum shrivelled to something that looked like a walnut.

She giggled. "That always gets me, man!" she exclaimed. "The way them little fellahs jess run back indoors. Let's see ef'n we cain't coax 'em out to play, huh? Come on, guys, li'l Ebony wants to play wid ya!" And she opened and closed her fingers like flower petals at sunrise and sunset, raking their nails with feather lightness over my scrotum … until, to my amazement, the two fellows *did* at last come out to play. And the walnut-shell skin went all stretched and flaccid again. And the thrills it sent throughout my body were just electrifying.

My hardon responded to this stimulation by swelling and stiffening still further, until it was just brushing against my belly with each pulse — and let me say I have a slim figure, so my gut wasn't hanging down to meet it.

"My-oh-my," she said again, taking it gingerly in one hand while the other continued the good work they had both started. "Ah don' often see 'em as stiff an' hahd as *this!* You sho' he won't snap right off ef'n ah was to brang him down toward mah mouf?"

She tried it gingerly, as if she truly were afraid of such a tragedy. "Now *this* one could hurt a gal," she went on. "So you jess hol' yo'seff good'n still, y'all heah me now? No jabbin' an' no stabbin'." And, just to make sure, she spread her hand flat, fingers splayed over the lower half of my belly and wedged her elbow between her torso and my knee. " 'Course," she said, relenting a little, "yo can move a *li'l* bit. I reckon yo' 'sperienced 'nuff round gals to know how much, huh?"

I gulped and croaked that I hoped I was. And then I watched in fascination as she started a tantalizing little mime down there, holding my joystick like a ... well, like a joystick, wagging it around in tiny circles, reaching for it with those stupendous lips and her big, hot, succulent tongue. Sometimes she made sure she succeeded. Other times she made equally sure she failed. Never in a predictable sequence. So the ardent, pulsating tip of my tool was only sometimes rewarded with the thrill of warm, moist contact — and the corresponding thrill of cool air on the wetness when contact was broken. At other times there was the subtler thrill of thwarted anticipation.

You know how your body anticipates any sort of contact, not just the erotic kind? How you wince *before* you turn on a cold shower ... how your flesh cringes just before someone hits you ... how your heart turns over just before your lips meet those of a girl you love? Well, my fellow thrilled in the same sort of anticipation every time those lovely lips and that tremulous tongue came near him. And when she failed to make contact, in that knowingly teasing way of hers, he was left with a thrill of a different kind — spiritual, non-physical, divine. And Ebony knew, to the last tiny palpitation, exactly the degree and duration of each and every one.

Only when she gauged that I was firmly on the first plateau of my fellatricious pleasure did she progress to the next stage. In this she would briefly raise her head and take the whole of my knob inside her mouth, sometimes sucking, sometimes curling her tongue slowly, lazily, all around it, sometimes giving me gentle little bites that sent a thrill of fear through me — reminders of that ancient nightmare of the *vagina dentata,* the 'toothed vagina,' which runs through the folklore of even the earliest civilizations.

It made a difference, knowing that this was no mere foreplay. My mind was not looking half ahead, anticipating the glory of measuring Ebony's insides with the appropriate measuring rod. This was *it* — the real thing for tonight. It concentrated my mind and will on every little nuance of what she was doing to me down there.

The world of sexual pleasure holds more riches than Aladdin's cave. But among its brightest and most precious jewels is the sensation that arises when a skilled young girl runs her tongue, slow and snakelike, back and forth, back and forth — swaying like seaweed in the push and pull of the waves — over the exquisitely sensitive crown of your knob — and most particularly on the underside, where the ridge of the frenulum tucks up into the dividing bulge of the glans. For a time there I feared the pressure in my brain would blow the top of my skull right off.

"Gimme a pillow, now," she gasped as she paused to draw breath.

As I hastened to obey her, the cool air of her inhalation, rushing in around that part of me which had been so deliciously hot only moments earlier, was yet another sort of thrill.

Back went her mouth, clamped firmly around me. And now there was no more touch-and-tease, no pulling away. Holding me in her there, she grasped my hips and encouraged me to move gently this way and that, from side to side and round and round. And in and out, to be sure — but not too far in (for her sake) nor too far out (for mine).

Each of these stages was a new plateau of pleasure, so by now I was within sight of the long, inevitable rise to my climax. She, with her years of experience, must have known it, too, for, having brought me from 'within sight' to 'within touching distance,' she stopped abruptly, wriggled out from beneath me, and, giving me a friendly slap where it wouldn't blind me, cried, "Okay — on yo' back, mistah! We goin' fo' gold, y'hear me?"

I expected her to take the pillow away but instead she added another. I discovered why as soon as I lay across them, for not only did it thrust my joystick as proud as it would go, it also lifted me so high that my balls were now dangling free of the mattress — where those nimble fingers could wreak their delicate havoc with my senses.

When she said we were 'going for gold' I assumed she meant to work for my climax as swiftly as possible. Instead she began a whole new series of amorous games between her lips, her tongue, her teeth, and that quivering, passionate rod of gristle she held in her one free hand.

She licked. She licked in little darts of her tongue, here, there, everywhere except where I might expect it. She waggled the mobile tip of it every which way, including loose. She licked in long ice-lolly strokes from bottom to top, from top to bottom, all round the top. She curled the tip of her tongue in baroque corkscrews all around the furrow where knob meets shaft.

She bit. Little love nips all up and down the shaft … long, relentless, gentle, chewings round and about the top, sometimes pretending she was about to crack it between her back molars, the way a dog would crack a marrowbone, grinning slyly at me as if to say, 'Go on — dare me and I will!'

And, of course, she sucked. Man, did she suck! She could close her mouth around me and move her tongue inside there in ways that words could never capture. Fast as a hummingbird's wing, slow as a lizard's tail on a cold day, soft as melting marshmallow, hard as a man's knuckle … that tongue was a cast of thousands, a will-o'-the-wisp, a narcotic, an elixir, a fount of indescribable rapture inside the hot, all-embracing cavern of her mouth.

Somehow — and here she showed how supremely skilled she was at this marvellous game — she took a pleasure that usually went straight up to the pinnacle of a climax and turned it into something that rose in cycles, like an upward spiral. That, I find, is the hardest of all to describe.

A series of little thrills … no, not little. There were no *little* pleasures in anything that happened with

Ebony that night. A series of *big* thrills would build up to something stupendous, when she would take me deep into her throat and swallow hard, so that I almost passed out at the ecstasy of it. And then she would begin again on the next cycle of bites and sucks and licks, a little higher up the scale.

At last the inevitable happened — and I'm talking now about a full thirty-five minutes after she first started coaxing my balls back out of hiding. I gave out a wordless cry of rapture, strained to lift my backside off the pillows, and shuddered all over from head to foot. At once she took me deep into her throat again and started swallowing like mad. I tell you, when they make robot whores that outperform the real thing, they'll give them vaginas that do to a man what Ebony's gulping throat did to me that night; but even then they'll never equal the living thrill of it.

She knew exactly, and I mean to the microsecond, when the gusher was about to erupt. And she'd hold her throat clamped tight-tight-tight around my glans until she felt it pulsing up the tube, and then she'd relax so utterly that it would shoot out with as much freedom as it would have in empty air — at which moment she'd swallow hard and clamp her tonsils tight again, ready for the next mighty spurt and the next release.

I've heard whores say that men's orgasms are purely mechanical. Well, maybe they are in the sense that a man can be raped — that is, made to come against his will, simply by applying the right mechanical stimulus to the appropriate region. But that's at the very lower end of the scale. At the rarefied upper end, where skilled workers like Ebony operate, it's quite another thing. A ho-hum orgasm, erupting into the vagina of a ho-hum partner, will coax, let's say, half a millilitre of sticky out of a man's balls. By contrast, I'd not be surprised to learn that Ebony stimulated and swallowed *five* mils out of me that night. Okay — scientifically impossible — I know all that. But it sure felt like five big juicy mils went out of me. I mean, my balls were *drained*. They *ached* with their emptiness. My whole body felt limp and exhausted.

I was revived by a cry of triumph from her, a simple, happy, "Ha!"

I lifted my head and glanced down to see her fingers holding up my limp little two-inch dick and letting it drop back to vanish — hide in shame, perhaps — among the hairs of my bush. "That's the fusst time ah done seed it *whupped,*" she said.

"It's where you girls get nearest to making us hate you," I said.

"Huh?" She dropped my dick and looked at me in alarm.

"Not to worry." I laughed. "I'm reconciled to it by now. Good luck to you, I say. But I can remember how, when I first started enjoying you ladies of pleasure, and I'd be lying here all exhausted and drained out like this, and the girl would start making well-darling-that's-that noises and movements, and it would occur to me that she might very well be back on that same bed in less than ten minutes, doing it all over again."

"And?" she said, implying (rightly) that it was not a very extraordinary discovery to have made.

"Well, a man would sacrifice one of his balls if the other would let him enjoy half a dozen women every day. And get *paid* for it! You lead in reality the sort of life men can only fantasize about — and you don't even *enjoy* the sex! Can't you see that would make any young man angry? Especially an unthinking young man like me, in those days."

She thought it over a moment and said, "Yeah, I guess." Then she smiled archly. "Who says we don' enjoy the sex? Okay, so we fake the orgasms. So what? Ah kin enjoy the sex without all that. Ah enjoys meetin' diff'rent men an' all. Talkin' an' stuff. I kin enjoy *their* pleasure. Ah git a kick outa thinkin' they'll go a long ways afore they gits another ride as good as what I done give 'em. Ain't that the truth, now? Didn' I jess done give you 'bout the bes' blow job evvah?"

"Oh, Ebony!" I took her face between my hands. "That was no blow job. I mean the word does not *begin* to describe what you just gave me. That was way up with the best sex I ever enjoyed. Ever! That was the gates of paradise opening to let me in."

She grinned, happy yet again. "Jess you wait till tomorrow night!" she said.

"Thursday," I said hastily, rubbing my aching balls tenderly. "Definitely Thursday."

Leaving her to tidy up and get ready for the next lucky man, I limped back to the salon and settled for half an hour's recuperation at the bar.

A line-up of fourteen girls was in progress. The last three introduced themselves as I sat down but the man was having difficulty making up his mind. While he dithered, two more men came in and the girls started introducing themselves again. One of the newcomers, a tall, rangy, cowboy type, picked Desirée the moment she spoke her name. His companion chose Fern. The slow guy looked daggers at them but they just grinned back as the girls led them away up their own respective corridors. The girls were beginning to show their impatience when Ebony returned to the salon. The ditherer pounced on her at once. "A black gal," he said. "Now *that's* what I come a-lookin' for."

So I sat there and sipped my drink while the only three girls I knew in the house were spreading their legs under three more samples of today's dirty dozen.

One of the girls joined me, introducing herself as Lorey. Knowing I'd spent the best part of forty-five minutes with Ebony, she knew also that I wasn't in the market, so to speak. She was relaxed and easy. "Well, Riley," she said after I introduced myself, "that Ebony's quite a gal, eh?"

"She got my vote tonight," I answered.

"She got more than that out of you — by the look of things." She laughed.

I pulled a jokingly glum face and agreed.

"Pity about her phoney Southern-belle accent," she went on. "Fan mah mouf, honeh, ef'n y'all don' look jess plum tuckered! 'Course you, as an Englishman, wouldn't realize it but *this* is the farthest south that gal ever went — Reno, Nevada."

"Tell me, Lorey, what's your *real* name?" I asked.

It took her aback. She was half affronted, half scared.

In an American accent I said, "You get the point, huh? What if my being a limey is all put-on, too? This is a house of illusions. Shoot, honeh, y'all know that, surely?"

She laughed then and said, "You'll do, Riley. You're pretty cool, man. It's a house of illusions, all right, and not too many laughs."

English again, I said, "You do all right, I expect?"

She piled all of her lips over on the left side of her face. "Not like I should. All the girls say I should pull more men than I do. I mean ..." She leaned toward me and lowered her voice. "Look at Cindy there — the fat one."

"Chubby," I said.

"And past forty, too. Well past. Yet she pulls as many as me. Why?"

I hesitated, not knowing if she was asking for real.

"You know, don't you," she accused me. "Go on, speak. I won't scream or faint or nothin' like that. I truly want to know."

I drew breath and reluctantly prepared to answer. It's always tiger country when a girl begs you to speak out and promises not to scream.

"I do a good job, too," she put in. "Once we're alone on the bed, skin to skin, y'know, I do a fucking good job, to coin a phrase."

"Funny," I began. "You're only talking to me like this, Lorey, because you know I'm spent as far as tonight goes. If you thought I might have another shot in my locker ..."

"Do you?" she interrupted hopefully.

"No, listen, this is the answer. Or my answer, anyway. We're animals, too, all of us humans. And the sex drive is about the most universal thing there is, right across the whole animal kingdom. So even the most moronic man who walks through that door — even if he's dragging his knuckles and you can't see any forehead above his eyebrows — even he is the honed product of two billion years of sexual evolution. He can read sexual signals. Maybe he can't spell his own name but he surely can read sex signals."

"You say I give out the wrong signals?" she asked belligerently.

I shrugged. "What's wrong in one place could be absolutely right in another."

That checked her. "Go on," she said after a pause. "I saw you watching me in that line-up. You *know* something, don't you."

"Your smile said, 'I'm a pal.' Your eyes said, 'I'm the ice maiden.' Your tone of voice said, 'Don't mess with me!' Not crudely — the way an actress would do it if you asked her to do it. But subtly, the way even a two-billion-year-old Neanderthal would feel it."

Her eyes were blank, or at least unreadable. "You said something about being wrong in one place and right in another," she reminded me.

"Okay. Those confusing signals would be absolutely right if you were offering sm — you know, strict discipline."

She turned from me then and slumped on both elbows on the bar, staring vacantly at a small pool of spilled cola.

"Have I shocked you?" I asked.

She shook her head slowly but said nothing.

"Well, then?" I prompted.

She heaved a huge sigh and turned great soulful eyes toward me. I felt I was peering through them into her self, her true self. "You're right," she said. "Funny thing is, I've known it all along. That's my personality. I hate sex. Or this kind of sex. I hate the men who come here and demand it. I only do it for the money and that's why I'm no good at it." She stared hard at me. "And you really think these Neanderthals can sense that?"

"I did. So why shouldn't they?"

She smiled the first real smile I'd seen. She really was very attractive when she did that — and it was genuine. "You're no Neanderthal, Riley. Believe me. The trouble is, I hate hurting people really. I won't even eat meat. Nor fish."

"You could at least try," I suggested.

"I did. I ate meat until I was ..."

"No! You could try the other thing — SM."

She laughed. She was even more attractive then. "It's not on the menu here."

"Then go where it is. There must be somewhere. This is America, right? Where no demand goes unmet for more than twenty-four hours?"

She was seriously considering it. She returned her attention to the little cola pool while she spoke. "Know what?" she told it. "Know what I'd like to do? I'd like to finish up here — this Saturday, say — the management wouldn't exactly break its heart, I think — and take two weeks' vacation up in Utah. Bryce Canyon or one of those parks. And then look for one of those specialist houses. You wouldn't care to join me for a couple of weeks, would you, Riley? No strings."

Did I ever say I love American girls? And need I explain it now?

I was trying to think of some witty way of accepting this amiable offer but she must have thought I was stalling. "After all, what's two weeks?" she added. "And if it doesn't work out ..."

"If it doesn't work out, well, I don't even know your real name, right?"

She rolled her eyes heavenward. "Gertrude," she murmured. "Gertie. Hear enough?"

"Okay," I said. "It's a deal. You're right. I need a vacation."

"Not from sex, I hope."

"There's no such thing as a vacation from sex — or heartbeats."

She looked at me in amazement. "What was with that old Eartha Kitt song, 'An Englishman Needs Time'?" Then, glancing at me shrewdly, "You know anything about this SM stuff? You into that?"

"I tried it once," I said. "In Paris, France. I was alone there one Christmas and I saw this ad for a *dominatrice très sévère*. So I called her up and made a date ..." I lost myself in the reverie.

"And?" she prompted eagerly.

"I'll tell you all about it," I promised. "It'll be my bedtime story in our first motel."

"Wowee!" She gripped my arm and hugged me deliriously.

She was going to be fun to be with. Sometimes you have to make decisions like that. Sum up a person's character and say yes or no.

Another line-up was called. Her happiness carried over and the man picked her without hesitation. As she passed me, leading him to her bedroom, I raised both hands in a gesture that, I hope, said, 'See!'

Desirée's customer returned soon after that, looking about six inches shorter and a year or two older. "Not pickin', pal?" he grunted at me as he sat at the bar to await his friend.

"I picked. I'm recovering still," I told him.

He grinned. "Know whatcha mean. If you ever come back, that Desirée is some hot bitch lemme tellya."

He ordered one of those undrinkable American beers but when he saw his friend approaching he downed it in a few deep gulps, burped several times, and swept the poor fellow out by the door, saying, "C'mon, we're late enough already."

Desirée herself appeared soon after.

"That man just paid you the highest compliment," I told her as she sat at the bar. "What's your drink?"

"Coke," she replied, letting out an exhausted sigh. "What was that?"

"The cowboy — the guy you were just with ..."

"Cowboy!" she sneered. "He manages a floor of one-arm bandits in Reno — and I had to tell him three times to go easy. He was *hurting.*"

I understood the man's choice of the word 'bitch' then. "He said you were the hottest little kitten," I told her.

"Oh, good!" She bucked up a lot at that.

"Apart from him, how's it going generally?" I asked her.

Now her face split in the broadest grin. "Pretty good. I've done" — her eyes rolled upward and vanished for a moment — "seventeen tricks now. Not bad for a beginner, huh? Including six Japanese. They fly them in, you know."

"From Tokyo?"

"No! From Reno. It's a ten-minute complimentary flight." She glanced at the clock, which was coming up to eight. "The first one's due any minute now. 'Course, you were here earlier yesterday. Anyway, the plane just hops back and forth all the time, bringing anyone who wants to come, ha ha. And the first one brought a planeload of Japs, and one of them picked me, and then there were eight more on the next flight, and they must have spoken to the first lot, especially the one who picked me, because five of them insisted on me after that. So I just lay in my room for about three hours while they came and did business, one after the other. And you know what it was?"

"What?"

"You should be proud of me — your star pupil. Remember teaching me about anal?"

I did. And very pleasurably, too.

"Well that's what they like, those little guys. Because it's tighter round the back, see? And they've got dicks to match their stature. We all prefer them, actually. God, I've seen enough of big dicks, let me tell you!"

"You've had your fill of them, eh?"

"That's not considered funny in these parts, Riley. That last guy *hurt*. So we like the Japs, even if they all want it round the back. All except this one guy." She looked all about her, as if she really shouldn't be telling me this, and went on, "He brought out this ... this ... I dunno what you'd call it. A condom, I guess, except it had walls about a quarter-inch thick. Honest, I had a fight not to laugh. There was this big rubber dick — milk-white column, blood-red knob, like in those dirty Japanese woodcuts."

"Erotic Japanese woodcuts."

"Okay. Anyway, being hollow, it had this vagina inside. Not just a hole but a vagina with a soft, stretchy lining. And a proper cunt all modelled round the bottom, with labia and all. It's made of silicone or something. And there's fluid between it and the stiff-dick part. And the top bit of the dick, just by the knob, is made of this stretchy, telescopic stuff. So when he pokes into the vagina part, the dick gets stiffer up there and sort of grows an inch or so into me! Talk about weird! Also, he strapped it on him kinda loose, so that when he thrust back and forth six or seven inches it went the full way in and out of me — my vagina, of course — he used the proper hole. Anyway, although it went all the way in and out of me, he only went three or four inches in and out of *it*. Because of the loose straps, see? But four inches was like the full length of his hardon. Get the picture?"

"Vividly," I assured her. "Why did he bother? Having you there at all, I mean?"

"Well, of course, I asked him the same, only a mite more tactfully. 'Honourable Japanese man cannot pleasure himself without also pleasuring lady,' he said."

"And did he?"

She looked at me scornfully. "What do you think!"

"It's more a question of what *he* thought."

"Oh, *he* thought he did." She laughed. Then, serious again, she touched my arm and said, "No, but I'm more grateful to you than I can say, Riley. I don't think I gave you anything like a thousand dollars' worth of pussy last weekend — not now I've seen what a girl has to do here for ..."

I stayed her with a finger to her lips. "I'm the judge of that," I told her.

"I'm going to pay you back five hundred dollars at least," she promised.

"I didn't teach you anything," I told her. "If I could just pass on what Ebony did to me yesterday and tonight ... d'you know, I haven't even been *inside* her yet!"

She stared open-mouthed at me.

"And yet — saving your presence — she's done things to me with her hands, yesterday, and mouth, tonight, that almost took me apart."

Her eyes gleamed at that.

"I wonder ..." I said speculatively.

"What?"

"I'm coming back again on Thursday night, for a full, gourmet session with her. What if I made it a twosome — her and you. I wonder would she show you all those tricks. No, they're more than tricks. They're skills. Arts, even. Yes — she's an artist, all right."

She thought it over. "You'd never deceive her into doing it. You'd have to be straight with her. And even then she mightn't. Perhaps if I offered her my share of the fee?"

"I'll leave it to you," I said. "She'd do it for me but maybe not too willingly. Approach her right and she might be glad to help you."

When I parked my car outside the Mustang at nine o'clock that Thursday evening, my trembling fingers could hardly grasp the steering wheel, which was, in any case, all slippery with my sweat. And my erection actually *hurt* as I waddled up the path to that adorable door, beyond which lay so many paths to paradise that a man could die for choice. But my choice was Ebony, of course, sweet and willing as ever. I glanced at Estelle but she just shook her head, almost imperceptibly. I gathered there was no deal on a twosome and it might be best not even to mention it. So I didn't.

"Poor Limey," Ebony said as she closed the door of her room behind us.

It was *her* room, too. The Mustang girls slept and worked in the same room. I often wondered what it must be like for one of those girls — knowing the attitudes that most of them have to men and sex — to settle down to sleep in a room where anything up to a dozen men grunted and thrust their way to paradise inside her that day, and then to sleep, and then to wake up and look around and remember — 'Oh yes, this is where it's going to happen all over again today!' How does she get up? How does she put even one leg out of the bed? And how do they manage to smile and joke and generally be so pleasant, the way they do? They are true heroines, every one.

Anyway, Ebony said, "Poor Limey! Yo' ain't jess got two trick eyes. Yo' got a third trick eye down there, right in the end of yo' dick. Ain' that a fact?"

And when I ruefully admitted it was so she yanked the pants off me and said, "Why, it's lookin' at me right now, thinkin' tonight's the night, man! Tonight I gets me a taste of hot, black pussy! Y'all had a taste of black pussy afore, I reckon?"

"Mm hmm," I said.

"Mm hmm?" she mimicked. "Yo' sound like yo' didn' think too much of it."

"Well now," I replied, "let me just tell you I thought a *lot* of it at the time. But that was before I came through that door there last Monday evening. And let me tell you this, too — in this room I've known black *fingers* that were better than the best black pussy I ever had. And the best white pussy, too. And yellow pussy and brown pussy and green pussy and … you name it."

"Yeah, man!" Her beautiful, sexy grin almost split her face and she looked like she was flashing a whole white cliff full of six dozen teeth at me. "Mah fingerzzz!"

At which she reached slyly out and coiled them round my prick, giving it one of her special squeezes. We were both naked by now, sitting side by side on the edge of the bed.

"Gonna fly me tonight, huh?" She waggled it around. "Gonna put this joystick in my sweet li'l cockpit and flaah me to the moon, huh?" She pulled back on the joystick.

"Yes, ma'am!" I just leaned right back on my elbows and luxuriated in her skill.

"Gonna flaah me down, down, down into one o' them sinks of iniquity the preachers love. All them naughty places!" And she thrust the joystick hard forward, making me sit upright again.

"Yes, ma'am!"

"Gonna do lots o' naughty things in lots o' naughty little places, ain't we? ... Gonna flaah me on mah side? ... Gonna flaah me on mah *othuh* side? Gonna land me on mah back and on *fayah!* And gonna put out mah fayah wiv a flood like yo' never shot befoh. Ain't that so?" Each of these 'questions' was accompanied by appropriate movements of the joystick.

And to each I replied an ecstatic, "Yes, ma'am ... yes, ma'am ... yes, ma'am!"

She worked this erotic catechism up to a glowing finale, at which point she let go her grip. Blood rushed into my erection, twitching it into life as she leaped on the bed, landing on all fours with her working parts gleaming moist and pouting pink, almost in my face. "Feed her, Limey!" she cried. "Feed her yo' gristle like yo' never put it to no chick befoh. Ride me to the stars!"

Well, of course, after that build-up, the closing of her soft, warm, supple vagina around my tool was a sensation quite out of this world. It's a beautiful moment in any session with a girl but Ebony turned it into something far beyond even that.

And I think, too, that the way I had built up to it over the whole of that week had turned me into a kind of challenge for her. I'd asked her to demonstrate on me how she'd started by doing hand jobs and had become the best fricatrice on the block; then how she'd graduated to blow jobs, and had become the best at that game, too. So now she just had to show me how superb she was at the nicest game of all.

And did she ever!

I don't mean she ran through a whole Kama Sutra of positions. But even in the most common ones — the doggy ride, and even the good old missionary position — she managed subtle little variations of posture or rhythm that made it seem quite new — especially when she flexed and squeezed with those vaginal muscles that some girls can control at will. She caught the rhythm not just of every thrust but of every withdrawal, too, responding with some little counter of her own that was its perfect compliment.

And, greatest of all, she showed no sign of sexual pleasure in herself — no sighs, no little palpitations, no moans. She just lay there alert, watching me with those gleaming eyes in her glossy black face, responding with the speed of a cat, and making it clear with every gesture that this was *my* party. The sex was mine and *her* sex was mine. She was a skilled and perfect pander to *my* smallest pleasure — the way a sporting girl ought to be.

Then, toward the end — and this was the cleverest touch on her part — she started giving out little gasps of surprise. And I mean little. A catch of her breath. A little puff, as if she were blowing a tiny feather off my shoulder. The suggestion it conveyed, almost subliminally, was that I was doing something right — very right. I was getting under her professional armour and startling her into a genuine sexual response. Of course, I don't believe it for a moment — not here in the cool of my memory. But at the time … well, that was a different matter.

She timed it perfectly, too, rising to a little crescendo of surprises just as my buttocks tightened like iron and my pelvis strained to pack every last millimetre of gristle inside her — then, in that magical moment just before the first great gusher of juice gave me a near-death experience, she let out her breath in one long sigh of ecstasy and I felt her vagina clench tight around me, turning my climax into a spermspouting battle. My tool felt like some hydraulic machine rammed tight into some cervice, injecting into its depths against huge resistance, which the actual force of each squirt caused to fall away.

It's a rare orgasm, one in a thousand, when mind and body are so united, especially with sporting girls. A good one will give you all the time you need but even so, you know she's impatient to see the back of you and light up her shingle for the next man. She may not show it, not by the flicker of an eyelid, but that doesn't stop you from knowing it's there in her thoughts. So, no matter how mind-blowing the orgasm you have with her, some little part of your brain is aloof from it all, watching her and waiting for one little sign of impatience. And that's what Ebony managed to overcome with me — she put that vigilant little watchman to sleep, which let me surrender totally to the sensation.

I wish a grand orgasm meant one would be free of that demanding tyrant down there. But it doesn't. An indifferent session with an indifferent sporting girl can free me for as long as a week — understandably, you may say, except that equally ho-hum sessions have seen me walk a hundred yards and up the very next steps that led to a room with a light in the window saying MODEL. And I've enjoyed total-relief sessions like that with Ebony and, equally, gone a week before desire returned. And that, too, would be understand-able, you may say — except that equally intense enjoyment has found me weak and trembling next day, with the little tyrant down there hoisting himself erect three times an hour and shrieking (in blood and nervous energy, not words), "Get me some! Get me some!" until I've been driven out to relieve him yet again. There's just no telling.

And there was no telling that night, either, as I stepped into the shower with Ebony at the Mustang. It felt as if I'd be going a week without wanting more. But when she picked up the shower handset and turned it to its most stinging spray and started training it on that particular organ ... well, as she said a moment later, "It looks like this fellah's got one mo' shot in his locker!"

She was still creamy and well lubricated down there and, as I slipped inside her once again, she murmured in the most tender, loving tones, "Cost'ya 'nuthah fifteh bucks, man."

A humorum encounter in Meard Street

These casual memoirs of a decade and more of devoted
cunny-hunting in the flesh warrens of the world
inevitably concentrate on the unusual, the outstanding,
the memorable. But behind each of those encounters,
if I were writing a true chronicle, I should have to
record a dozen of those ho-hum sessions I mentioned
just now for each of the more memorable ones. A
couple of dozen, in fact. So, just for the record, they
tend to go like this:

It's midafternoon on a sunny summer day. I'm
walking along Meard Street in Soho. This is back in
the days when all those houses on the north side are
sporting girls' cribs and the one at the eastern end is a
brothel with the sign GIRLS GIRLS GIRLS scrawled on
the window. Two girls, usually stoned, sit in the windows
there, beckoning men in. I pass them by and look for
one of the freelance 'models.'

I find her sitting out on her windowsill, one floor up,
about halfway down the street — a petite blonde with
short, curly hair. She's wearing a thin, floral-patterned
dressing gown. Her legs are stretched along the sill
and she's resting her back against the brick reveal. She
has her eyes closed and her face to the sun. If she falls
asleep, she'll slide off and break her neck. It's hot. All
the girls in London, not just the pros, are in skimpy
clothing. They all relish the power of sexual attraction
— also how they can double it by saying no, push off,
get lost. And I'm going quietly berserk down here,
looking up at one girl who isn't going to say no.

She stirs in her sunny dream and the dressing gown falls away to reveal a few inches of the underside of her right thigh. My hand could be there. My lips, too. The thought decides me.

Rosie, says the little ticket above the bell push. But it said the same two months ago, when 'Rosie' was black, and last summer, too, when she was a tall brunette. My erection cranks up a few more degrees of stiffness as I push the button, remembering happy times in that room up there. A buzzer blows a muted raspberry above me. A short leg in high heels shows briefly above as she scrambles to get back indoors. My tool feels stiff enough to snap right off by the time I get to her door. She pulls it open as I approach. Her nostrils flare and her tight-pressed lips twitch as she stifles a yawn. She has no maid or minder.

She sums me up in half a second, sees no difficulty, stands back to let me in. Her face is rather plain but her body is good — the thin cotton dressing gown, now tied tight around her waist, conceals nothing important.

She hands me a card and goes over to the window to draw the curtains. The card says: "Massage. Hand job. Blow job. Straight sex. Short time. Longer time. Positions. Anal. Dominance. Fantasies." There are no prices.

"Well?" she says, looking at the card, holding out her hand for it.

"Straight sex," I say. Why does my voice shiver still, after so many hundred sessions like this? Why is it still so compulsively exciting? "Thirty minutes. Various positions but nothing athletic. It's too hot. Isn't it hot?"

"Thirty quid," she says, holding out her hand.

I count it out and give it her. "The name's Riley," I say.

She puts the money in her handbag and she puts the handbag back in a drawer. She slips off her dressing gown. She's wearing nothing but her shoes and a watch. Her body *is* good — high breasts with big, soft nipples, trim waist, curvaceous bottom, lean thighs. She drops the gown on the chair beside the bed and sits on the towel there, elbows on knees. She checks the time on her watch and then just stares into space. I hang my jacket over another chair. Then my shirt. "I guess you're busy this weather," I say.

"Bit more than usual," she agrees.

Carefully I drape my trousers over shirt and jacket. My tool is thrusting my briefs out like a tent on its side and I have to lift the waistband right up to get it over my knob. She doesn't look at it.

"The heat gets this fellow feeling pretty desperate," I say as I hop on alternate legs to take off my socks.

"Uh huh," she says to the floor mat.

I waddle over and put it near her face. "Say hallo to my best friend," I tell her.

"Hallo." She reaches out and gives it a few gentle squeezes. Skilled ones, too. She knows what she's doing and what effect she's having on me.

"He's a good friend to you, too," I point out. "Without him you wouldn't be thirty quid richer than you were five minutes ago."

"He's good and stiff," she says, staring in the right direction but not, I think, actually looking at it. "About ready to pop inside. How d'you want me first?"

Oh, Rosie! I could tell you the answer to that! But I won't because it's quite clear that you think your part in this little contract begins and ends with your making yourself available to me without protest. In fact, without any expression of feeling at all, real or simulated.

"Kneeling here at the bedside," I reply.

She turns round and kneels on the bed. I'm about to protest when I see she's just reaching across it for three little scatter cushions. Coincidentally she gives me an eyeful of the two fat lips that guard the portals of paradise, red and engorged with chronic wear and tear. Other girls would wag their tails a little at this point and grin back at me over the shoulder and make some provocative comment and even pretend they were hot for it, too. But not Rosie.

Rosie just grabs the cushions, drops them beside the bed, picks up a finger of cream from an open pot beside the bed, kneels on two of the cushions with her thighs apart, and says, "Okay."

As I kneel down behind her on the other cushion I see her finger come stealing between the upside-down vee of her thighs and smear the cream into her crevice.

I kneel there a moment, relishing the sight of my swollen red knob, throbbing to the thump-thump-thump of my heart, only millimetres from those swollen red lips. Other girls would give another delicious little wriggle at this point and, maybe, a little squeal of anticipatory delight. Not Rosie. Rosie checks her watch again and remains available.

I grab my tool low down and push its knob just an inch or so into her cranny. Then I begin to move it slowly up and down, picking up her lubricant.

Rosie, now able to guess the level at which I'm going to penetrate her, pulls a pillow under her belly. And remains available.

Well, with or without cooperation, that idyllic moment when your knob glides up and down between a sporting girl's labia, feeling every little hair and wrinkle, remains magical, unique, compelling. And when you slither it inside — slowly, slowly, slowly … wow!

The fact is, the tyrant down below isn't too fussy about the personality of the girl who owns that crevice, nor her acting ability, nor anything else at that high level. 'Groove not grooviness' is his motto. As long as he's being accommodated inside a hole that's warm, slick, alive, and yielding, he doesn't care. And, when the only commodity on offer *is* that same hole, then 'warm, slick, alive, and yielding' isn't a bad bundle to be getting along with. Rosie's hole has all of those qualities so it and my tyrant get along just fine.

As soon as I wriggle deep into her, in to the very hilt, she makes one small adjustment of her hips and holds herself there, not moving again, not sighing, not speaking … just being available.

"You're so soft and juicy!" I say.

"Good," she replies "Tell me when you want the next position."

So I enjoy several minutes of leisurely poking before I withdraw and take her gently by the hips, intending to turn her over.

"Don't paw me, tell me," she says.

So I have to say it. "I'd like you on your back, across the bed, feet on the floor, thighs wide apart."

She picks up the cushions and throws them back where she got them. Then she assumes the required position and stares at the ceiling. The tyrant doesn't care. With his one red eye he stares at wide-open pussy and implores me to get him in there. As if in collusion with him, Rosie slips a hand down, spreads her labia between index and middle fingers, and goes on counting the cracks in the ceiling.

I slide into her and luxuriate once again in the tight, juicy clench of her vagina. "You have a fabulous cunt," I tell her. "I go with a lot of girls and I can tell you — most of them would envy yours."

"That's nice," she says. And remains available, and available, and available …

I reach forward and caress her breasts. She just lies there and makes them available, too.

"Where are you from?" I ask.

"All over. Tell me when you want the next position."

And so it goes on for another twenty-odd minutes — not grisly minutes but not memorable ones either.

Such encounters are, as I say, more usual than the interesting and more personal ones I've tended to record in these memoirs. Maybe they are essential to the proper enjoyment of a full, rich sex life with the willing girls of the world. I mean, if you dine every single night in a restaurant with three Michelin stars, you'd soon lose all the finer points of your appreciation. I haven't proved that, mind, but if someone's willing to put up the money, I'm willing to give it a try. I guess you'd need the odd trip to the Burger King and Happy Eater to fill out the supreme experience.

And that's what girls like Rosie are — the Gammon Queens and Happy Muff-divers of the sex-sporting world. I'll tell you a little trick I've tried with them. It doesn't always work. In fact, it doesn't often work, but when it does — about one time in five — it's quite amusing.

Most sporting girls avoid orgasms by faking them —
that's well known. By concentrating everything on the
performance they close their minds off to what's
actually happening down below. So what I do is this.
Actually, I tried it on Rosie that day, now that I come
to think of it — and it worked, too.

I postponed my spermspouting until she drew breath
to tell me time was up. I could tell that by the way she
kept checking her watch. Then she wasn't going to let
me soak it, even though she could feel it, still stiff as a
ramrod, inside her. So when she started trying to
shuck me off, I said, "Hold on, pet. I'm going to give
you another thirty for a second go — another half
hour. Okay?"

She sighed and lay back and let me soak it properly.
It was the first time she'd looked at my face since that
half-second glance at me, right at the beginning. Then
I withdrew, paid her the thirty quid, and told her I
wanted her to lie on her front, fully stretched, bum in
the air, while I poked her from behind.

As soon as I was deliciously notched inside her once
more, I put my lips close to her ear and murmured,
hypnotically, "Now I'm just going to poke you in this
one position — nice and slowly — for the next half
hour. And all I ask of you is not to move. Don't wriggle.
Don't sigh. Don't gasp or catch your breath. Above all,
don't fake any kind of response. Go to sleep if you
want as long as you stay absolutely still, okay?"

Of course, I was describing exactly the way she had
behaved during the previous thirty minutes. But —
human nature — it's one thing to carry on like that
when your client wants you to behave quite differently.
You're showing him that his money can buy your

vagina but nothing else is included. And if you're really determined to show him, like Rosie, you don't even bother to fake an orgasm, either. It's quite a different thing to behave like that because your client has paid you to and now *commands* it! I could feel how it riled her to be commanded not to fake an orgasm when, only five minutes earlier, she had most pointedly refused to do so.

She just stiffened underneath me and fumed with anger.

After a while I murmured, "That's good. You're doing it perfectly." And her anger rose again. And then, from time to time, I'd throw in something else, equally complimentary. Like, "I don't do this with many girls, you know. Most of them aren't equipped like you. You were born with one of those vaginas that feels excitingly, subtly different with each new thrust." And, "You belong among the stars, Rosie. You're one of the all-time greats." Or, "You're the Rolls-Royce of your noble profession."

All of which stoked her anger to close on fever pitch. At one point, near the end, she was actually shivering with it. I stopped at once and uttered a cautionary, "Uh-huh!" — which, of course, made her more furious yet. So, what with all these stirred-up emotions and being forced to concentrate for thirty minutes on a rod of good firm gristle slipping inexorably, monotonously, in and out of her vagina ... the inevitable happened. I wouldn't say she had a full-blown orgasm, mind, but she was down there in the foothills, giving out little gasps of surprise and struggling hard not to, catching her breath while trying to force herself to breathe regularly, shivering with the effort of trying not to go

all the way and the double effort of not shivering at all!
And I had the delightful reward of observing two small
strawberry patches flush their colour into the skin of
her back — something she could do nothing to control.

Who was she really — young Rosie? What was her
real name? What thoughts flitted through her mind as
her vacant eyes stared out toward Wardour Street
while she waited for tricks, or up at the ceiling while
she gently, uncomplainingly let them do what they'd
paid for? When the bell startled her from those reveries
and she heard the tread of an advancing male upon
her stair, what hopes, what fears passed through her
mind? Her very passivity forced these questions upon
me — and denied me any chance of an answer.

But maybe the last laugh is on me because, although
I set out to record an example of a humdrum, *un*-
memorable session with the run-of-the-mill sporting
girl — the sort of experience that makes the gourmet
session so memorable for me — I find that, between
us, Rosie and I managed to make something memorable of it, after all! It was, indeed, a happy hour in
Meard Street in the good old days.

Courtenay of Leamington Spa

I was doing some work at Coventry University and staying in Leamington Spa. It was going to last a week or two so I was in no rush to seek out the best of the local talent on the very first night. What I usually do in situations like that is enjoy a leisurely dinner before walking around the town and seeing what's on offer, chatting up a few girls, maybe hiring one but more usually going back the following night after a thorough survey. But then I found this escort agency's card in the Gideon Bible. Someone had scribbled the names Debbie, Laura, and Courtenay on the back, plus the comment, *Phworr!*

Never being one to look a gift horse in the mouth, I got an outside line and dialled the number. A silken-voiced girl answered with the name of the agency. I asked how bookings were going and she wanted to know how I'd got their number.

"Mister Gideon gave it me," I told her, giving the name of my hotel and room number. "He lives in one of the drawers beside the bed."

· She cottoned on fast and asked me to wait — while she searched her records for the last client that Debbie or Laura or Courtenay pleasured in that room. It must have checked out because she came back with, "That's fine. We can arrange a dinner with one of our young ladies but please understand that any other arrangement is between you and her."

"Mister Gideon was very taken with Debbie, Laura, and Courtenay — but not all at once, I trust."

She didn't say yes, she didn't say no, she said, "Laura's on holiday. Debbie already has a date. But Courtenay, now ...? Yes! Courtenay *is* available."

I should have paid more attention to the hint of suppressed mirth behind her tone. "What's she like?" I asked.

"Good question, sir! No, joking apart, she's a platinum blonde, twenty-two, medium height, and slim. Well, fairly slim."

"Specifically?"

Rustle of paper. "It says here that she's five-six tall, bust thirty-five, waist twenty-two, hips thirty-six. She could be with you by half-past-seven?" She made it a question.

I said I could just about wait that long.

She was there at half-past-seven on the dot, dressed as if to take the floor on Come Dancing — off-the-shoulder ballgown in fluffy tulle, gauze stole, jutting breasts, near-shoulder-length black lace gloves with no fingers — that is, with her own fingers free. Her fine platinum hair was combed back into a strict ponytail and then encased in lacquer. The ponytail was tied with a black velvet bow and she had a choker of the same material around her neck.

But if she was twenty-two, I was sixty. I had a queasy feeling she was, in fact, barely legal. Still, if the hotel had raised no objections to her previous sessions here, who was I to quibble?

I doubt her waist was twenty-two, either, especially once she shed the corset she was obviously wearing, but I wouldn't quibble about that, either. A pneumatic inch or two never did a girl any harm; I cannot understand the allure of those anorexic catwalk freaks.

She ordered a Manhattan and then offered the barman the choice of adding more gin or mixing up a new one, with less vermouth in it this time. Their eyes locked and the steely glint in hers won.

The waiter followed us to an alcove with our drinks.

"Mud in your eye," she said, taking a good slug of hers. Then: "Let's clear one thing up, Riley — to save a good deal of hassle later. I *do* — just in case you were wondering."

"I thought that was implicit, Courtenay, in what the agency girl told me."

"No," she said almost belligerently. "She told you the arrangement with us escorts is for dinner only. Anything else is between you and me. I'm taking a chance on you. I usually tell my gentlemen I *don't* do it, especially if I feel the *least* bit dodgy about them. Maybe I relent later and say okay, if I decide they're cool, after all."

She had a peculiar accent — refayned with a touch of Brum. Her diction — indeed, her whole manner — was precise and determined. I couldn't imagine anyone talking her into or out of anything she'd set her mind on.

"Which brings us to the matter of my fee," she said.

"Ah, yes?"

"I'm expensive, but let me tell you what you'll be getting. We'll go in to dinner at about eight and finish at nine. During that time we'll have conversations on a wide variety of subjects. I'm well informed on most things and gentlemen tell me I'm a pretty good conversationalist, too. My special interests are financial."

I prepared to laugh but she wasn't joking. Boy, she was *not* joking, but I didn't know that then.

"The one thing I draw the line at is any smutty talk at dinner because I'm also, as you can see, a very refined young lady. Anyway, if you skip the dessert — I never take dessert myself — we can be upstairs in your room by nine. And then you've got until midnight to have your wicked way with me."

"And, if I may ask, how much ..."

She cut me short again. "There are very few things I draw the line at, Riley. And I also expect to enjoy it as much as you do, if not more. I don't mind a little pain, as long as it's kept within bounds, either giving it or taking it. If it's giving it, I can dish out all you want. If it's taking it, I enjoy a little spanking with the bare hand on my naked bottom. I draw the line at bondage for me when working solo, for obvious reasons."

"And, if it's not too mercenary to ask ..."

"We can get up to a lot of lascivious tricks in three hours. And you can have as many goes as you like. So, all in all, taking everything into consideration, three hundred and fifty pounds is not unreasonable."

I just gaped at her.

"I know," she said sympathetically. "A lot of gentlemen are shocked by that at the beginning. A lot of them complain. But only before. Never after. I've never had a complaint after a gentleman has had his wicked way with me."

"No, no," a little devil made me say. "I'm amazed — considering all those tricks you've just promised — I'm flabbergasted that you *only* charge three-fifty for it. I expected more like five hundred. In New York, of course, I'm used to forking out even more than that."

Her eyes flashed angrily. She was furious with herself for having pitched it so low. "Well," she said, recovering with admirable speed. "I have been given tips well above that basic level, of course. My feeling is that I should set my fees at rock-bottom and then leave it to the gentleman to give me my true worth."

"After he's had his wicked way with you?"

"Exactly!" She leaned forward, spilling her big, soft breasts onto my arm. "So really, all I'm saying to you is that it can be *your* usual fee, right? *If* you think I'm worth it — which you will, I promise."

"You," I told her, "are a remarkable young lady, Courtenay. May I ask your true age? I'm sure you're young enough for that to be more of a compliment than an affront."

She smirked. "I'm sweet nineteen, actually. The agency has to say we're all over twenty-one. And most of us are, of course. Some of them are quite jaded, but not me. I'm still very fresh."

"May I ask how long ..."

"Two years," she said complacently.

We finished our cocktails and went directly in to dinner. She ordered oysters and steak, the one raw the other almost raw.

The 'wide variety of topics' on which she could discourse intelligently included: pensions planning, offshore tax havens, high-yield versus high-growth funds; the comparative advantages and drawbacks of BUPA, PPP, and the HSA; and the benefits of paying income tax on income from her kind of work. I tried her on music (any kind), literature, fashion, *my* work ... no joy. Holidays produced a brief lecture on avoiding raw food abroad, but that was it. Somehow the talk always crept back to pensions planning, offshore tax havens ...

She wanted to know all about my investments, too. Not so much the actual figures but questions like how did I decide when to buy and, even more difficult, when to sell? And did I think a market-driven system, like London's, was better than an order-driven system, like most of the other stock exchanges in the world? Her manner of eating was much more fascinating than her talk.

If you've ever seen small carnivores at feeding time in the zoo — a mink devouring raw fish, say — you'll know how she ate. Actually, you'll have a perfect picture of it if you ever saw *Barbarella* and can remember that scene in which a small posse of little-girl dolls with razor teeth crowd Jane Fonda in her nymphet days and bite little chunks out of her legs. (And all the men in the movie theatre say, 'They didn't need to build those little robots. *I'd* have done that for nothing!') She didn't eat like that all the time, thank heavens; but whenever she mentioned some particularly slick financial deal she'd pulled, she smiled while continuing to chew. She smiled with open lips, ear to ear, which revealed little bits of bloody meat being crushed between her razor-sharp molars. Moments later her mouth would be closed again and she was eating like a prim young angel — almost apologizing for the need to do something so distressingly physical.

After parading her own astuteness she turned the spotlight on *my* pensions. I fell several miles in her estimation, I'm sure, when I told her that my way of dealing with my pension had been to mug it all up intensively for a month — become the world's leading expert on the topic — make my decision, buy the damn thing, set it all up, and then forget about it until the time came to retire. She thought that was dreadful. She'd already taken out five one-shot plans, which would mature at different stages of her life, and she was always on the lookout for more.

"All right," she said. "You claim you're not married just at the moment, but you will be one day. What's your wife going to think of you with an attitude like that? What sort of woman's even going to *look* at you without a continuously developing pension spread?"

I tried to lighten the conversation by muttering I'd be more worried by middle-age spread by then, but she'd have none of it. "A generous pension is the noblest way in which a man can tell a woman he loves her. Take my tip. If you want a wide choice of available females when you come to settle down, forget the bouquets of flowers, give them a bouquet of annuities and maturing investments."

I asked her what she was hoping to do with her life. Wasn't she afraid she had already weighed it down with so much financial baggage that it would never take off?

She looked all around to make sure no one was eavesdropping (for she was about to break her own no-smut rule) and then, almost whispering, she explained: "I'm going to keep this up until my mid-twenties," she said. "I've read somewhere that women don't get to enjoy you-know-what — n-o-o-k-y — fully until they're in their thirties. But I think that's talking about real, loving s-e-x with just one man. The sort of s-e-x *I* enjoy now is" — and now, for the next three words, she did lower her voice to a whisper — "promiscuous and kinky." She grinned naughtily. "I think I'm at the perfect age to enjoy that sort of s-e-x and I hope it'll go on until I'm twenty-five. By which time, with careful investment, and a good spread of risks, I'll have getting on for three quarters of a million in assets. Not all liquid, of course. If the world economy picks up and inflation stays low, it could be over a million." She grinned. "And I'll have had all that fun, too!"

"And then?" I asked.

"I'll get married, of course."

"To someone with a good spread of maturing assets?"

"Right! I've already had offers, good ones, too. But it's much too soon. When I hang up my French knickers, I'll marry a nice, sweet, rich businessman in his fifties and give him the longest, happiest retirement he could ever wish for."

"Not to say the happiest death!"

"Yes," she agreed seriously. "It would be an excellent way for a man to go, don't you think?"

We skipped the pudding — or 'dessert' as she insisted on calling it.

On our way out of the dining room she returned to her earlier theme, saying she really was surprised at me for being so lax about my pension. And as for my stock-market system, whereby I bought a whole basket of shares every June and sold them regardless in January — she thought that was dreadful. I pointed out that I usually made a couple of thousand that way, but she said it went against the whole spirit of the thing, which was to outsmart all the other punters.

But the moment we were in my room, the most amazing transformation came over Miss Courtenay. I don't know what arrangement of buttons, poppers, zips, or what-have-you held up her dress but they were no match for her deft fingers. In a flash she stood before me, pink, curvaceous, and ostentatiously feminine. The pink was mostly corset. It did nothing to hold up her big soft breasts — which was okay because they needed nothing to hold them up, beyond their own firm fruitiness. It also did nothing to hide her pale muff and the the two fat rolls of her labia. Nor did the pink French knickers she was going to hang up one day; for they parted in an upside-down vee with its apex just below her navel and its lower edges sewn to what you could call the shortest, laciest pants at the tops of her thighs — two-inch strips of broderie anglaise. And in case anyone doubted she had hips, they protruded naked as well, as raunchy and titillating as any I remember.

"Come on," she said breathlessly. "All that talk has got me dying for a poke. Give us a quick one and then we can get down to some serious sex." She could say the word now.

By way of preparation she raised her right hand to her mouth, still wearing the arm-length but fingerless black glove, and carefully extruded about 5ml of glutinous saliva onto the tip of her middle finger. This she then equally carefully ferried to her cleft, where she rubbed it in with a sticky lasciviousness and gave out a huge sigh of satisfaction. Then she lay right back and spread her thighs wide. Even that did not part her labia, which now gleamed like the white pastry of two glazed but uncooked croissants.

I have never, before or since, been so simultaneously excited and repelled by any girl. Even if her portrayal of a sex-glutton was all part of the act, it made no difference. It was a consummately convincing act. I could not get out of my mind that image of her mouth — which, in memory, seemed to be all incisors — rending raw steak with such delicate savagery. It was all part of the same whole. On the outside she was a prim, pompous, petty-minded little bourgeoise, all the worse for being so young, so disgustingly self-satisfied; but lift the lid, shed the dress, spread the thighs, and she was revealed as a raw bundle of the most primitive urges, consumed by appetites that Gargantua himself would have been hard put to satisfy. What hope had I?

And yet what hope had I of escaping the attempt, either?

"That's right — no finesse!" she gasped as I lumbered, naked, on top of her. "Full throttle. Thrust away. Quick as you can."

I just fell inside her. A drunk with the world's smallest dick couldn't have missed. Those big, fat lips were made for steering the long and the short and the tall between them. And the moment I was inside her, a strange kind of suction seemed to take over. Some girls with small, narrow vaginas can make your tool feel like an intruding giant; but Courtenay's, which was a huge, soft, feather bed by comparison, somehow made mine feel expanded, enlarged, drawn out not just to twice its length but twice its thickness, too, as if — as I say — by suction of some kind.

I began to thrust away at once, pulling almost completely out of her with each stroke, so that just the tip of my knob stayed snug between those chunky, glistening labia, and then thrusting in again with a force that would have made any osteopath wince. The walls of her vagina, for all their softness, seemed to pluck at my tool on each withdrawal, clinging with a loving, lingering grip that blew my mind. It is hard at such moments not to believe in magic — that some kind of magical powers do not dwell in those few square inches of incredibly subtle flesh that make up a girl's vagina.

She writhed and gasped beneath me, lifting her Venus mound up to meet me as I went in; wriggling a little sideways as I went out. Every half-dozen thrusts she'd throw her legs up around me and beat a tattoo on my backside with her heels, giving out little girlish shrieks of pleasure at the way it got me even deeper inside her *and* jiggled about unpredictably. At those moments I could feel the tip of my knob against her cervix and the top of her love canal.

It didn't take too much of that treatment to get me spermspouting away. She felt it coming about half a minute before it happened and she abandoned herself to her own private *orgia* beneath me. It was a fairly massive outpouring, too, for, being rammed tight against the blind gullet of her, I could feel the hydraulic shock of each squirt as it slammed against those membranes. Then came that most delicious sensation of all — the feeling of your own hot milt as it oozes back down over your still twitching spermspouter, driven out by the massive swelling of your tool and the gripping spasms of her hole in their combined ecstasies.

There's always that moment of anxiety when you've finished a really fine poke, and there's time for more — lots more, in this case — and you *want* more, and you wonder if your best friend down there agrees. Usually, thank heavens, my libido and I see eye to eye — that is, I look down and there's his one eager eye staring right back at me, *badoing!* Ramrod stiff. Begging to be hidden somewhere warm and wet.

Sometimes he's even more eager than me. I'm tired. I've been overdoing it lately. I've already overdone it twice with this girl in the past hour. You'd think I deserve a bit of rest. But those six stiff inches of solid libido don't agree. *More! More!* they cry while I, with aching back and weary bones, slip him once more between the gates of paradise and bury him in the old magic.

At other times I cannot wait to get back on the old fork with this or that girl — gorgeous, young, and willing though she is — and *he* says, 'You want her? You've got her. But count me out!' And nothing will rouse him from his flaccid torpor. A hardoff, I call it. Such humiliating moments are rare but no doubt they will increase with age. Gather ye rosebuds while ye may — I'm sure Shakespeare was nursing a hardoff when he wrote that.

Anyway, the point is, you never know which one it's going to be. Especially with a girl like Courtenay, who half fascinates, half repels.

So I was as surprised as she to pull out of her and to feel my hardon go *thwack!* up against the taut skin of my tummy. She was delighted, too, though I was less certain.

"What a gorgeous fellow!" she exclaimed, pulling it down to make it go thwack again. "Hee hee! We mustn't waste it."

And before I knew what was what she had leaped out of bed and pulled my feet onto the floor, leaving me sitting on the edge of the mattress. Then, without waiting to explain, she pulled a chair up until it touched the bed about a foot to my left, and threw herself across my lap, bottom in the air, head resting on her folded arms on the chair.

"I'll bet you were angry with me just now," she said, "when I made you give me a quick poke like that. I'll bet you wanted to explore me all over … kiss me all over … lick me all over — things like that — and really work yourself up into a fine old shiver. Be honest now."

"Well …" I began hesitantly.

"No point in denying it," she said. "I'll bet you wanted to smack me quite hard, no?"

All the while she spoke she kept wriggling herself into ever more comfortable positions, arching her back, pouting her bottom up at me, and squirming until she got her Venus mound onto the top of my thigh so that every twitch of my muscle gave her a vibratory massage there.

I tried a couple of twitches and she let out little yelps of delight, saying, "Oh, you wicked man!"

When she said it for the second time she went on, "Still, you're not half as wicked as me — the thoughtless way I behaved. I really do deserve a smacking, don't you think? Quite a hard one you could try. I can't resist you in this position."

I gave her a half-hearted pat on the right cheek of her bottom.

"Go on," she said, as if I hadn't moved yet. "You can start any time."

The curious thing — well, curious to me, because I'd never gone in for any spanking before, never having been attracted to it, not even to the idea — was that even that mild smack gave me quite a powerful erotic thrill. Her pale, taut, girlish bottom, so smooth, so young, so defenceless, roused something inside me that I had never suspected was there. (It roused something on the outside of me, too, but I'd always known *that* was there.)

I'm sure it wasn't the first time it had happened to one of her partners. I saw her watching me in the mirror, smiling that smile people smile when they watch you discovering something they've set you up to discover. "Go on," she murmured, wriggling excitedly in anticipation.

I gave her one hard smack — well, it seemed hard to me — it certainly made the palm of my hand smart and it left its print on her round, white cheek. She explained to me after when, slightly ashamed of giving in to her demand, and even more ashamed at having given way to the lust her demand aroused in me, I tried to apologize. "There are lots more nerves in your hand than in anybody's bottom. Anyone who smacks someone's bottom with the hand and says, 'This will hurt me more than it hurts you,' is telling the absolute truth."

At the time, though, when the smack and her muffled squeal of joy were still ringing in my ears and the smart of it was stinging my hand, all she said was, "Again!" the way children do when you give them a ride to Mars or an extra hard push on the swing.

And that's what it was for her. An infantile regression into a violent but safely threatening stimulus. She could not enjoy sex unless it skirted the edge of danger every now and then. She asked for several more smacks, which I duly gave her. And then I noticed she was breathing in gasps, writhing slowly, eyes shut, mouth

open, saliva running, and there were angry red blotches
up and down her back — in short, she was close to a
climax. Fascinated, I slipped one hand down into her
furrow and, with the other, found her breasts where
they dangled freely in the space between my lap and
the chair she had placed so carefully. Her pussy was
wet-wet-wet and her nipples hard-hard-hard. When
the tip of my middle finger found the swollen bud of
her clitoris it was as if every ounce of power drained
out of her. She simply collapsed where she was and lay
there like a warm, wet cloth.

Men have died in the throes of orgasm. They have
collapsed. They have strained muscles that took weeks
to mend. All this I can understand. But I cannot imagine
a man lying as still and as drained of muscular power
as that. What a different thing it is, this *orgasm,* in us
and in them! If I'd had the gift to *see* it in her, I think
the whole of her body would have been aglow from
the top of her scalp to the tips of her fingers and toes.

Another difference is that when an insatiable young
thing like Courtenay gets going, the appetite merely
feeds upon itself. The orgasm does not satisfy, it merely
craves more.

I lifted my hand and said the word she had said a
dozen times before she collapsed like that — only I
made it a question: "Again?"

"No," she said, jumping up as bright as a button.
"Something new now." And she unpeeled the lower
half of her corset; I had not realized until then that it
was in two pieces, held together with Velcro. She
unpopped her suspenders and dropped them beside
the bed. "O-o-o-h!" she sighed, as she caressed the
newly revealed skin of her belly and rubbed her

knuckles into the small of her back. "Here, you can do this better than me."

I spent a minute or two proving it while she stretched and writhed and luxuriated in my caresses, which were sometimes fingertip gentle and sometimes fingernail fierce. Suddenly she said, "I want to be poked again. A different way. I've got an idea." And she crossed the room to where my dressing gown hung on a coathook beside the door. A moment later she returned bringing with her only the silken cord, which was of gold-coloured thread. "Tarrah!" she exclaimed, holding it so that a large gold tassel appeared to swing from each of her nipples. "Sex is best when you improvise, eh?"

I wondered what sort of improvisation was coming when the first thing she did was to tie one end of the cord to the left side of the chair back, at the top — that chair which seemed to feature in all her sex romps. Then she passed the loose end around her waist as she bent herself forward over the back of the chair. She spread her legs until her tummy was hard against its upper curve. "Now," she said, passing the cord once around the top bar of the chairback to her right so that, when drawn tight, it pinned her to the chair.

"Here," she said, flapping the tassel at me. "Take this and pull on it."

Of course, in coming close enough to do that I inevitably came close enough to get the tip of my erection — which was back at full power and ready to thrust for England — in between her inner labia, which blushed red and frilly between her pale, pouting outer lips, held apart by the wide spread of her thighs.

"Ooh!" she squealed. "You naughty boy! Who told you you could do that?"

"I see a mouth with ruby lips that spoke the words unto mine ear."

She gave out a low, dirty giggle. "I think they spoke to some organ much closer than your ear, Riley. Now what I want you to do next is pull the cord tighter and tighter and at the same time slowly push your joystick into my cockpit. Try it."

I did. I tugged at the cord and, as I watched it bite deeper and deeper into the flesh of her waist and the small of her back, I slowly eased myself right up inside her until, at last, my arms were trembling with exertion and my tool was rammed to the very hilt of me.

She let out one long, breathy moan and wriggled delightfully. "Again!" she whispered. "That is so absolutely fantastic. Don't you think it's fantastic?"

"Yes," I whispered while I still had the faculty of speech.

I let the cord relax at once but withdrew as slowly as I had gone in, while she used the freedom to wriggle her bottom in little darts, sometimes thrusting me out, sometimes trying to entice me back.

I lost count of the number of times we repeated this delicious manoeuvre — and losing count is rare with a sporting girl; even the good ones are so concerned to give value for money that they hasten you through every page in the Kama Sutra, not staying on any one thing for long. Then I had an inspiration. I realized I could wrap the cord several times around the palm of my hand, close my fist around it, and then a simple rocking motion on the top of the chair was enough to tighten and loosen it the way she liked. Then I stopped moving in and out of her but leaned right forward, over her, instead, and wriggled from side to side.

My hardon, levering against her pubic bone, pressed the sides of her vagina alternately, in time to the squeeze I could now apply through the cord with a simple tilt of my fist. But it was when I reached the other hand under her and began again to squeeze and tickle her nipples that she began another swift ascent to orgasm, uttering little cries of astonishment and catching her breath whenever the sensation proved especially thrilling. What she liked best of all, I discovered, was having my fingernails scratch as gently as possible on the outer sides of her nipples.

This time her orgasm was more muscular than the last. A great spasm passed down her, from her tethered waist to her tiptoe feet. Then at a moment when any man would have collapsed in erotic exhaustion, she, of course, sprang up again, saying, "This cord has given me another idea. D'you want to unzip my corset?"

"No," I said, leaping to a position in front of her. "I've got better things to do with my hands while yours are busy."

And while she fiddled with the hooks behind her, I caressed her breasts as gently as I possibly could with the tips of my fingers, starting with them lying flat on the smooth, soft skin and ending with all ten nails on the big pink areolæ of her nipples, which started her on a new frenzy.

"Wait! Wait!" she begged. "Save it until I tell you. You'll see."

The moment the last eye was unhooked she flung the corset aside and raced out of her stockings. But her adorable nakedness did not last long. One swift dive into her bag and it was covered by an even more adorable pair of harem pants — of gauze as fine as woven air, open right through the crotch, from waist-band to waistband, and with black floral silhouettes woven into the open seams around that divine opening. The waistband, also embroidered, was low around her hips, just level with the top of her beaver, and the bottoms were gathered in to a broad elasticated band above her calves.

While I was on my hand and knees before her, admiring these delectable features at close quarters, she was covering her upper half. Actually, covering is hardly the word. You know those circles of gauze with lacy fringes weighted down with beads, which you put over milk jugs in summer to keep off the flies? Well, she was covering her own 'milk jugs' with something very like them — two semicircles of lace and gauze arranged like the upper half of a strapless bra. From where I was, with my eyes around the level of her waist, the brightly coloured glass beads in the lace spilled over her proud nipples and scintillated as they swung.

By the time I rose to my feet to examine these new delights at close quarters, too, she was tying a yashmak around the lower half of her head. "Now," she said, taking one tassel of my cord between her hands, "pass the cord twice around my wrists and then bring it through from the back — between the wrists — yes, that's right. Not too tight. Slack off a bit — I'm only going to hold it and pretend it's actually tied. Okay? I'm a new slave for your harem, where you've been screwing the tails off your concubines until they all complained of overwork and went on strike and they told you they wouldn't perform again unless you got one more girl to share the ..."

"Hold on. How many of these concubines do I have?" I asked. I always like to get other people's fantasies right.

"It doesn't matter. They're not part of it. They're just background."

"Pity. I thought you were going to impersonate them, one by one."

She stared at me in amazement. "Fabulous!" she cried. "Save it. We'll do that one later. I've never done that one before. Don't go and forget it now. Anyway, in this little game, I'm your new slave girl and you're taking me back to the harem to try me out."

"You're on sale or return?"

"No. I please you or I die! Don't keep interrupting. So here I am, lying on silken cushions in the harem with all the other slave girls and we're all trying to sleep except that we can't until our master, that's you, has come in and made his choice. Sometimes he picks six girls, sometimes just one and tonight they say he'll pick only one — me — because I'm the new one."

"You're still bound at the wrists — is that ever since the slave market?"

"Yes. I can't be unbound until you've deflowered me. It's symbolic, see? You're liberating me into the world of sexual pleasure. Which I've never tasted yet."

"You're a virgin?"

"Tight as a drum, never been done. They always were, you know — fresh young girls from the slave market." Her voice broke on the words and an erotic shiver ran through her. "So come on, choose me. D'you know the way you choose me? Or any of the slave girls?"

I shook my head.

"Feel in my bag there. You'll find a pot of ointment. Sort of oriental-looking with an onion-shaped ... yeah, that's it. Well. Turn down the light. On the dimmer. Bit more. That's it. So here we are — all your slave girls, all lying down here on the floor, pretending to try to sleep and actually just waiting in feverish anticipation for you to come in and pick one of us. So, go halfway back to the bed and then pick your way towards me over all their bodies. Remember there are half a dozen girls between you and me. What are you doing?"

"Turning this one over with my foot to see if she's you."

"Eek! I like it! You play *good* games. Also you've still got that hardon. Very few of the men I go with can keep one going this long."

"Shut up, slave girl! You speak when you're spoken to. You're supposed to be a virgin, anyway."

She grinned, bit her lip, and nodded encouragement at me. But the excitement proved too much for her. She wasn't enjoying *being* the slave girl, she was enjoying *thinking about being* the slave girl. A subtle difference but it came out in her next words. "I tell you what even a virgin would be thinking as she lay here looking up at your joystick there. From this angle it looks absolutely *humongous* because I can actually see the bit between your legs, which you don't usually see from above, but which from here looks like the rest of it. And I think a virgin slave girl lying down here and looking up at that great long horny hungry monster, questing among our eager feverish bodies would feel such a wave of female desire rising up all around her and filling the room that she couldn't help wanting to reach out like this ... to touch it ..."

"How dare you!" I said imperiously and pushed her flat on her back again with my foot. I needed no further instruction in the act of choosing her; the ointment was clue enough. I took a good dip of it with the long finger of my right hand and, kneeling before her, thrust her thighs apart with my knees and massaged it gently in where it would do most good — though she was already delightfully warm and wet down there.

"Oh, I submit, O Master. I submit!" she murmured, rising again and grasping my tool, kissing it and licking it all over. If she hadn't already milked it once, she'd have had a full-force tribute all over her face.

"Enough of that," I said gruffly and gave the cord a jerk. "There's some time to go before we get to that. First I want to see what I got for my money. Sit there on the middle of the bed." I jerked the cord again to hurry her. "Right underneath the canopy."

It was one of those twee imitation antique beds that hotels choose when they want to bump up the bill a bit, a half-tester rather than a four-poster. I stood on the mattress in front of her and pulled the cord right up, raising her arms above her head. Then, passing the loose end over the frame of the canopy, where the two little excuses for curtains met, I tightened it until her arms were as vertical as they'd go and then tied it in a simple knot. She could, of course, let go of the tassel in her hands at any moment and get free; she did not mix her fantasies with real-life folly.

But now, pretending she was trussed and helpless, she looked up at me with piteous eyes and begged me to be gentle with her.

"Tell me, little girl," I said, "is it true you never lay with a man before?"

"Yes, Master," she whispered, swallowing heavily.

"Well, let's see if you have all the right assets to please a demanding master like me. You do desire to please me, don't you?"

"Yes, Master." She lowered her eyes demurely.

"You have the most graceful arms," I murmured caressing them and raking them lightly with my nails, from her wrists down to her armpits. "And the most delectable neck and ears." I kissed her neck, blew in her ears, tickled them with the tip of my tongue.

She closed her eyes and shivered — and would have snuggled back against me if she had not been trussed.

"And these …!" I spidered my fingers down to the swelling sides of her plump young breasts. "These are absolutely divine!"

She sighed and shivered and moaned as my fingertips roamed at random over the soft, swelling flesh — always advancing to the very edge of her areolæ but never actually touching them. My lips continued to nuzzle her neck and graze her ears while I murmured sweet nothings, telling her how provocative and sultry she was. When she could bear it no longer she began twisting her torso this way and that, trying to get her nipples into contact with those maddening, teasing, tantalizing fingernails.

But I was always ahead of her and so the voluptuous contact — the contact she now longed for above all else — was denied, though I could look down her chest and see how hard and swollen they were; they thrust the beaded fringe of lace aside and poked out from beneath the seductive semi-coverings she had donned earlier. She let out little animal whimpers, begging me to relent. But I did not. The whimpers rose to a piteous moan interspersed with sighs of "No!" and "Please!"

I stopped her mouth with a kiss and — at last — set my fingernails gently roaming over those hugely swollen nipples. They were so hot, so engorged with blood, you could almost call them mini-breasts in their own right.

She let out a long, tortured sigh and begged me to untie her. I relented there, too, and pretended to undo the knot she held in her hand. She collapsed backward into me but I slipped out from under her and then straddled her with one knee on either side of her hips and my hands pinning down her arms above her head. She fell into a half swoon and just lay there, staring down with hooded eyes, her chest heaving with powerful emotions.

"Now keep your hands above your head," I commanded. "I want to explore your charms without help or hindrance from you — understand?"

"Yes, Master," she whispered.

I placed my hands on either side of her breasts and squeezed them togther, thrusting her swollen nipples up and bringing them close enough to dart swiftly between them, licking them, suckling them, nipping them gently with my teeth. Her thighs parted wide over the backs of my calves and she lifted her pelvis until her bush began to tickle my dangling balls.

Evetually, though I could have supped at her breasts for quite a while longer, I could resist that open invitation no longer and so kissed my way down until my lips could graze among the pale, spicy fuzz at the top of her Venus mound. My tongue snaked out ahead of me, down into the folds and nooks around her clitoris. She sighed and spread her legs wider yet. But I played the same tantalizing game as before, running the tip of my tongue up and down and round and round but never quite touching that most exquisitely tender spot of all. I've read somewhere that the clitoris has more nerve endings per square millimetre than any other flesh in the entire animal kingdom. I could believe it from Courtenay's responses to my tongue that night.

The more I teased, the wider she spread her thighs and the more she arched her back and reached her pussy up for that most thrilling touch of all. But I, with my nose firmly pressed into her beaver, could ride every twist and turn and still deny her the ultimate sensation.

Now she was past the use of actual words like no and please; all that emerged from her lips were incoherent moans and whimpers and whines. Then, taking pity on her once again, I ceased all movement and simply pressed my tongue, not too hard, against the rosebud of her clitoris. I say I ceased all movement but — as you'll see if you open your mouth and watch yours in the mirror — the tongue is quite incapable of staying still. It ripples. It heaves. It twitches. It fidgets. And the most nerve-rich tissue in the entire animal kingdom is ideally equipped to appreciate those subtle, un-programmed movements of a soft, warm, wet organ pressed against it. There was an embarrasingly loud cry of joy and then another soft, warm, wet organ, not inches from my tongue, became warmer and wetter than ever.

She forgot my command to keep her hands above her head and, instead, grasped my head and seemed almost to fight to thrust the whole of it inside her. I hadn't the heart to complain, somehow.

When her latest orgasm had run its course she remembered her role in the fantasy and meekly asked me what my pleasure would be next. I went and sat on the chair and told her to go down on her hands and knees and crawl backward toward me. It was a most delightful view. The gauze of her harem pants fell slack and open, offering no hindrance to that glorious vision. When her feet were level with mine I leaned forward, grabbed her round the hips, and lifted her to her feet.

I made her stand there while I caressed her hips and buttocks through the fine gauze and stroked the insides of her thighs through the gap her pants so obligingly offered. Gently I pulled her an inch or so toward me, slipping my knees between hers while I continued to fondle and stroke her hips and bottom. She caught on quickly and continued to inch her way toward me while I went on enjoying those oh-so-feminine curves and the promise of what they enclosed.

My best friend down there certainly enjoyed it as he wagged his head to my frantic heartbeat, as if saying, "Yes! Yes! Yes!" to the ever-increasing nearness of those hot, wet folds and tucks of flesh around his ultimate goal.

The nearer she came the more I moulded her hips, bending the small of her back so that her lovely curvaceous bottom pouted toward me. I spread my thighs wider and yet wider, which — naturally — parted hers wider, too, but, more importantly, it brought her lower, lower, lower until her sex and mine were a thrilling, vibrant millimetre apart.

They touched! They trembled. They shuddered as if some voltage fused them.

They parted again, held only by threads of her juice.

They touched again. Throb, throb, throb … he nuzzled and grazed and edged minutely inside her. The palpitations of his beat fluttered the hanging curtains of her frills until the moment came when she could stand it — indeed, simply stand — no more. Then with a great sigh of joy she lowered herself upon me, arching her back as far as it would go, and thrusting the perfectly aligned canal of her vagina down upon me.

Never mind that I had been there but half an hour earlier, it was as if I had never been inside a girl before. That long-delayed consummation to our fantasy foreplay was one of the most wonderful homecomings I had ever experienced. As the vigorous clench of all that was warm and wet and sweet closed about me, I flung my arms around her, pulling her tight to me, caressing her breasts, feeling again for her clitoris, kissing her neck, nipping her ear with my teeth … until my spermspouter gushed so mightily inside her I was surprised she did not rise on that pale, milky stream and balance near the ceiling like a pingpong ball at a shooting gallery.

Actually, that's what it felt like, but she had milked me so voraciously the first time that I doubt there was enough there to lift a pingpong ball half an inch, let alone a big fleshy girl like Courtenay. But a big fleshy girl like Courtenay had a lot of flesh to feel with, especially as her kind of orgasm seemed to possess every part of her. "Don't stop!" she gasped. "I'm on a wave. Keep me going. Hell, I *am* a wave! Surf me!"

"I can't," I confessed. I could already feel my hardon turning into my softoff.

So could she. "Let's do this, then," she said urgently as, casting aside our roles, she grabbed me by the wrist and arm wrestled me onto my back on the bed. She cast aside her harem pants and the things over her breasts, too, before she flung herself, stark naked at last, upon me. Then she began a slow, sinuous writhing all over me. I don't mean she physically moved all over me but at one point or another every delightful inch of her came into contact with every delighted inch of me; her actual physical movements were little more than an inch in any direction — but she found directions that navigators are still looking for.

After a while I lifted my right thigh, pressing it lightly into her fork.

"Ooh … y-e-s!" she murmured and snuggled down against me to concentrate on that sensual area of contact between us. And every now and then she'd hesitate for a moment while a profound shudder ran throughout her body, making every part quiver and shattering her breathing.

During one of these episodes I began to run my fingertips lightly up and down her back. Her disordered breathing turned to a strangled gasp and she stretched herself taut all over me as she pumped her bottom up and down frantically, turning a minor thrill into another full-size orgasm with her pussy rubbing a hot, moist stain upon my thigh.

Around then my nether friend woke from his slumbers and began to take a renewed interest in the enticing proximity of his ancestral home. He stirred, stretched, raised his sore and weary head, wavered, fell, tingled, stiffened, rose again from the dead, and, at last, ascended into heaven once more. As the creamy glow of her vagina closed all about him again there was a kind of internal thud as the full vigour of my racing blood rammed into him, turning him from pliable gristle to inflexible bone.

"Oh you d-a-r-l-i-n-g!" Courtenay murmured as I lowered my thigh again to let her stretch out full upon me. She closed her eyes, settled her head on my chest, and, to my amazement, I saw her hand steal up to her face and her thumb slip neatly in between those adorable lips.

And that was all we did for the next ... I have no idea how long. I don't even know what time we started this final act of loving copulation. We just lay there, notched in glory, with her luscious bottom rising and falling gently and her soft, warm vagina clinging to my hardon, squeezing and massaging with every wanton stroke. Every so often she would pause and a tremor would pass through her, shaking every part of her body.

Slowly, quite imperceptibly, my excitement mounted, too. My breathing grew disordered. My heart thumped audibly — it must have been deafening to her, with her ear pressed tight against my chest. My hands trembled uncontrollably as I fondled her back, her hips, her adorable bottom with ever-more ardent caresses. And because she could hear my heart's increasing lustiness she knew exactly when I was rising to my third and surely final crisis. At just the right moment she cried, "Yeah!" and rolled over, pulling me with her, ending with me on top again. At the same time she flung her legs up around me and dug her heels into my buttocks, straining with all her might to pack more and yet more of me into her for that ultimate throb-throb-throb as I pumped my emptiness into her once again — as thrilling a ferment of pain and pleasure as I ever enjoyed.

When I had drifted gently back to Planet Earth I found she had Mister Softee in her hand and was squeezing him with gentle affection. "There's more life in him yet if you want to make a night of it?" I suggested.

But she just laughed and let go rather quickly. "I like to quit when I'm ahead," she said. "You know what to do if you want another romantic evening with me."

She rose and dressed — and modestly accepted the five hundred I gave her. The most I've ever paid, I think, but I didn't begrudge it one bit. The only awkwardness came when she couldn't find her brooch. I said I was pretty sure she hadn't been wearing one, at which she gave up hunting for it. "It may be at home," she said.

"And if not?" I asked, thinking she might give me an address to send it to.

"If not" — she kissed me on the nose — "I'm insured to the hilt."

Fondly I watched her go down the corridor. Slave-girl Courtenay was nowhere to be seen; smack-loving Courtenay was packed away, too. In their place, every bit as sexy and curvaceous as they, was insured-to-the-hilt Courtenay, dripping with pension plans and portfolios and clutching another half-K to add to the stockpile. I tried to feel jealous or resentful but it was a no-go. All I could think was that if she had given to all those hundreds of men whose fees had created her securities the same value for money she had just given me, she was worth — and welcome to — every penny.

Moscow with Natasha

I'll bet I'm the only man who ever picked up a sporting girl with Mikhail Gorbachev and the entire Soviet Politburo looking on. Actually, now that I say it, now that I remember the way Natasha worked, I'm not so sure which of us did the picking up. This was back in those heady days of *glasnost* and *perestroika,* when there was still a bit of law and order in Moscow and prostitution 'didn't exist.' I was in Russia to use up my roubles. They had abused one of my patents and, rather than pay me in hard currency, had told me I could visit them and spend all my roubles there. So I was going to return, laden with East German Leicas, Beluga caviar, and stuff like that. Also, I was going to have a lot of fun among all those nonexistent prostitutes.

On my first day in the city I did the usual thing — I went out for a stroll first to find then to evaluate the local talent. I brought along a couple of bottles of vodka because I'd heard it could make one welcome in lots of places and get one out of lots of scrapes. I didn't even mean to go into Red Square, because I figured that if their boast about prostitution was true anywhere, they'd make sure it was true there. But there I was suddenly, swept up by the crowd, all watching a parade of some kind. It couldn't have been May Day because it was still very cold, with snow on the streets. But it was a parade of some kind and all the bigwigs were there, as I said, from Gorbachev down. And I ended up right beneath the podium, where they all stand.

I don't suppose they were actually looking at me, and even if they had been, they wouldn't have seen much. In fact, all they'd have seen would have been a man in western-cut clothes standing behind a young lady in furs, both hemmed in by the crowd, both apparently watching whatever was going on out there — which I couldn't even see because of the fur hat the young lady was wearing. The other things she was doing were all taking place out of sight.

The pressure of the crowd was so great that at first I did not notice the extra push from the girl in front of me — just that she had rather good perfume for a Muscovite of those days. Soon, however, the rhythmic wiggling of her bottom against a part of my anatomy especially attuned to respond to a wiggling female bottom was too marked to ignore. Moments later she must have realized I was rising to the occasion for she leaned slightly backward and murmured in my ear, in English, "Fifty dollars in your hotel room, okay?"

Well, I was still nervous. Everyone knows that, in all countries, the security services recruit their agents from among businessmen who go on visits to police states like Iraq and the USSR, as it was then. I knew it back then and I knew the Russians knew it, too. In fact, the British security services had never approached me but the Soviets weren't to know that. As far as they were concerned, *all* visiting businessmen were potential spies. And so they blackmailed them all — or gathered material with which blackmail could be applied if it became necessary. Somewhere still in Moscow there must be thousands of feet of film and videotape of all our most prominent businessmen — Lord this and Sir somebody that — all enjoying what seemed like amazingly cheap sessions with the most gorgeous sporting girls.

Natasha was gorgeous, too. No doubt about it. With big dark eyes in a gazelle-like face and long, lustrous, jet-black hair spilling out like a shampoo ad all round her light-gray persian-lamb hat. So, tempted though I was, I also had warning bells ringing loud and clear. My escape was to turn the temptation around, onto her. "I was looking for somewhere to sit and drink a bottle of vodka," I said. "With one or two amiable companions."

Either she was under pressure to get me near a camera or she was genuinely promoting the oldest profession.

Her eyes gleamed at the mention of vodka. I never met a Russian whose eyes didn't. So, I decided, my fears were probably groundless. It was a bit of a letdown — obviously I wasn't considered important enough to blackmail.

"You have vodka?" she asked.

"Two bottles," I said. It was a good part of their month's ration then — back in the days when they were trying to cut down on alcoholism and rationing systems still worked.

"Ssh!" She put a finger to her lips. We were already attracting attention. "I take you somewhere good."

The parade lasted another thirty minutes — the longest half hour of my life, standing pressed up against a willing girl, feeling as much of her body as can be felt through two heavy fur coats, two sets of stout outer garments and heaven knows how much underwear. Still, it's amazing what imagination can do to fill the gaps in reality. By the time the crowd began to disperse I could almost *see* her thighs in the dark under her unseen skirts inside her all too visible fur coat. And it didn't stop there, either. My fantasy had X-ray eyes that saw, not washed-out shadows on transparent film, but flesh, coloured flesh in the round — just the bits it was interested in, the rest being a kind of shadowy suggestion. And those eyes saw the pale skin of her Venus mound half obscured by whorls of gleaming black hair; they saw her labia, blushing pink veterans of a thousand welcomes; they even saw what unaided eyes could never see — the squat, quiescent tube of her vagina, which, at the promise of action, would spring to life, engorge with blood, and stretch to receive ... me! I needed little fantasy to imagine my excited spermspouter nosing up on its first probe into that empty, unknown sea.

I was in a delirium and was already regretting that I hadn't accepted her opening offer, KGB cameras or no. But from the gleam in her eye at the mention of vodka I knew I'd never wean her off the evening she now had planned for us. I wondered what was going through her mind. She was obviously going to give me a go with her in exchange for the vodka rather than money; that was part of the implied deal. Did she think about it at all? Probably not. The sweet gift of limitless sexual indulgence is wasted on women and particularly on sporting girls, who have the perfect excuse for it.

We men think about it all the time but can't do it; sporting girls do it all the time but hardly ever think about it — even while doing it! I ask you — weren't the Greeks right to believe that the gods made mankind for their amusement?

Anyway, the parade was over and the crowd had thinned considerably.

"Come," said Natasha, taking my hand. "We ride two buses and Metro."

"Are we going to your home or what?" I asked, falling in step with her.

"Friends to me. They live near."

"Do they speak English?"

"They sing. They dance. We all sing. We all dance. We drink vodka."

"And then?"

"You know what then. We go to bed and have fun."

"Do the buses run all night? How am I going to get back to my hotel?"

She grinned at me, a sexy, gamine grin. "Tomorrow morning. Okay?"

A whole night with this gorgeous creature who could smile like that when she promised it to me — and all for the price of two bottles of vodka, twenty quid! "Okay," I said.

We were the centre of attention on the buses and the underground. Western clothing stood out in those days and so did Russian styling of the kind Natasha wore. A gorgeous, young, well-dressed Russian girl and a slightly bemused westerner — no doubt with a smug smile on his lips — it took little imagination to work out what was going on.

It was dark by the time we left the Metro station. We were in the middle of one of those vast, gloomy satellite suburbs of high-rise apartment buildings from the days of Stalin. We had to pick our way across a wasteland of wrecked concrete, mangled iron, and litter that was knee-deep in places. Perhaps she was luring me into a trap, I thought. If someone were to murder me for two bottles of vodka and a handful of dollars, who would know? Who would care?

Perhaps Fate has some mechanism whereby, if you think of things like that, they become less likely. It seems to work the other way round; every time I wonder if a girl will drop her knickers for me, it's the likelihood that drops instead. Anyway, nobody jumped us and we arrived at the entrance to a concrete stack-a-prole tower unscathed. Her friends, Ivan and Lana, lived on the eighth floor. He was thin, and there was something about him that said 'cancer' straight away. He chain-smoked all the time and told lots of jokes; unfortunately, they were all in Russian so all I could do was laugh when Natasha laughed and feel happy for her. She seemed to be having a *genuine* good time and I hoped it lasted when the lights were out. She had a face and figure that could have commanded a thousand a night in London. Lana, by contrast, was the fattest, ugliest, jolliest woman I'd seen in a long time; but she clearly adored Ivan. He clearly adored her, too.

They had little English and I had less Russian but it didn't matter. Vodka is a great uniter of nations. We played some poker for matchsticks, danced jolly Russian dances, put out all the lights and sat around a candle on the floor, singing mournful Russian dirges. We cried at the memory of some mythical golden age — or perhaps at the way the vodka was vanishing out of the bottles. And at one in the morning, when it had all gone, we blew out the candle and went to bed.

That is, Ivan and Lana went to bed while Natasha and I lay on the sofa, fully dressed, beneath four thick fur coats. For a while we listened to the other two making gargantuan love next door, full of laughter, sighs, and huge, overflowing cries of joy. Then Natasha prompted me with a little wiggle of her bottom.

"How?" I asked, for we were both fully dressed.

"Feel," she said.

Mystified, I obeyed — and discovered that part of the back seam of her long black velvet dress, from the waistband down to the knees, was held together with Velcro. His lordship down there grew so excited at the discovery that he burst out above the waistline of my pants in his eagerness to get home between those warm but unseen (and probably never-to-be-seen) thighs of hers.

Her pussy was already juiced up and she received me into her with a happy sigh. It was like a dip in something hot and spicy. There was little room for manoeuvre on the narrow sofa but she suited her action to mine so that I got most of the length of me in and out with each thrust. Her vagina was beautifully tight — warm and smooth.

I felt for her breasts, hoping to find she had similarly obliging seams under her armpits, too. I was not disappointed and, moments later, felt her shiver as my fingers and thumbs started toying with her nipples, which swelled and hardened in response.

"D'you mind if I take this rather slowly?" I asked in a whisper. "The vodka won't allow me a second shot, I think."

"Go as slow as you like," she said. If she'd been a cat she'd already have been purring.

It was the darndest screw I ever enjoyed — and, against all the odds, I truly did enjoy it. The room was below freezing. The couch, as I said, was narrow. We

were both fully dressed for a Russian winter — the
only naked flesh in contact was that of her vagina
around my spermspouter and her hot, swollen nipples
between my fingers. And we were both slow-drunk on
vodka — in that precarious state where you can lose it
at any moment.

But, thank heaven, it did not happen to either of us.
For the best part of an hour we held that one position
while I slipped gently in and out of her and she equally
gently wagged her tail in strict time. Every now and
then, as I felt her rising to a little thrill, I'd give her an
extra-deep plug and fondle her nipples with extra
finesse, and she'd reward me with a shudder that
brought me one step nearer my own climax.

I was waiting for her to have the big one but it always
stayed frustratingly out of reach. At last I became
aware that her hands were no longer plucking at my
wrists or encouraging my fingers at their work on her
breasts. I thought she was perhaps rearranging the
furs over us but soon twigged that she was opening a
seam in the front of her skirt, matching the one she
had opened for me at the back.

It took no genius to divine her purpose, which was,
indeed, a purpose most divine. As soon as I heard the
Velcro part, I stretched my left hand to work on both
her nipples and slipped my right hand down to that
little bud of pleasure which lay all snug and hidden in
the front of her cleft, a tantalizing inch or so away from
my tool.

At least, it should have been hidden there but she
was now so gone in her arousal that it had swollen to
the size of a marrowfat pea and had thrust aside the
lips that usually concealed it. I did not rub it as they do

in the hard-core movies; if those girls were *really* turned on, they'd be screaming with pain at such treatment. Instead I eased the full length of my middle finger into her cleft, so that the tip of it touched my hardon, while the padded ball at the base, where palm and finger meet, lay snugly against that swollen button of lust. My hardon, as it slipped gently in and out of her, imparted the teeniest motion to my finger, most of which was cancelled out by the movements she was still making with her pelvis. But just enough was left to agitate and inflame her clitoris to start on her long, unstoppable climb to the heights of orgasm.

When a woman lets go like that it really is awesome. The equivalent in a man is all concentrated in that one place, in the leaping, throbbing, bucking head of his spermspouter as it gushes in ecstasy. But with a woman it's everywhere. Her nipples catch fire, her limbs melt to a jelly, her scalp and the tips of her toes burn, and her whole frame shudders and shakes as if there's a massive earthquake going on a hundred miles down inside the earth.

Natasha cried out and shivered and jerked as if shocks of a thousand volts were shaking her. Then — the effect of the vodka, I suppose — she fell fast asleep while I was in the throes of one of the most massive gushers of my life!

I, too, fell asleep soon after. My last thought was that I must try to wake sometime in the small hours and poke her once again, through that obliging seam in the front. In fact, I awoke at nine to find Natasha gone and Ivan standing over me with what he must have thought was an appetizing breakfast. It was the effect of the vodka, I suppose.

Eva, Ulla, and Rosa in Stockholm

Troubadours sing of winning the heart of a fair young maid. Well, there are other parts of a girl that can be won in fair contest, too. I've seen it happen — at the *Get Lucky* sex-club in Stockholm, to be exact. It was well named as far as I was concerned.

'Sex-club' was a fancy name for a fairly standard European-style brothel — a discreet-looking house in a slightly run-down suburb at the northern end of Döbelnsgatan, the street where most of the city's pavement hookers hang out. It offered a choice of six girls most days, nine or more on Mondays, Fridays, and Saturdays. The Monday rush surprised me but I got the explanation before I left there that night — which was, incidentally, a Monday.

There was no sign outside (brothels are not quite as legal in Sweden as they are in Germany) and no suggestive lights or pictures hung in the windows. Only the swish of Volvos and Saabs as they arrived or departed showed that traffic inside the house was brisk, too.

The owners justified the name 'club' by holding an event every now and then, and I happened to visit Stockholm — and *Get Lucky* — on one of those appointed occasions. As a matter of courtesy I had asked Nils, the engineering director of the firm I was acting for, out to dinner. He said he'd prefer to be taken to *Get Lucky*. I didn't mind, not only because I *never* mind going to a brothel but also because dining out in Sweden is about the most expensive in the world. An ordinary £4 bottle of plonk can easily be charged at £25; for a fine wine it's a case of, 'If you have to ask the price, you can't afford it.' Fortunately, the same is not true of their girls, who, though far from being the cheapest, are certainly among the most stunning in the world.

The 'event' they were staging that night was a suck-off/jerk-off contest between three men and a girl. It started about ten minutes after we arrived — perfect time to let us pick a girl each, enjoy the contest, work up an appetite, and then enjoy working it off on the girl. Or *in* her, actually. Although a couple of dozen men had already arrived, there were still two girls available: Nina, a Hungarian gypsy-type with dark, curly hair, flashing eyes, and breasts like a figurehead; and Ulla, a tall, svelte strawberry-blonde with a willowy body and small but beautifully formed breasts.

I asked Nils how come they were still free and he explained that most men would book an appointment and come back later, after eating out somewhere. He chose Nina and I got Ulla, whom I would have picked anyway. You don't go to Scandinavia to enjoy brunettes, right? I also bought a bottle of champagne, which was the entry price to the contest, or to the spectator part of it. We sat, the four of us, at a card table in 'the salon,' which was an ordinary sitting room, about three metres by six, with sofas all around the walls and occasional tables and chairs like ours.

The way Ulla explained it to me was that, in a short while, three men and a girl called Eva, all naked, would appear in our midst and we would have a few minutes to inspect the men's tackle and then place bets as to which of them would come first (and that's *come* as in hand, vagina, or mouth), which would come second, and which third. The men would stand side by side; the girl would crouch before them and suck the middle man's prick for twenty seconds, while doing a hand job on the other two. After twenty seconds, they'd rotate clockwise for another twenty seconds. Thus, for every minute that passed, each man would get her right hand, her mouth, and her left hand in turn.

When the first man came, he'd drop out, naturally, leaving the other two to fight it out. The one who held out longest could mount her then and there and finish off inside her.

"You also write how-long-time to each," Ulla said. "Like, you write 'Man One will come first after five minutes, twenty seconds. Man Two is being second after seven minutes, ten seconds.' Et cetera. And the spectator who guesses right, or nearest, gets a free hour with Eva." It sounded pretty tacky to me and I was in two minds about entering at all, even for a lark. What killed off one of those two minds, and left the other as hot on the idea as I've ever been hot on anything before, was the sight of Eva.

She was in her early twenties but looked about seventeen — that is, she cultivated the appearance of a willing but shy and inexperienced teenager. She had a round face, a longish, pointed nose, cherub lips, and big, baby-blue eyes. You could see her among the sixth-formers getting off any school bus — adorable and adored, confident of her sexual attraction. To cheers from all the males she came tripping into the room, all elbows and awkward legs — hands clasped over her large, soft breasts to stop them jiggling all over the place — and smiled an embarrassed but delighted smile at her 'unexpectedly' enthusiastic reception. Her body tapered to a slim waist before swelling to a delightfully curvaceous bottom. Her legs were long, slim, and gangly; her disproportionately large knees and ankles gave them an adolescent appearance. I had a one-in-twenty-something chance of winning her for a free hour of bliss between those slender thighs and, tacky or not, I wasn't going to pass it by.

A moment later the ribald cheers were renewed as the three contestants entered the room, too. I guess there can be few sights more comical than that of three naked young men marching solemnly into a smallish drawing room, each holding his erection in his hand as if it were a weapon in some kind of duel. But no one laughed. They must have been overawed by the sheer size of the man who led the little column — the size of his prick, rather. The man himself, aged around twenty-two, was your average six-foot-two Scandinavian — nothing remarkable — but his prick must have been all of eight inches long and all of two inches in diameter. It made him wobble slightly as he walked, like the tail that wags the dog.

Behind him was a slightly older man, about five-eleven in his bare feet, with a pretty average-looking prick, six inches long and an inch and a bit in diameter. And behind him came another six-footer with a prick under five inches long and less than an inch in diameter. No way were they chosen by accident. In fact, I believe, they were chosen deliberately to exploit our male prejudices — at least, that is the thought which flashed through my mean, suspicious mind the moment I saw them. I don't recall their names, though they were introduced to us individually by the madam, together with lots of coarse jokes in Swedish. I'll call them Big, Medium, and Small.

They stood in a row facing us, with their backs to the huge porcelain stove in one corner of the room. Big was in the middle. Madame and Eva put two chairs facing each other, one in front of Medium, the other in front of Small. And there they stood for us to guess their prowess and place our bets.

I decided that Small was going to win and Big was going to lose, with Medium, of course, getting the silver medal in between. I did so because I always suspect these things are rigged, anyway, and it looked as if the management wanted us to bet the other way. I did not believe that the size of the prow denoted the prowess.

"What d'you think?" I asked Ulla.

"Go by their balls," she murmured. "Not the dicks."

Advice from a pro! Fortunately, it concurred with my own choice, for Small had big balls while Big's seemed to be hibernating up inside his body. I bet Big would come in five and a half minutes, Medium in seven and a quarter, and Small would hold out for ten and three quarters.

I showed my bets to Ulla, who looked at me pityingly. "I warned you — go by the balls," she said. "Small" — we used their proper names, of course — "has the biggest balls, he will finish first."

She had meant the advice in precisely the opposite sense to the way I had interpreted it! Still, I let the bets stand, pitting my amateur intuition against her professionalism. I was to be in the city all week, so I reckoned I could always come back another day and enjoy Eva for her regular fee — or so I thought then.

When all the bets were gathered in, Madame sorted them into three piles, according to first choices. Most of the betting, she said, was on Small to finish first. The rest of us leaned forward eagerly to watch. I don't know why voyeurism has such a bad name. When you think of it, it's an uniquely *human* activity. Study monkeys in the zoo or apes in wildlife films. When a couple are copulating, you don't get crowds gathering to watch. The only one who takes any interest is the dominant male, when he thinks a female in his harem may be getting a bit on the side. We humans watch because we're the only animal with enough empathy to make us want to.

When pretty, gangly young Eva went down on her knees in front of Big, with her pretty little rosebud lips just inches from his knob, empathy stiffened every prick in the crowd behind her. When she rested her elbows on the chair seats and closed her well-lubricated hands around Medium's and Small's erections, empathy gave every man there a little tingle of joy. And when she closed her lips around Big's massive tool, a huge sigh rose from two dozen throats and there wasn't a prick in the place that did not twitch and shake under its burden of this wonderful empathy.

"Good technique," Ulla murmured to me. She was praising Eva for holding her head at an oblique angle to Big's prick, which protected her from excited accidents. If Big lost control and gave her a wild pelvic thrust, he'd merely turn her head slightly rather than push the full length of that magnificent organ down her throat — or out through the back of her neck, which it looked quite capable of doing.

"When you have two hands," Ulla added, "you can hold so." She grabbed an imaginary erection in both hands and sucked the air where the knob would be. She sucked with love and apparent ecstasy, by way of promising the delights she had in store for me when this tedious charade was over.

Big just stood there, his eyes closed, an ecstatic smile playing on his lips, and his face raised skywards. The beating of his heart sent tremors down the skin of his belly. To his left, Small stood with folded arms, legs apart, watching in detatched fascination — like the rest of us — while her supple and well-lubricated fingers writhed like baby snakes all over his diminutive but iron-hard tool. On the other side, Medium fucked her hand while she held her fingers in a tube for him.

The twenty seconds went quickly enough. Small — who was not a small *man* — pushed Big aside in his eagerness to get his prick in Eva's mouth. I noticed she took him head-on, with no fear of a stab in the throat. I began to wonder if I had chosen wisely after all. Small seemed very eager to finish. Or perhaps he was just supremely confident of winning. I hoped so. The sight of her fingers crawling so lovingly and teasingly all over Big's huge erection was as stimulating as the thought of all that meat inside her mouth had been earlier.

After another twenty seconds Medium barged Small aside and began an eager series of pelvic thrusts into Eva's mouth — until Madame warned him it was against the rules. He could thrust away at her hand all he liked but when he was in her mouth he had to stand rock still. There was a bonus for us spectators when she sucked Medium. Since he was shorter in height

than the other two men, she had to lean forward more
— just enough, in fact, to expose the labia between her
thighs. They hung down like the fleshy petals of some
exotic tropical blossom, or the opened heart of some
delicious pink fruit.

Another twenty seconds went by and her gorgeous
mouth closed lovingly round Big's vast tool again. A
collective sigh of envious empathy went up at the
sight. And so a minute had gone by.

And then another.

And then another.

The little drama taking place in the corner of the
room now held no sense of strangeness for me — nor
for anyone there, I think. The sight of a beautiful
young girl sucking off one man while she jerked off two
others was as everyday as street theatre in Covent
Garden. For me the excitement began to build up
again when five minutes had passed and Big got his
fifth suck going. He was visibly excited now and I felt
sure he'd come during the next twenty seconds —
which would put my estimate only ten to fifteen seconds
out. You can imagine my keen disappointment when
Madame called out the end of his suck and he still had
not come.

And you can imagine my delight when, ten seconds
later, he let out a gasp and ejaculated a great, thready
blob of semen — in fact, two blobs connected by an
eight-inch thread of sticky. The fluid went whizzing
past Eva's fingers and orbited each other a couple of
times before they hit the carpet some three feet in
front of him. There were belated cheers and cries of
excitement as three or four more salvoes followed,
each with decreasing force, until Big collapsed and,

with a happy shrug, withdrew from her hand and the contest.

Madame threw away the piles of those who had bet one of the other two would come first. Only four of us spectators were left in the contest, which was now between Medium and Small only. I began to suspect that Eva's left hand was more deadly to male hopes of prolonging the pleasure than her mouth was. I watched particularly the way she'd toss a man's prick five or six times and then slip the knuckle of her thumb underneath it for a couple of strokes, pressing it hard under the glans. It might not be especially pleasant but, as I know from certain private experiments I've made with various artificial stimulating devices down the years, some stimuli in sex need not be pleasant to produce an orgasm. A vibration of 600Hz, for instance, is almost *un*pleasant, but it can provoke an orgasm inside ten seconds — and a very unpleasurable, unsatisfying sort of orgasm it is, too.

I noticed that Eva used this knuckle-kneadiing technique more often with Medium than with Small, so — if it was a speeding-up technique — she wanted Small to win, too. I didn't blame her, mind. If I had to let half a dozen or more foreign pricks rut away inside me every day, I'd want most of them to be like Small's, too.

However, my guess of seven and a quarter minutes came and went with no result -- just as did two other guesses of six and three-quarters and seven and a half. In fact, Medium started coming at seven minutes, fifty seconds, into her mouth. She sucked and swallowed, sucked and swallowed, while he giggled like a schoolkid and stamped his heels ecstatically on the floor.

And wouldn't you know it — one of the spectators had guessed *exactly* seven minutes and fifty seconds!

I had no particular desire to sit among two dozen other men and watch Small enjoy the fruits of his continence with Eva. I allowed my dreams of enjoying her to fade, for tonight, anyway. "Okay, *chérie,*" I said to Ulla, "let's go upstairs and get down to some *real* business."

She was shocked. Partly because it was bad manners but mainly because I was throwing in the towel before I had definitely lost. She now explained that they added up the errors on *all three* guesses, in seconds, and the one with the lowest score was the winner. So the other guy, a portly Italian sitting among a voluble group of his fellow countrymen, and I were now the only two left in contention, for at least I had got the order right, if not the timing. I sat down again and allowed my dreams of Eva to revive.

It worked out like this: I had been spot on with Big and thirty-five seconds out with Medium. My nearest rival had been twenty-five seconds out with Big and spot on with Medium. He had guessed ten and a half minutes for Small while I, remember, had guessed ten minutes forty-five. So if Small held out for at least ten minutes forty-three seconds, I would have won.

The rule now was, it seemed, that Small had to lie on his back, as still as possible, while Eva tried every trick to make him come. And believe me, over the next two minutes she tried. She sucked him. She straddled him and impaled herself on him and wriggled her gorgeous young bottom in every imaginable direction. She pumped her haunches up and down on him. She lay flat out upon him and treated him to a merciless flutter of pelvic thrusts ... And through it all he lay there, eyes closed, a seraphic smile upon his face.

But somewhere around the ten-and-a-quarter mark a change came over him. His whole body tensed up and his breathing became irregular. He opened his eyes and looked about in a kind of panic. His eyes pleaded with her. He had obviously nerved himself for something like half an hour and she was bringing his plans down in ruins. The Italian was beside himself, jumping up and down and shouting, *"Si! Si! Venite! Venite!"* and holding out fistfuls of cash. Cash solves all problems in Italy. But his cooler-headed pals saw that his behaviour was distracting Small and thus reducing his chances of winning so they hauled him back and held him still — or as still as any Latin ever can be.

But for that feverish intervention I believe he might have won. It startled Small long enough to bring him back off the boil. Eva could feel it, too, and redoubled her efforts to make him come — at which she eventually succeeded. At ten minutes fifty seconds, to be precise.

The Italian came over and good-naturedly shook my hand. Everybody cheered. He tried to strike up a conversation, asking me what I did. For the sake of his ego I told him I was a sex therapist specializing in the problems of impotence and premature ejaculation — which, when translated to him, allowed him to retire unbruised.

I asked Ulla if she would be there tomorrow, too.

"Yes," she said.

"Then so will I," I promised.

Eva, clad in a silk dressing gown, slipped her now dry fingers through mine and led me away.

The much-vaunted 'sexual revolution' has revolution-
ized very little. The sex wars, which have been going
on for the past ten thousand years, still have their
ancient verbal battles, even though the actual words
may have changed. For most of that time a boy was
hung out to dry on will-she-won't-she hooks. And any
attempt at intimacy met with 'Gerroff! What d'you
think I am? Don't you ever think of anything else?'
Today, things are subtler. The modern Ms's keep-off-
the-grass manoeuvres tend to be those of the old-
fashioned Mrs's — slight headaches, amiable tiredness,
and fluttering eyelashes that promise, 'soon but not
quite so soon as you'd hoped, pet.' In short, the put-
offs are softer but they're still there. So one of the
great pleasures of walking upstairs hand-in-hand with
a sporting girl is as undimmed now as it ever was: A
man's mind is not ringing with ifs but with hows.

Specifically, on that night in Stockholm, how was I
going to enjoy Eva?

Ulla, already engaged as tomorrow's treat, was
definitely a girl for all positions. With her slender,
willowy body and almost boyish hips and buttocks, she
was a girl to be on top of, underneath, beside, standing,
sitting, kneeling, and lying — curled or full-stretch ... a
girl to keep your hands busy. But Eva, with her younger
and more voluptuous figure, was, I felt, one to snuggle
down with and experience slowly, lovingly, intimately.
Besides, I could not banish from my mind a picture of
Small's sticky still lodged there at the top of her vagina. I
have always relished the thought — and the act — of
poking up into a vagina filled with another man's seed.
(This was, of course, in that glorious decade and a half
between the Pill and AIDS awareness, when the word

'precautions' meant squirting the occasional tube of antibiotic up your prick and all sporting girls let you ride them bareback. Ah me!)

Here's a project for a third-year engineering course in hydraulics: Design a benign tool one man might use for removing another man's recently ejaculated semen from a woman's vagina without damaging the female tissues. Extra marks will be awarded if the tool can achieve this purpose without alerting the female as to what it is doing.

Actually, there'd be no point in setting such a question because Mother Nature, disguised as the Selfish Male Gene, has already come up with the most superb instrument for the job. Speaking as a student of hydraulics I have to admit that the erect human penis could not be bettered as a scavenge pump for old semen and a depositor of new stuff. Any first-year student could tell you you'd need a shaft with a slightly bigger head for the job — something like a tall mushroom with a small cap. How would it work? At the end of the inward thrust the dome of the cap would press against the top of the vagina, forcing the semen downwards. It would then collect under the rim of the cap and be pulled out on the next withdrawal. The next inward thrust would leave it smeared way down near the bottom of the vagina. To the sperm it would be like taking a cross-Channel swimmer to Galway Bay and saying, "Okay, brother — there's the Atlantic. Good luck!"

So far, so good. Unfortunately, from the scavenger's point of view, that mushroom dome would squeeze a dangerous amount of the previous ejaculate up through the cervix and send it on its merry way toward the egg, which is the last thing the selfish male gene wants to happen. A small rethink is called for. The designer must obviously consider the mechanics of the operation more closely. Start with the fact that humans, unlike other apes, fuck face to face. So let's remove the rim of the dome on the side that runs up the back wall of the vagina — the wall that is crowned by the cervix. And let's put all the pleasure nerves on that side of the organ so that its owner will have every incentive to press that underside against the vagina and not the less sensitive top side. Let's call it the thrust side — as with any other sort of piston. Next let's *tilt* the dome so that the rim runs back and down at an angle from the top of the thrust side. And let's streamline it a little, too, so that the semen scooped up by the almost rimless thrust side is streamed back down to collect under the rim on what we can now call the scavenging side — as far from the cervix as possible. Make the rim, or glans, extra big there to accommodate as much semen as possible.

There now! Is not the resulting organ a marvel of hydraulic engineering! A thing of beauty and a joy for ever — *and* a selfish, dedicated rooter-out of rivals in the game of life! One more refinement: Arrange for a flap of skin to close over the scavenged semen and trap it in the glans during the withdrawal stroke but to fall back and pull out the sticky with it on the next thrust. Now the marvel borders on the miraculous. Finally, arrange for the nervous system of the owner of this miracle organ to require between four and five hundred thrusts before it, in its turn, ejaculates in ecstasy. By then the scavenging of any rival semen will be as complete as the most selfish gene could desire.

For me one of the pleasures of poking up into another man's sticky is the mental picture I get of my own sturdy organ ramming all the way to the hilt of the girl's vagina, pushing his stale stuff back over my knob and into the recesses of my glans and yanking it back down toward Galway Bay. And I know I'm not alone in this. Eva confirmed it — not in so many words but by the look of tender exasperation she gave me when, on entering the bedroom, she got out a vaginal douche and I gently took it from her and put it back in the drawer.

"'Men!' she said. "Okay. At least I wash you first."

I broke all records for getting undressed.

The room was very Scandinavian in style, what you might call luxuriously clinical. Furnished from IKEA probably. Clean duvet covers for every client. All-round lighting that did not flatten everything and make it dull.

Certainly nothing about Eva's body was dull. Close to — and I mean side by trembling side — she was even more luscious and appealing than she had seemed downstairs. There was something so juvenile and innocent about her that you could not believe those cherubic lips had just sucked Big, Medium, and Small in public down there; you could not believe that hundreds of hands had caressed those superb breasts, so girlish, so unmarked, so soft and full; your mind rebelled at the thought that hundreds of pricks of all shapes and sizes had slipped in between those petal-like frills of her labia, which looked so pink and fresh and dainty.

And yet the skill of those gentle fingers as they washed my erection — and added several degrees of hardness to its excited condition — belied her appearance of adolescent innocence. I surrendered utterly — and fortunately without a shot being fired. Not at that stage, anyway.

A sex session with a sporting girl is a peculiar thing if you compare it to one with a regular girlfriend. In some ways it is — or can be — even friendlier and more intimate. It all depends on the attitude of the girl. All sporting girls have one thing in common — they all know they have to get on with it. But from that point on they differ. For some, duty begins and ends right there — they just get on with it, coolly and clinically. At the other end of the scale are those who seem to realize that although this session will be one of half a dozen or more, all of which they will have to 'get on with' that evening, for their partner it may be an experience he will remember for weeks or even months. So he might as well remember it — and her — with joy and gratitude.

Eva was such a one. Without losing her professional distance she nonetheless radiated a friendly warmth that utterly captivated me. She could have said, "You have an hour," and left me to make the most of it; instead she kissed my neck, close to my ear, and said in a voice that bubbled with promises of fun, "We have a whole hour, darling, so don't rush. You can fuck me twice if you wish."

What did it cost her to put it that way? Nothing.

What did she gain by it? A good tip, of course, but also a very pleasant, gentle, loving hour in bed.

I picked this career (I kid myself) because it allows me to travel the world, see the most fantastic places, meet interesting people, sample unfamiliar foods in their native haunts ... et cetera. The truth is I am dragged from one exotic location to another by the old Tyrant-in-the-Trousers who wants to measure the insides of as many exotic girls as possible and who knows that, no matter where we go together, we will find dozens of them who, in return for a bit of monopoly money, will let him measure away ... and away ... and away ... until he has no more strength to stand.

With Eva, though, the session turned out ever so slightly different. No standing gropes and caresses. No lifting her arms above her head and fondling her breasts, her waist, her hips, her bottom. No spreading her out on the bed and feasting my fill at her fork. No bending her over chair or chaise longue and ploughing my knob up and down her crevice, picking up her juices and cranking up my excitement until it forced me to thrust all the way in. No sitting and cuddling with her impaled on my erection, wriggling her agile hips and bottom to the peril of my sanity. In short, none of the usual sporting-girl tricks — to start with, at least.

Perhaps it was the effect of that crude and public display, back there in the salon? All I knew was that I wanted something warm with her, something intimate and almost domestic in its simplicity. And, in a way that's hard to explain now, I wanted it for her sake as much as for mine. She ought to feel valued for *herself*, for her glorious body, which seemed so young and virginal, not for her good-natured willingness to accept something as crude as that public exhibition back there. I did not want any more exhibitions, not even private and exclusive ones for my benefit alone. So I turned the lights down low and guided her straight into bed. And under, not on, the duvet.

"Really?" she asked in some surprise. "Like I said — we have an hour. We can spend long time fore-playing, no?"

"Maybe later," I murmured, turning her on her right side and snuggling up behind her, spooning myself tight in against her. "But for this first one I can't wait."

"Mmh — nice!" She murmured as she lifted her left thigh to let me inside her; but she would have said that to whatever I'd suggested, of course.

Instead of going in, I slid my tool along the full length of her crevice and groped my arm around her to catch the knob of it as it emerged at her front, right beneath the hot little nook where girls hide their clitties from just any old roving priap. I pressed it into that nook and teased it with a couple of almost imperceptible thrusts.

A moment later her hand slipped under mine and took over. Whether she intended it or not, she thus left both my hands free to fondle and caress the rest of her, from the sides and tops of her buttocks, round her slim, supple waist, up her sinuous back, round her ribs, under her arms, into her armpits, and on along the sides of her breasts. There, while she and I cooperated to vibrate my knob against her clittie, I teased her nipples with touches and caresses that were invoiced but never delivered.

Round and round her areolæ roved my fingernails — indeed, all over the big, soft paps. I touched and teased everywhere except the by now swollen cherries of her nipples themselves. To add to the tease I slipped my tongue in behind her ear and tickled her there with it, and suckled her lobe, and ran the tip of it around the shell-like whorls of her ear itself.

At some point she decided either to let herself go with me, genuinely, or to pacify me by letting me think she had. I did not care either way. If it was a simulation, it was faultless — and a faultless compliment to me. If it was genuine, it was a compliment to me as well. But it serves no purpose for a man to speculate in this area. It's fruitless for any man to say, 'If I were a sporting girl and a really skilled and dedicated lover bought an hour of my time and clearly *wanted* me to turn on with him, I'd do it.' Any man *would* say that, wouldn't he! We can have no idea what happens to sexual feelings and responses when professional demands turn the very act into an endlessly repetitive process.

However, there are a few rare sporting girls who have learned to take that process full circle, to the point where the sensations and responses that time and repetition have dulled can occasionally be restored to it at will — yet without losing sight of that same professional process. I believe Eva was such a girl and that she made just such a choice that night with me. Either that or it was an amazing display of professional control when she coolly made her body break out in a sweat, and coldly scrabbled my hands onto her breasts, and unfeelingly gasped and shivered as they cuddled her nipples at last. And even then, why she craned her head round and pressed her burning lips to mine and kissed me with such passion would still baffle such explanation. Did the fact that no money had passed between us have something to do with it? Who can tell?

I was certainly in no mood for questioning why sporting girl and client had so unexpectedly turned into man and woman.

After an age of such play she wriggled round on her back, lifting her left thigh to let my tool continue with the good work, now from an oblique angle. She continued to guide, I carried on jiggling up and down with the tiniest movements. At the same time she threw off the duvet and flung her other arm up behind her head. She was panting hard and bathed in sweat. Our eyes met in the gloom, full of questions. I was thinking, *Is this really genuine?*

And what was going through her mind? *Isn't this dreadful? What must you be thinking of me? What can we do now that it's started and is looking unstoppable?*

And I'm sure both of us were thinking that thought which any two complete strangers must think in such circumstances — *How far can I trust you?*

I put all my trust in biology. Good old Mother Nature. I closed my eyes and snuggled my nose into her armpit. Girls on the Continent don't shave under there; it's wonderful. I sneaked my right arm under her, around her waist, to pull her to me and caress her breasts and body with my left. She took the hint and pushed the tip of my prick down to where it nuzzled in between the gates of paradise. That moment when the soft flesh of a warm, wet vagina starts to engulf the hot, naked tip of a randified phallus, stiffened almost beyond bearing by erotic sights, lascivious caresses, wanton feelings, and sexy aromas, is a moment of sweetness that nothing else can match. It happens a thousand million times a day, all over the world, and yet to each randy man and every turned-on woman who experiences it, it is unique.

Even to me, as I let my tool linger there, one inch hot and five inches cool ... there where it had lingered thousands of times with hundreds of other girls, that moment with Eva was unique. Her vagina was as slim and smooth as the firmly rounded adolescent bottom she now offered me as, once again, she rolled on her side, away from me. I lay still and waited for her to move for, even now, my prick was no more than that first inch inside her. She caught on quickly and arched her back a little more, getting me another fraction of an inch deeper into her. Smooth, smooth, smooth all the way. I began to jiggle slightly now as she continued to arch her back even more, slipping me into her millimetre by millimetre.

It took us a full minute of this heavenly cooperation to get me all the way inside her. Arching her back was enough to get only five-sixths of me there. For the last ardent inch she had to wriggle and squirm her bottom tight into my groin. But once she was there she could make the same sort of pelvic thrusts a man would make to get me in and out of her. It was painful for me, of course, but in a thrilling way, because, as she thrust away from me, the firm tube of her vagina moved almost to a right angle with my erection, so that when just the tip of it was left inside her, the rest of it was almost tucked back inside her furrow again.

I would have protested at the pain and suggested some slight variation if it had not become clear to me that the pressure of my knob against the front wall of her vagina was highly stimulating to her. She lingered over it, moving slowly, holding her breath until I was almost out of her. Then she would breathe out almost explosively, something like a whispered imitation of a dog's bark. And she'd experience one of those petty thrills that lead up to full orgasm. It came with a violent shiver that shook the whole of her body. The fascination of it set my pain at nothing.

After a few of these ecstatic strokes she lifted one hand and swept her hair off her ear, plainly inviting me to return to teasing it with my tongue. On its way back down, that same hand plucked mine from their perch on her hips and raised them to her breasts. As soon as my finger closed around her nipples she let out one long, "Ja-a-a!" and started hyperventilating, the way an athlete might before a race. Her hand stole down into her crevice and she pretended to be tickling the underside of my prick as it went in and out of her — or, rather, as her pelvic thrusts uncovered and engulfed it. She did, indeed, tickle me there, but I knew what she was really doing with the fleshy bottom-most joint of her long finger, which never lost contact with her clitoris.

For fully twenty minutes we kept that up — or she did. I just lay there and marvelled at the human female's capacity for erotic pleasure, and my luck at being privileged to witness it. Eventually, when it was clear she could go on passing in and out of orgasm for ever, I took over again. I thrust against her so that she rolled over onto her stomach. At the same moment I got one hand stretched wide across her breasts, touching both nipples with my thumb and middle fingertip; the other hand went down to her crevice and took over from hers.

Something within her had been waiting for it. For her final release she needed movements she did *not* control. All that had happened so far had been a superior form of masturbation, practised on the body of a complaisant living manikin. What followed now was the real thing. My gristle, piling in and out of her with an urgency her pelvic muscles could not match, must have been as familiar to her as blood to a surgeon — and should have been as unemotive, too, it being her trade. But she had taken herself beyond that point so that when I got the insteps of my feet beneath the soles of hers and pressed up hard, and slipped my tongue back through the sweet disorder of her hair into the shell-like whorls of her ear, and massaged my fingers over and round her nipples, and stroked her clittie with delicate finesse, and thrust-thrust-thrust deep into her, pulling far enough out each time to let cool air rush in between my sweating groin and her perspiring buttocks ... well, she let out one long scream of agonised ecstasy into the depths of her pillow and, for a second or two, passed out entirely.

She came round a moment later to feel my tool going berserk inside her, leaping and squirting like a manic water cannon as four days of sexual continence deluged out of me and filled her belly. If anything ought to have recalled her to a professional frame of mind, it was that old familiar gush of semen. But she just lay there gasping, winding down from her own Everest of pleasure even as I slid down off mine, which, relatively speaking, was no higher than Ben Nevis.

What with those four days of continence, my prick did not go limp — nor even threaten too.

"Oy-oy-*oy!*" she murmured, jiggling her bottom a bit to encourage me.

The excess of my sticky was oozing out of her now, with little crackling noises at her every movement. I whipped it out of her and flung myself on my back. My tool, still gloriously stiff, waggled in the dim lamplight and a delicious coolness surrounded it. I promised it that when it felt cold I'd find somewhere nice and warm for it to hide again.

She sprang from the bed and went over to douche her vagina into the bidet. When she finished she wiped herself on several paper towels and came back to the bed with a tube of KY-Gel, which was warm from its shelf above the radiator. She lay on her back and brought her legs right up so that her knees were beside her head, clamping them tightly there by folding her arms behind them. This thrust her vulva out like some giant, tropical oyster. I squeezed the tube over it and trailed a thin transparent snake of gel down the rilles of her inner labia. I teased her by taking an age over screwing the cap back on. And then, kneeling over her, I used the tip of my tongue to spread the gel on the inner sides of her labia. The sight of her lying there with her eyes closed, her lips parted in a seraphic smile, and her bosom heaving her thighs up and down was powerfully erotic, even though I knew that from now on she was a professional girl again. Now it was all for me.

I thought I might segue smoothly from this tongue-massage into full-frontal copulation, but she had other ideas. As soon as the gel was spread to her satisfaction (and mine, though by different criteria) she rocked herself upright and rolled off the bed. She went over to the handbasin and returned with soap and flannel, a towel, and a bowl of warm water. She set them down beside me — I being flat on my back again by now — and gave my tool the most tender, loving wash it had enjoyed in years. Her soapy fingers did things that, if I had not shot my bolt so recently, would have made a whale-hunter cry 'Thar she blows!' It was the sort of treatment she had given Medium and Small out there in the salon; my respect for their resilience, in holding out as long as they did, rose several leaps and bounds. She could even dry a man's prick to distraction.

She returned from emptying the bowl and settled her body between my thighs. "Now!" she said gleefully as she nudged my legs wider apart and took my erection between her gentle fingers. Somehow she managed to suggest that she had never seen or touched anything quite so wonderful before.

"French," I said.

"Swedish!" she corrected me. "Even better."

And so began what I can only describe as a love-ballet between her mouth and my erection. It was many minutes before she did any of the usual things — the kissing, the licking, the little bites, the full-mouthed sucking. First she held it firmly, down near the root, and thwacked it repeatedly against her cheeks, her nose, the point of her chin, her mouth, moving her head around this way and that as if each part of her face would complain if it were denied that especial favour. She did not look to see the effect of this play upon me. I guess she didn't need to, though. The throbs and tics of my rigid flesh were giveaway enough, even without the gasps of pleasure I could hardly help emitting. She kept her eyes gently closed and that happy little smile continually twitched at the corners of her adorable lips.

In between those meaty thwacks she held it tight to her cheek, or neck, or the side of her nose ... or wherever it happened to be when the mood took her, and rubbed it gently back and forth across her flawless young-girl's skin, or massaged it with up-and-down movements of her head.

By the time she progressed from this to the more usual techniques of fellatio it was like taking an old friend indoors out of the cold. I closed my eyes and tried not to faint with the almost unbearable pleasure of it. She was the most skillful fellatrice who ever went to work on me — at least, I could not recall a better just at that moment. *Remember this ... and this ... and this,* I thought as she did one magical thing after another to me — tricks I did not want explained in case the magic died. But I knew there was no way for me to preserve the precise nature and quality of that ecstasy and convey it unchanged into the realms of memory. All I can remember is the *fact* of it — that she did things to me which would, at any other time and with any other girl, have had me gushing at the ceiling. But Eva, without curtailing the ecstasy one bit, kept me just below that danger line and saved me for a further and even more delightful experience.

Maybe it's an old wives' tale but they say we've got seven layers of skin — three dead and four living. Well, Eva made me feel as if all seven layers were alive. My prick *never* felt so peeled, so vibrant, so dynamic, so eager ... so *greedy* as it did in her mouth and throat that heavenly evening in Stockholm.

After a while she sort of edged over until she was lying on my right leg. I crooked it a little until I got my instep into her fork, where I jiggled it about gently until she moved on. There came a moment when she was lying at a right angle to my body and playing my prick like a mouth organ. Then the sight of her curvaceous young body was too much for me. That *greed* in my loins spread to the whole of me and I reached eager hands to grasp her hips and pull her fork up to my even more eager mouth.

She threw her thigh up and forward over my shoulder, stretching and spreading her fork for me. I savoured the glory moment — my head nestling on the inside of her other thigh and my vision filled with the folds and involutions of her blessed sex. It would have been glorious even if she had not still been doing the most marvellous things to me down below. What an embarrassment of riches! Which should I wallow in first? Her clittie, hot and swollen in its snug little bower? Her dainty bumhole, puckered and enticing between the parted cheeks of her buttocks? Or paradise itself, that deliciously smooth, delightfully firm tube of her vagina?

Or all three?

I curled my hands around her buttocks, pulling her to me, me to her. She curled her fork into my face and jiggled the end of my nose up and down her crevice while my tongue sought and found the little button of her joys. My hands, of their own volition, caressed their way all round and over her bottom, worshipping her unblemished silkiness. Round and round they strayed, renewing my amazement at her perfection with every pass. Then round and *under* her buttocks to the tops of her thighs at the back.

And there my fingertips, still with a will of their own, discovered the lush complexities of her sex and dabbled in among them. She stiffened. I felt her hold her breath. One long finger found her bumhole, the other wriggled its way into her vestibule, that beautiful anteroom to her holey-of-holeys. In they slipped, a mere half inch, slick with her juices and the gel. The fingertips trembled and fluttered.

She let out a gasp. She had stopped doing anything to me down there. The fingertips snaked farther in and wiggled again. Again she gasped. Her hips shivered. She lifted her thigh off me in an attempt to spread her fork wider, to invite me, provoke me, to do more, more, more. Her foot wavered aimlessly above me for a moment and then settled on my shoulder where her thigh had been. She could not have been more wide open to me, nor more rapturously inviting.

I slid my fingers in as far as they would go and fluttered them lightly, the way you'd trill two notes on the piano. But this was a three-note trill because my tongue was doing the same to her clitoris. For 'trill' read 'thrill'; because it started her off again and she lost control of her body once more. The thigh beneath my head stiffened and twitched; the other thigh lifted itself high in the air, like a ballerina's during exercise, and thrashed around wildly. Sometimes her heel stamped my shoulder. Once it banged my head.

She kept crying, "Ja! Ja! Ja-a-a!" — which meant she was doing nothing to reward my prick for all this pleasure. *But never mind,* I thought, *his time will come. And so will he.*

Why do we do it? I was paying this girl — or would have been in any other circumstances. I was/would have been paying for the privilege of driving her wild with pleasure. And yet I would have paid good money to do just that. It was a far greater pleasure to me to be a confidential witness of that most awesome phenomenon — a gorgeous young girl in the throes of sexual frenzy — than to get my end away in the belly of yet another paid houri. Never mind that I was lying in some mild discomfort, flinching from her flying heel and wishing her thigh-pillow beneath my head would just stay still for a second, this was a reward beyond all price — and a rare one, too, in the sort of encounters I usually experience.

The time came, inevitably, when she flopped from sheer exhaustion. Then it was clear that the long, long foreplay I had hoped for — the gourmet feast of her delectably sexy body — was again postponed. I rolled her on her back. She flopped there, too, panting hard, bathed in sweat — a powerless doll. I could have put her in the most bizarre positions and she would have lacked the energy to get out of them. But I simply arranged her with her thighs lightly parted, her arms lying loose, and I straddled her body on my elbows and knees.

Keeping the merest gossamer contact between our bodies, I swayed gently from side to side, up and down, round and round. She sighed a long, low moan of exhausted pleasure. The strongest pressure on her came from my prick, of course. In that position both gravity and anatomy combined to press its knob hard against her, between bellybutton and beaver. There it traced small, slow circles in her perspiration while the rest of me made larger ones all over her.

"In! In! Go in!" she whispered after a while, encircling it with tender, loving fingers and gently coercing it toward her centre of bliss.

I obliged, but when the knob reached her clittie, I paused to see what she would do. She had let go of me but she grabbed my gristle back and used it as a vibrator, all around the top end of her slit and down into it, pushing at her clittie far harder than I would have dared. She gave a shriek of pleasure and collapsed again, still holding me tight down there and pressing hard. Her body went into spasms, as if her muscles were convulsing with minor seizures.

"No more," she gasped when this series of orgasms had run its course. "Please! Go in now. Right in — hard as you can. Fuck me hard."

Her vestibule was like warm marshmallow but the tube of her vagina was as smooth and firm as before. A proud vagina. A pliant milker of pricks. Some girls' vaginas are soft and clinging — they provide grip without pressure. Young Eva's, by contrast, applied pressure without grip, a perfect degree of all round pressure. I've never been able to decide which of those two kinds is preferable, so I just have to keep testing, testing, until, one day, I'll get the answer; my main trouble is that whichever one I'm enjoying seems best at the time.

Eva's certainly felt like the best *ever* — at the time. If it had been any tighter or any firmer, it would have been painful. But it had that quality of perfection which meant that a long, slow, deeply penetrating thrust yielded thrills every millimetre of the way. She liked it slow, too. Slow and regular. Quite by accident — helped by my long and varied experience, to be sure — I found *her* particular rhythm. Every girl has one, a pace her body can latch on to — just as every swing in the playground has its natural period of oscillation. Once I found it, her whole body became once more a playground for the jolts and shocks of orgasm, but now they were deep and vaginal.

At the height of them she put her right hand under her breast and squeezed it to a cone, with her areola and nipple swollen to something that looked tender, almost painful. Her other hand pulled my mouth down to suckle and lick her there. My hands took over from hers and my mouth darted rapidly from one breast to the other. She dug her nails into my back and clawed so hard I feared she might draw blood. I cannot remember any other encounter with a sporting girl quite like it. I think I came in self-defence, before she ripped the flesh off me in her frenzy.

Then it all turned weird.

The theory is that women take a long time to come down off the mountain. Men, by contrast, turn over and fall asleep at once. Eva obviously hadn't read those books. She let me soak it to the last tiny squirt. No complaints there. But then she jumped up, bright as a button, and tripped across to the shower, which was a cabinet in the corner. Big enough for two, of course.

I joined her at a more weary pace — mainly to show her that my prick was still proud enough for one final go. All it needed was a little tender, loving soaping from her firm, girlie fingers. She performed the service willingly enough — and my prick responded magnificently — but she refused to let me have another go. My free time was up, she said.

"I'll pay for this one, then," I promised.

"No. It's enough. I must go back to the salon now."

"Must? Why? Is there another exhibition?"

"No, I must fuck with another man."

"But isn't my money as good as his?"

"That's not the point," she said.

"What is the point then?"

"It's none of your business. Look! We had good time together, no? Be thankful. Don't ruin it."

We left the shower and started to dry ourselves and each other. "I'll come back tomorrow," I threatened.

"Okay," she said. "But I am not here."

"Wednesday, then."

"I'm still not here. Only Mondays am I here."

I gave up. "Okay, Eva," I said. "You win. By next Monday I'll be gone. We'll probably never meet again. So don't you think you could spare me just a tiny little explanation."

It took a bit more cajolery of that kind but eventually, by the time we started dressing again, she agreed. "I am poet," she said simply.

"So?"

"So! You know any poet who can live by writing only? Monday nights I make ten thousand crowns here [which was then around a thousand pounds] with exhibitions and fucking. I fuck all night, eight ... ten men. Then I not even *think* upon sex all week. Only Mondays." She chuckled. "Monday nights! Phooo!" She fanned both hands toward her pussy, as if to cool it off.

"So you won't have another go with me because you *want* sex with lots of *different* men?"

"Just that. If I did it every night ... pfft! No more fun. Mondays only — lots of men — lots of fun!"

We were dressed again by now. "Why Mondays?" I asked as we left the room. "Isn't that a slack night in sporting houses here?"

"No. Very busy. Married men have to spend week-ends with their wives. They can't wait for nice sex. Also

many businessmen come to the city on Monday. Maybe
they finish their business by Tuesday lunchtime.
Monday night is their one chance for nice sex with a
nice girl … we *are* nice girls, no?"

"You all look very nice to me!"

"'Well, this house has six nice girls most nights but
Mondays it's nine. Ulla — that girl you were with
before — she is also Monday-only. Or Monday and
Friday, sometimes."

So it's tonight or never with Ulla, too, I thought.

But it was not so. Ulla also freelanced. We made an
arrangement for her to come to my hotel the following
evening at seven.

She was there on the dot. She said she had till nine,
so there was no rush. Actually, she wanted to practise
her English, which is the international language of her
business as it is of any other. She wanted to see the
world before she settled down. I told her what I knew
of the sex business in various countries — places
where she could probably work freely, others where
she'd have to be careful. My vast cosmopolitan experience impressed her. She asked if I could remember
any of the girls especially. I asked how many clients
she could remember.

"More than you'd think," was her reply.

I said I could remember practically all of them,
except, perhaps, when I went for an endurance record
in Bangkok — to see how many I could manage inside
twenty-four hours. "I only remember some of them," I
said. "Actually I gave up after just over twelve hours
because it became boring — you probably know the
feeling. If you took out the time when I stopped for
meals, it was less than twelve hours."

"And how many girls?"

"Fifteen. But that was nothing. The hotel porter told me one man, a Norwegian, managed thirty girls inside twenty-four hours."

"Fifteen!" she exclaimed. The Norwegian's claimed record didn't impress her at all. Actually, Swedes and Norwegians don't impress each other at anything very much, anyway.

"I don't want to try it again," I said, for she had a certain gleam in her eye.

"How many times could you do it, or like to do it in a night? With just one girl."

"Eight?" I guessed.

"This *I* would like to experience," she said. "I would like to tell my boyfriend what's possible. Sometimes he says twice is too much. He blames the tap water."

"Tonight?" I asked dubiously. Eva had taken more out of me than I had supposed — which is why I agreed so readily to her next suggestion.

"Tomorrow night. I come the same time — seven. We enjoy a little candlelight dinner together. I know a nice *tête-à-tête* restaurant by the water. Then we walk back here and I stay all night and you fuck me eight times — more if you will but not less, okay?"

"Er ..." I made the international sign for money.

She turned pale. "I will not pay you."

I took her hands between mine and said, "The moment I saw you, Ulla, I knew I was the luckiest man alive. But even I did not think I was going to be *that* lucky."

She blushed and giggled. "It's for nothing," she said. "I will enjoy it more if it's for nothing. Dinner will not be cheap."

We left it at that. She still had half an hour to spare before she had to leave for her next trick. I asked her if she knew the man she was going to.

"Not man," she replied. "Men. And I know them both. One at nine, one at nine-forty. Both in the same apartment house. Neither one is knowing the other and both are ignorant they fuck me. One is bachelor, never speaks except hallo, stand so, lie down so, goodbye. The other is married and I must join him and his wife in bed."

"Good heavens!"

"Sex is bizarre, Riley. The wife does not like for her man to … how d'you say for oral sex?"

"Cunnilingus for licking a woman's pussy, and …"

"Licking pussy!" She clapped her hands. "I like. I like. The other I know — it's suck off, like what Eva did last night. So, yes! I lick this wife's pussy. Same time … No, I tell you from beginning." She eyed me curiously. "Funny. Were you Swede, never in the lifetime would I tell you these things!"

"So why *do* you tell me?"

"Because I like. Because I am proud, not ashamed. I want that people shall know. So! It begins with I give them little theatre — me and my vibrator. She took it out of her bag and showed it to me — one of those very expensive ones made of some black ribbed plastic, which allows it to squirm gently in a corkscrew spiral as well as vibrate; it also had a tickler attachment for stimulating her clitoris.

"I have my own orgasm then, too," she said. "But quietly, so they don't notice. Then I simulate — that's right? Simulate? I simulate a big, *big* one for them. Mainly for the wife. She's very pretty. Very sexy. Soon

I suggest we meet for some fun one afternoon. D'you know what Eva and I do for fun some afternoons?"

"Don't stimulate my imagination!" I begged. "Not if I have to wait until tomorrow night now!"

She laughed. "We go out with just very long tee-shirts on. No panties. Then we go in the Galleria and stand near the edge of the balcony to see how soon we get a crowd. And the same in the central station. And in old bookshops, where they have ladders for high shelves. One goes up the ladder and the other watches the men fiddle in their pants. It's fun, no?"

"And that's what you want to do with the wife?"

"No! I want to have sex with her, which I do, anyway, but without her husband. He's not bad. He fucks me every Friday lunchtime, too. But I fuck many men and not many women."

"So — after you've done your little bit of theatre for them, what then?"

"Oh yes. I lick her pussy and he licks mine. Then she licks my pussy and I suck him. Then ... well, they like it different each time. This time ..." Her jaw dropped and she put her hand to her mouth like a schoolgirl who's forgotten to do some homework. "It's my turn to suggest. Thank God you asked, else had I forgotten! What can we do?" She grinned broadly. "You suggest something."

Bangkok must still have been on my mind. Not the marathon but the time when I took four girls (only!) up to my penthouse. One of the ways I enjoyed them was to get two of the girls to lie on their backs, on the bed with their feet on the floor and their thighs apart, and then the other two girls lay on top of them, face to face, with their thighs outside the underneath girl's —

therefore even wider apart. That way their crevices lined up perfectly to make one single heavenly groove, almost a foot long — or tall. And the idea was to plunge my gristle deep into one girl, thrust it all the way home, withdraw again, run it up or down the crevice until I could do the same with the other girl. Up and down, up and down, never breaking contact, keeping that most sensitive and exquisitely ticklish part of my anatomy in unbroken contact with that delectable and most heavenly part of a girl — of two girls, indeed — from first plunge to final squirt.

Ulla thought that was brilliant.

"If the wife likes it," I said, "tell her you could introduce her to the man who told you about it. Bring her tomorrow night."

She laughed at that and told me she was too selfish. She wanted to experience this eight-fuck marathon without having to share. However, there was a gleam in her eye which suggested she was teasing me and that the wife would, indeed, join us on the morrow.

Being Swedish, Ulla was there on the dot of seven the following night. Alone. So much for my intuitions! She was right about the dinner — it was not cheap. But then we had fillet steak. I love watching girls eat rare fillet steak, especially if I know we're going to have sex soon after. Their teeth and lips are so delicately savage and the warm, pink meat is so like an excited vulva.

We arrived back at my hotel just after nine-thirty, which, if your stomach is pleasantly distended by steak, *crème brûlée*, and burgundy, is a perfect hour for some slow, gentle, passionate frolicking in a nice, warm bed, in a dimly lighted room, with a gorgeous and experienced young girl and a top-of-the-range vibrator.

"First we shower, yes?" she suggested. "Together?"

"I'll tell you in a moment," I replied as I started unbuttoning her blouse. She either had a gossamer-fine bra or nothing at all under there.

She had nothing at all. Nothing between my lips and those adorable little breasts, whose nipples covered almost half their surface. Resisting the temptation *they* offered, *I* offered my nose up to her armpit. It was the smell of a woman's bed on a leisurely awakening — plus that excitingly indefinable musky perfume shared by all redheads and auburn or strawberry-blondes. "I would prefer you like this," I said.

It pleased her. Women like to be liked for themselves but they have no self-confidence about their own body aromas.

"What about the other place?" she asked archly, standing with her thighs apart and hitching her already short skirt up a revealing inch or two. She was wearing nothing beneath there, either, apart from her sex and her craving.

The moment my nose got near her bush I knew I'd pay her a hundred quid *not* to wash down there just yet. Later, sure, when our debauchery had sweated its gluepot reek out of our pores.

"You've been standing on ladders in bookshops today," I accused her.

She giggled, but denied it. "But I did see several men at nearby tables in the restaurant who found conversation quite difficult. And there was one who could *not* stand up straight, poor fellow!"

"You enjoy it, don't you!" I accused her as I removed her blouse and started on the belt of her skirt. "Being able to exert this power over men. Power at a distance."

She deftly undid my shirt and trouser buttons in one swift downward traverse of her hands. "I often think about that, sitting in *Get Lucky* waiting for a man. I never think, 'I wonder *if* it comes a man?' Only *when* it comes a man. Always it will come a man sooner or later — usually sooner. Men cannot stay away from a place where it is willing girls for them."

Her fingers closed round my erection as my pants fell to the ground. "We do it standing up first?" she asked.

"What we call 'a knee-trembler'," I told her. "Maybe. But I want to do something else first. I just want to admire you. D'you object to being admired all over?"

She had a lovely, infectious giggle. "Where?"

There was a chaise longue by the window. A padded French thing that didn't go too well with the prettified Scandinavian-line stuff, but I wasn't going to complain to the management. "Here," I said, patting the seat.

I used to think that men hunt for sex and women yield when they're cornered. No longer. The main difference is that men will screw almost anything warm and wet with hair around it, women are more choosy. But once they have chosen, their hunting is a thousand times more single-minded and undeflectable than any man's. If a woman is determined to do you the Favour and you don't want her to — emigrate. Even joining a monastery wouldn't save you. By the same token, once they know they've got their man and they're about to get their helping of sex from him, their pleasure at the conquest is commensurably greater than ours, too.

Ulla already had that dreamy little smile glued to her lips and she moved with the steamy languor of a woman caught up in the toils of wantonness. She sat on the chaise longue and waited, being used to doing what men desired of her. I knelt in front of her, grasped her ankles, and lifted her legs up onto the seat, too. She leaned against the backrest, which was at an angle of forty-five degrees. I pushed her thighs together and lifted her arms up to entwine them above her head. Eager though I was to begin, I could not help pausing to admire Nature's work; the naked body of a beautiful young woman is surely the most glorious thing in the whole universe. She came out of her stupor a little and stared up at me. "Your eyes," she murmured. "They are nicer on me than other men's hands."

She meant, 'so let's see what your hands are like!'

I was in something of a stupor myself by now, drugged with the juices of my lust. The precise mathematics of the night ahead — eight, nine … a dozen times — no longer mattered. Between now and tomorrow's dawn this beautiful young creature and I, shorn of polite civilization and reduced to our elemental urges, were going to explore her sexuality in the profoundest degree. Yes, *hers*. A woman's sexual pleasure, because it has no set bounds and is potentially infinite, is always full of delightful surprises.

I ran my hands over her skin, gently, hardly touching her. She sighed and moved her body this way and that, now flinching from my touch, now seeking it more firmly. I rose and went to stand behind the head of the backrest, where I let my hands slide up and down the undersides of her arms, which were still linked behind her head. She must have thought I meant her to move them because she hunted for my prick, which was standing mighty proud over the velvet above her head.

When she found it she pulled it down onto the cloth, which both prickled and teased.

I leaned forward, bending over her body, which was now utterly relaxed and stretched out beneath me. I massaged her shoulders, her ribs, her waist, exploring her smooth and flawless skin. I moved my fingers beneath her breasts and ran them up over her nipples. She, still straphanging on my prick, raised her elbows high, throwing her breasts out and up at me like two firm pears. I licked my lips and leaned farther down to suckle them.

Her nimble, experienced fingers fondled my prick with consummate skill, now light as thistledown, now virgin-tight. I had to fight for breath as I thrust it toward her for more. Her nipples hardened and swelled between my fingers. I could feel my pulse shaking the whole of my body. We stayed like that for a minute or two, kissing and licking and fondling each other, each lost in the other's erotic pleasure.

After several unhurried minutes I raised my head from my feast of her breasts and nipples and went back to stand beside her. With gentle hands I parted her legs and got her to sit astride the seat. Her body was still leaning against the backrest. The dreamy smile was still on her lips and she surveyed me through hooded eyes. I sat astride, too, facing her. I edged toward her, slipping my knees under her thighs when they touched. This, naturally, spread her thighs wide open, and for the first time I saw the lushly complex folds of her vulva, spread for my delectation. She had a big Venus mound, richly covered by a bright auburn bush. The dainty shroud at the front of her cleft was parted by a visibly swollen clittie.

With a wicked smile, Ulla lowered her hands to squeeze and caress my prick with her teasingly gentle fingers. Cleverly, she fondled the shaft of it only, just occasionally brushing my knob — knowing it would drive me wild but without risking a premature gusher.

I leaned forward and suckled one of her nipples while squeezing the other with my hand. At the same time I insinuated my other hand down into her fork, where I let the backs of my fingers graze softly in and around her shrubbery, making small circular movements over her Venus mound. She gave out an urgent moan and lifted her fork toward me. I moved the knuckle of my thumb down into the dark between her thighs and started doing things that made her sway and moan in a delightful blend of ecstasy and distress.

At length I left off suckling her and just sat there, upright again, caressing both her nipples with my widestretched right hand while I enjoyed her pleasure. She just lay limp, eyes closed, lips parted in that same dreamy smile. A little dribble collected there. Her hand was still holding my tool but forgetting to cuddle it. I gave a jig and she opened her eyes a slit, gave me a naughty smile, and started fondling me again. I leaned forward and kissed her gently on the mouth. She responded eagerly, sticking her tongue between my teeth and playing games there.

When our mouths parted, Ulla snapped a little love bite on my lower lip. I returned hungrily for more and we kissed for … who knows how long? When we stopped, I eased her farther down the seat until her shoulder blades were at the base of the backrest and only her head leaned against it. She knew what I wanted next and jiggled excitedly. When I grabbed two cushions she lifted up her bottom and let me slip them under her. I pushed her thighs as far apart as they'd go and gazed with adoration at her wide-open pussy.

What a glorious convolution of fleshy oyster it was — blush pink with deep sepia shadows, all gleaming with the juices of her excitement. I grabbed up another cushion as a rest for my chin and went down to start feasting on her sex. Her whole body was seized by a paroxysm of shivers. She breathed in short gasps between moans and whimpers. And when I slipped my arms beneath her thighs and reached up to fondle her breasts I think she almost passed out entirely.

This position was tiring, however, so I pulled my hands down again and used them instead to massage her thighs even wider apart. My tongue and mouth continued their feast while my hands roved at liberty over the insides of her thighs. I noticed that she started to fondle her own nipples.

Again I lost count of the time. I feasted on her to repletion, until she was well on the way to orgasm. Then I rose and, taking her by the hand, led her over to the bed. There I lay on my back while she settled on her tummy between my legs and, without the slightest prompting from me, grabbed my prick near the bottom and tormented it all over with darts and nips of her teeth and tongue. Little love bites. Small, swift licks. Long, luscious, lingering licks that made me squirm and moan as she had done a few moments before.

The bit I liked best was when Ulla held the knob of it in her wide-open mouth and breathed hot breath all over it, and then closed her mouth all round it and swirled her tongue this way and that — and then, suddenly, opened her lips just a little and drew in a sharp, chilly breath … and then closed the heat of her mouth all around it once more. It almost drove me out of my mind — that hot-cold-hot-cold-hot treatment.

Next she tried to swallow my prick whole — or so it seemed. I moaned. I rolled my head from side to side and drummed my heels on the bed. Then panic! I jerked sharply out of her. We stared at each other and held our breaths as if we'd just heard a knock at the door. The crisis passed and we smiled at each other and breathed easy once again.

"That was close," I said.

"You promised the first one standing up," she replied, pretending to reproach me.

I swung my legs up, over her head, and down onto the floor. I took her by the hand, and led her back to the chaise longue. This time I got her to stand where I had stood before, on the floor behind the backrest. I bent her forward over it, pushing her down until her blonde hair spilled out over the seat and her delightful bottom was open and vulnerable before me. My prick, knowing what was now going to happen, beat the air eagerly, throbbing with readiness. To tantalize him I nudged him in among the wisps of auburn hair sprouting out between her buttocks. With my foot I nudged her feet farther apart, spreading her thighs even wider.

Now I could just glimpse the complex whorls and frills of Ulla's quim, spread like orchid petals and seeming to beg me to get in among them. I grabbed my prick again and thrust forward until the knob of it was just buried in the wet warmth of those 'petals.' I moved it up and down, quite slowly, and in and out, too, following the elaborate anatomy of her most intimate quarter.

She responded by tightening her buttocks, one after the other — wagging her tail, in effect. And what an effect!

I started to push it in, watching with an old, familiar amazement as her vagina just seemed to swallow and swallow and swallow my prick until the full length of it had slipped easily inside her. That vagina, so hot and engulfing, so soft and yielding, so tight and clinging, was the perfect counterfoil to Eva's and I immediately regretted I would have no time for a threesome with them. I even wondered, fleetingly, if I could not change my schedule so as to stay on until the following Monday.

My hesitation made her jiggle her tail impatiently. I withdrew and immediately thrust it all the way in again — wham! A way of saying, 'Be patient!'

The next time was slow again, and my withdrawal was slow, too. And I moved myself a little from side to side. I was exploring every little fold and cranny of her hole with the knob of my tool. No complaints from Ulla now! She just lay there, bent almost double over the back of the chaise longue, with a seraphic smile on her face, giving out little sighs and whimpers every now and then.

I moved in and out of her like a machine, lost to the world. For me the whole of the universe had shrunk to the currents of pleasure that spun themselves around the tip of my prick as I thrust and withdrew. After a while I reached for Ulla's shoulders and pulled her upright, clasping her tight against me. She raised her arms right up and back over her head, back over mine, pulling my head close and my lips closer. While we kissed, my hands stole round and fondled her breasts again. Then I slid one finger down in a ticklish line, over her tummy and into her bush. There it found the magic button that detonated her body once again.

I could have come then and there but I wanted us to be face to face for that first mighty gusher, and I wanted to be as deep inside her as possible. So I reached down and, grasping her left thigh, lifted it onto the backrest, which turned her sideways-on to me. She took the hint and lifted her thigh in a high circle between us, like a cancan dancer's high kick. This had the effect of twisting her round, using my prick as a pivot until we were face to face.

Now she realized what I wanted. She scratched my back lazily awhile, relishing the pressure of my pubic bone against her clittie, and then she lifted her right leg and threw it up around me. We were both steaming wet down there by now and every tiny movement made lovely sticky noises, the way you'd smack your lips before a good meal. The lips of her sex were about to be fed a pretty hearty meal, anyway!

She lifted her other leg and clasped that around me, too, resting her bottom on the very top of the backrest. I stood close and tucked myself right in under her, getting inside to the very hilt of me. Then, when I had her well impaled, I straightened up and stepped back. The top of her vagina squeezed my knob. It was all I needed to brim me over. And what a gusher that was!

I gave out a roar of ecstasy. She gave out a whoop of delight. For a moment I think I could have let go and she'd have floated on my spermspout like a pingpong ball on a fountain at a fairground shooting gallery. I squirted and squirted and squirted into her. I could feel the hydraulic shock of each outpouring, first in the pipe that runs up the underneath my prick, and then in the hot bath of sticky that poured out of me and ran back down between her soft vagina and my hot, hard knob. She must have felt it, too. Every little shriek of joy coincided perfectly with my ejaculations.

I went on soaking it and jiggling and trying to provoke more and yet more thrills, however minuscule, because, as my Bangkok marathon had shown me, the sooner you go through the pain barrier of an empty pair of testicles, the easier it is to keep it up and to keep going. I have never emptied my balls completely in just one fuck, but I got close to it that night.

My prick started to flag even before the last squirt was squirted. It fell from bone-hard to rubber-hose turgid. A phailing, phalling phallus, you might say. But in circumstances like that, with a sexually exciting — and excited — girl like Ulla around, it didn't take much to revive it. And, of course, she was quite literally around ... me! Measuring her arms, legs, breasts, and body, I must have had something like five *yards* of warm, willing sex-therapy entwined most deliciously around me. She unwrapped her legs by sliding them down and around me. At the same time she made a slow wriggling movement of her hips, which rubbed her Venus mound hard against me. All of which brought the notion of hardness back on the scene.

She slid down to where her bottom rested on the top of the backrest again. I pulled away slightly to see how quickly my prick had absorbed the prevailing ethos of hardness and was pleased with the result. It was gleaming with my come and her juices but the management would have no cause for complaint because it didn't once drop down to smear the velvet of the chaise longue. Nor did her pussy touch it, either, for she gripped my arms and leaned right back, stretching her luscious, long legs out horizontally, one each side of my hips. Maybe it was the delightful vision of her gleaming sex that put the iron back in my prick, or maybe it could feel the inviting heat of those red, swollen, excited labia, pouting for the kiss of that equally red, swollen, and excited knob.

Anyway, I slipped it back into her vestibule and made those muscular contractions one makes to nip off a piss, which had the effect of jerking my knob up and down among the soft whorls of her oyster.

She sighed, bent her legs around me again, pulling me back into her, and murmured, "First standing, then sitting. I get it. Next is kneeling, eh?"

I hadn't planned it that way. In fact, I hadn't planned it at all, but her words gave me an idea. "Both of us sitting," I said, pulling out of her and leading her to the other end of the chaise longue. There I sat on the very edge of it, just with the cheeks of my buttocks, and turned her face-away from me, standing up, with my knees just touching the backs of hers.

For a while I simply adored her body with my eyes, my hands, my lips, and my tongue — scratching her back, caressing her hips and the backs of her thighs, and kissing her bottom all over, getting ever nearer to the well of all happiness.

When the tip of my tongue slipped into the cleft of her buttocks, right up near the small of her back, she gave a little moan and started leaning forward. I clamped my knees outside hers to keep her thighs together for the moment. She desperately wanted my tongue to tickle her where it would please a girl most, so, being unable to spread her legs, she arched her

back and leaned even farther forward to thrust her
derrière toward me. This had the effect of unfolding
rather than spreading her charms for my savouring.
But oh what savour! The mingled taste of nubile girl
and fresh-shot come, stewed with rekindled ardour,
seduced my tongue to ever-more vigorous and auda-
cious explorations, each of which made her bend
farther and farther forward, delivering up to me more
and yet more of Cupid's furrow. She ended up with
her fingertips on the floor and the full length of her
excited vulva exposed to my questing tongue.

She giggled. "You're licking it out to put it all back,
no?"

I said I couldn't wait for that, she'd just have to
accept what she'd left me after the first go.

She said she couldn't wait for that and stood up
again, still with her rear toward me.

I released her knees at last and, insinuating my feet
between her ankles, pressed on them until I had parted
her legs wide enough to get my knees between hers. I
held her buttocks to stop her turning round, and
began massaging them lasciviously all over and right
down to the backs of her thighs. I slipped my fingers
between her thighs and ran my knuckles gently back
and forth in her fork, touching the hairs but not the
flesh of her labia. She responded with a gasp of
encouragement and inched toward me.

As she moved backward, of course, the long triangle
of my thighs forced hers farther and farther apart. My
prick was now throbbing with eagerness to be back in
her warm snuggery. At last its knob vanished between
her parted thighs, but I arched my back, pulling him
down — deliberately not touching that part of her

which must now be craving for the feel of him once
again.

Her fair, fine-textured skin was blotched with the
strawberry marks of the female letch and beaded all
over with a gleaming film of sweat. She was struggling
to breathe. It was time. I straightened up, getting the
tip of my tool back into her vestibule. She shivered
uncontrollably as my hands went up to her waist and
held her firmly there. At the same time I spread my
thighs wide apart with a suddenness that took her
unawares. It forced hers so wide that she collapsed
down onto me — *wham!* She gave out a yelp of ecstasy
and collapsed against me.

I slipped my arms around her and pulled her body
tight to mine. One hand caressed its way down over
her belly and into her bush, to tickle her clitoris and
enjoy a fumbler's feast; the other played with her
breasts, with my thumb on one nipple and my little
finger on the other. She arched her back again, which
bent her hole to fit the curve of my prick to perfection.

She wriggled her hips and tightened her buttocks,
pretending she could not endure the exquisite nuzzlings
of my fingers down there. The effect her writhing had
on my prick and its readiness to fire a second mighty
salvo is not hard to imagine. I was within a hair's-
breadth of that unstoppable rise to orgasm — which
was not what I wanted at all. I wanted to enjoy the
welcome massage of her vagina around my fellow for
a while this time. To get off that escalator before it was
too late I lay back along the seat of the chaise longue,
pulling her with me. I reached down and pulled her
thighs as wide as they'd go. Then I returned to my
former pleasuring — one hand in her crevice, the

other now spread across to two flattened jellies of her breasts.

Her lips found my ear. "Please!" she whispered. "Not yet. It's too nice, too soon. Later, please?"

I let go and she sat up again, bringing her left thigh round to join the right so that she was now sitting across my lap. I let out a gasp, for that delicious twirl of her vagina round my ramrod was all I needed to get back on that old escalator ride to frenzy. She saw — and felt — the effect it had on me and did another ninety-degree spin until she was facing me, with her heels in my armpits. Then another, so that she was sitting across me but facing the opposite way from before. Then another, bringing her back to when she started.

Each twist was another mighty leap up that launching ramp. It turned her on, too, I could see, for now she twisted herself around in the opposite direction, one complete turn. Then she turned right or left at random, sometimes ninety degrees, sometimes a hundred and eighty, sometimes a full turn — each of us encouraging the other with gasps and whimpers of ecstasy.

It happened at last, of course, and it was the painful one, when your spermspouting muscles, stimulated to squirt the full magazine, bite down instead on next to nothing and spit it feebly into the aching red tip of your prick. Even so, it's the sort of pain most men would rather enjoy than not. And I had the added benefit of knowing, from past experience, that I was through the barrier and a night of purest pleasure lay ahead.

Still in full orgasm, she collapsed forward on me and jiggled her bottom for more. My prick, limp at last, fell out of her. She gave a moan of disappointment. I tried to make up for it with my hands and whatever massage my pubic bones could provide and she responded for a while. But it obviously wasn't as satisfying as having her vagina stretched by a rod of twitching, sperm-spouting gristle.

She rose to her feet and pulled me up to join her. "Now we shower, yes?" she said. "It's funny," she went on as we wandered toward the bathroom. "Four years have I fucked men and never in life have I done that. Whee! Whee!" She did a couple of pirouettes, clockwise and anticlockwise. "Is it good for you, too? You like?"

"I like!" I laughed. "I wanted to fuck you a bit longer but it made me come."

She nodded thoughtfully. "That could be useful."

I doubt not that, from that night on, dozens of her regulars who were used to sneaking those few extra minutes at the end of an agreed session were surprised into finishing before time instead. However, I don't suppose even one of them complained.

A shower after any kind of hard physical exertion is one of life's supreme pleasures, but a shower after the exertions of happy debauchery crowns the lot. And when the shower is one of those Scandinavian jobs with needle jets all round you and more controls than a jumbo jet, it's the next best thing to debauchery itself. We began, however, with a gentle, copious rain from above — a rain of hot, soporific water, almost profuse enough to drown in. Then we switched off and, half-blinded by steam, rubbed gel all over each other's bodies. When the palms of her hands massaged my nipples she felt an importunate nudge in the thigh from what — when she had last seen it — had been a shrivelled little button, like a bleached raspberry, lost in my pubic hair.

"My, my, my!" she murmured appreciatively and reached a soapy hand toward it.

"No," I said, lifting both her hands back to my nipples.

"Yes?" she said, arching her eyebrows.

"Caress me there and just watch."

And she did — in amazement. She fondled my nipples as a man would a woman's and watched with fascination as, heartbeat by heartbeat, my fellow lifted his head in gratitude until he was once again staring eagerly at her out of his one weeping eye.

She lifted one long, lean thigh over him and got him back where he most loved to be. We held each other tight and began a slow, stately massage of each other with the full length of our hot, soapy bodies. It turned into the long, slow session I had been craving ever since we started — a combination of snaky massage and regular in-and-out thrusting, but never more than two or three pokes at a time. Instead of an escalator to the summit it was a long, long path that circled round the mountain many times. Each thrust was one small upward step, no more.

We did not change position, either, although I had planned to do so when we began. It was too hypnotically marvellous for either of us to risk breaking the spell. When our disordered breathing told us we were both nearing another crisis she reached out — without alerting me — and touched one of those jumbo-jet controls. And to call them that is no exaggeration, believe me — for what seemed like a thousand needle jets of hot water hit us from every delightful angle, north, south, east, and west as well as up and down. Actually, even the notion of 'up and down' began to have no meaning.

And now there was no more point in snaky massage, nor in gentleness of any kind. Those water needles had the curious effect of enraging us even as they spurred on a wild delight that surged through every limb. We fucked like two mad things, risking bruises and broken bones as our bodies thrust greedily at each other, hungry for the ultimate. I had intimations of a pleasure beyond anything I had ever felt before, something occasionally glimpsed but never before grasped.

The overload of stimuli on every exposed part of my skin ensured that when I came it was not just in the knob of my prick but everywhere, all over me, from my scalp to the tips of my toes. A man cannot even imagine what a really big orgasm feels like to a woman, but that one I had in the shower with Ulla, is the one that most fits all the descriptions I've read. My body felt infinite and every extremity tingled.

I have no memory of getting out of the shower, nor of drying off, though I do vaguely recall that it involved standing in a mighty blast of hot air and rubbing each other's bodies to spread the dwindling patches of damp. I remember also that it left the skin feeling silky smooth. But the next memory that comes to me is waking up in bed, almost two hours later, with Ulla's wide-open eyes, two dark pools of peacock blue, only inches from mine. She must have been waiting for the moment because she immediately said, "Ooh! I forgot to say my prayers!" and leaped out of bed to repair the omission.

I was in the grip of a more basic need and went to empty my bladder in the bathroom. I returned to find her kneeling naked at the bedside, facing away from me but grinning at me in the mirror on the dressing table opposite. "You're not praying," I said.

"Part of me is." She giggled and wriggled her dainty, girly bottom at me. "Poor, sweet little pussy! D'you feel ready to answer her prayers?"

Doing-oing-oing! It rose like a prick in an adult cartoon, just at the sight of the two swollen lips of her vulva and the pale ginger fuzz of her bush peeping out between the writhing cheeks of her bottom. She watched the transformation with amazement. A sporting girl either sees them on younger men, hot and rampant and rearin' to go, or on older ones, feeble and slow to rise.

"Doesn't that hurt?" she asked. "When it goes stiff as quick as that?"

"Only when it has to go on supporting itself," I replied as I knelt down behind her and shuffled forward between her calves. "It's a natural-born parasite of the female flesh. Once it gets a bit of support all round it, the pain vanishes like magic."

It was magic, too, sinking my excited gristle into the hot, mushy clench of her hole and bending the rest of my body around her, so that we were in intimate contact from head to toe. She grabbed my eager hands impatiently and thrust them onto her breasts. And then we were away, our two bodies dancing the most ancient jig of all. My piledriver drove in and out, in and out, while her supple waist writhed up and down and from side to side, creating a slightly different pressure and friction with each ecstatic thrust.

Our breathing became increasingly disordered. My thrusts and her squirming grew wilder and wilder. Electric thrills played round my knob like the lightning in Dr Frankenstein's laboratory. It was pure pleasure for me now, dry-bob pleasure, orgasm for orgasm's sake, with no imperative to gush an ocean of sticky into the depths of her belly and flop out exhausted, no more use to my tyrant genes. I could feel the difference when I came — the dry, ecstatic tic of my hard in her soft, the lack of hydraulic after-swill and the absence of squirting pains all up the underside of my tool. I wondered if she detected it, too — or was she too abandoned in the whirl of her own orgasm to notice?

I soon had my answer. "Never did I fuck a man with no come in him," she said as we lay panting in terminal exhaustion. "It's fantastic, like a living vibrator."

"Not even with your boyfriend?" I risked asking.

"My boyfriend — ha! If he comes twice, must he wait two days before he can go again. I will tell him of this night and he must then do better. Lord God — you're still stiff!"

"It gets easier from now on," I replied. "But only if the girl is sexy enough."

She wrapped herself tighter round me. "And I'm sexy enough?"

I made my prick jerk. "There's your answer."

She squirmed again. "More?"

"Let's get into bed now."

We crawled between the sheets and I snuggled up behind her. She still felt as provocative to me as when we had begun. I spooned her bottom into my groin and jiggled my prick up into her fork.

"Am I *really* sexy?" she asked.

"One of the sexiest I've ever known. And, before you ask how many that might be, I'll tell you — somewhere between four and five hundred."

"Oy-oy-oy! All prostitutes?"

"Almost all. But there are over twenty million of you in the world, so I've got a long way to go. You are like lightning conductors, Ulla — you and the other twenty million sporting girls. You expose yourselves to the most powerful force in civilization — the rampant male urge."

"Twenty million!" she murmured.

"Over five thousand new recruits to the profession every day. It's impossible to imagine. But" — I jiggled a little with my prick firmly clenched in her crevice — "we can all do our bit to keep it going."

She arched her back and opened up to me. As I slipped inside her again she said, "You can do more than a bit to keep *me* going."

For a long, languorous quarter of an hour I poked her lazily, slithering in and out, neither progressing toward a climax nor slipping away from one, just holding both of us at the point of equilibrium between the two, where we could enjoy copulation for its own sake, not even thinking of climaxing and ending.

Then she said, "Now," and heaved at me, bearing me over on my back. I grabbed her hips and carried her with me, still firmly lodged inside her. She was then lying at full stretch on top of me with her head beside mine and both of us staring up at the ceiling.

"Now," she said again, lifting one of my hands to her breasts.

"Now!" She said it a third time, as she carried my other hand to her fork. My tongue began playing in her ear as she surrendered herself to me entirely, shivering all over and than going slack in every limb and joint. This was the position and these were the caresses she had begged me to postpone earlier.

If her previous orgasms had been awesome, the ones she now enjoyed were stunning, breathtaking beyond description. My own mighty release, which shook me quite a long while later, was feeble by comparison and utterly lost inside hers.

She then did that thing women usually complain about in men — she fell off me, already half asleep, and, five seconds later, was snoring profoundly.

And did I manage my promised eight goes with her?

It is impossible to say. We snoozed and screwed by turns the whole night long. The two activites merged into each other often, so that we would screw for ten minutes, during which she'd fall asleep, then I'd follow her — only to wake up fifteen minutes later to find her screwing me like a polecat. What is 'a screw' in such circumstances? I certainly had more than eight orgasms, and as for her ... well, count the blades of grass in a lawn — it's easier!

My final one was among the strangest I've ever enjoyed, I think. About six-thirty the following morning (knowing I had to go to work at eight-thirty), she slipped out of bed and into the bathroom. She returned with a steaming hot flannel, with which she wiped my prick (and, naturally, restored it to rampant health) before taking it into her mouth. I don't know what her fingernails did to my balls and the insides of my thighs but, between them — her licks, her suckling, her swallowing, and her caresses — she soon had my fellow throbbing and leaping in the throes of yet another ecstasy. Or not quite. What should have been the first 'mighty throb' of the traditional orgasm was, instead, more like the fifth or sixth. Or maybe like the sort of practice spasm a man gets from time to time in the middle of copulation, a single leap of the eager flesh on its way to paradise. Except that this was a sequence of those single leaps. It did not trail away, as an orgasm usually does, nor did it get stronger. It just went on and on and on ... for as long as she kept licking and sucking and biting and swallowing.

She felt it begin, of course, as my rampant gristle convulsed in her mouth, and she worked harder to thrill me at that vital moment for a man — except that this moment stretched itself to a continuous performance. Credit where credit's due, she did not stop. At last, though, it became so ticklish to me that I had to reach down and lift her head off me.

Just before she left she turned to me casually and said, "Oh, you know that couple I was with the night before last?"

"The ones you go to every Tuesday night? The guy who's going to fuck you at lunchtime on Friday?"

"Yes, well, it's about Friday, really. His wife, Rosa, asked me if I knew any man who might like to come and do her the same favour at the same time — Friday at midday. He doesn't go home until seven in the evening, so there'd be no hurry. I promised to pick her a good one. Are you interested?"

"Is she? In sex, I mean. I'm not interested in revenge but if she were interested in sex ..."

She grinned suggestively. "She won't disappoint you down there — that I can promise." Then her attitude changed. "God!" she sneered. "You really are ... what's the English? *Besatt.* You are *besatt* with sex, aren't you!"

"Besotted?" I suggested.

"You didn't ask is she old or young, is she tall or short, ugly or beautiful ... bad breath, pimples, scars. Just is she available?"

"It is the most important thing when time is short. Besides, didn't you tell me you fancy her yourself? I can't imagine you liking anything but the best. And don't tell me you didn't give and get the best last night."

She grinned again. "As long as it's old enough to have hair round it, and warm and wet enough to welcome you in, that's all you care about, no? Sometimes I hate men, but then I think, 'No! That's also why I love you all!' Eh?"

She wrote down Rosa's address, kissed me, and left.

On Friday morning a package awaited me in reception. Its shape was suggestive enough to make me open it in the privacy of my own room. It was from Ulla — her all-whistling, all-talking vibrator. With it was a note: 'Drive her wild with this.'

Rosa lived in a swell apartment block out on Lidingö, a select island suburb a couple of miles north of downtown Stockholm.

"Riley — Ulla's friend," I told the doorphone.

"Third floor, opposite the elevator," the doorphone told me. Its voice was shivering with nerves.

So was Rosa in the flesh — and what flesh! She could not have been a greater contrast with both Eva and Ulla: tall, built like an Amazon (but still possessing both breasts — very obviously beneath her thin cotton teeshirt), and with long raven-black hair caught up in a loose, straggly bun.

"You are Ulla's Englishman?" she asked through the crack the doorchain permitted.

"I can prove it," I said, showing her part of the vibrator.

"Oh my God!" She stared at it in horror.

"You've got cold feet ... had second thoughts, eh?" I said. "That's okay. We can go for a walk, instead. Go to a movie. Whatever you like."

She just stared at me blankly. "You don't mind?"

"Of course I mind. But I'd rather go for a walk in the park with you — willingly — than have sex with you unwillingly, just because, two days ago, you thought it might be a good idea."

It was a strange conversation to be having through a chained door. A man came out of one of the other apartments. Rosa opened up at last and let me in, saying something cool and formal in Swedish, loud enough for the other man to hear. Probably trying to give the impression I was selling insurance or something.

"You've had lunch?" she asked when the door was closed behind us. She was trembling all over — with lust, I hoped, though I feared not.

"Then we eat," she said. "But that is all. Just eat. We talk about it and maybe we have sex — only maybe. Okay?"

She took my coat and hung it in a cupboard, not with the others in the hall. In case friends called, I thought. I wondered which cupboard she'd bundle me into.

Lunch was a dainty spread of gravad fish, open sandwiches, fruit juice, and a kind of drinking yoghurt that's very popular all through Scandinavia. She became easier once she slipped into the familiar hostess role.

"You have done this before?" she asked.

"Never," I assured her.

"Oh God! And Ulla promised me she'd get an experienced man."

"I meant I've never helped a wife get revenge on her husband in this way. Or maybe I have, come to think of it. Maybe some of the sporting girls I've been with were only doing it to take revenge on mean or lecherous husbands, but they'd never have admitted it, of course."

"Sporting girls," she mused. "We call them *glädje-flickor,* you know — happiness-girls."

"Or joy-girls. Yes, I like that. I'll use it. Joy-girls!"

"You have been with lots of joy-girls, Riley? Ulla has told me your name." She had forgotten that I had told her, too.

"A fair number," I admitted.

"Oh God! And now you will compare me with them — and I have only had sex with twenty … thirty men in all the whole my life!"

There's no point in arguing with convictions like that. I tried to distract her onto a new tack by saying, "One of us ought to pay the other, don't you think? I don't mind which way but I definitely think one of us ought to pay, even if it's only a token amount."

Intrigued, she asked why. Her fears took a backseat for the moment.

"A simple adultery is just so ordinary," I said. "Maybe a hundred women are committing adultery at this very moment all over Stockholm. But how many will add the spice of a little money to the act? If you take money from me, it's like saying to your husband, 'You have to pay for it, darling, because no sensible girl would do it with you for free. But even the most virile and good-looking men have to pay me because I'm so valuable and desirable.' You can lie and tell him I was good-looking. I don't mind."

"Oh, but you are!" She raised a hand to my cheek and stroked it. Meanwhile the emotive possibilities in a straightforward little bout of *paid* adultery were beginning to tickle her. "Yes!" she exclaimed, her eyes now gleaming at the prospect. "How much shall I charge you? What d'you think he gives Ulla?"

I checked my watch. "They will start in ten minutes and she will give him exactly thirty minutes. So, if you want to make an effective gesture, we don't have much time to decide these things. I was going to say, on the other hand, that if you pay me, it's like saying to him, 'Two can play your game, darling. You're not the only one who can splash our money around for sex. And I got three hours *more* than you for the same money.' That would also be enjoyable, no?"

She laughed. "Three hours!"

"No," I replied. "Three hours *more*. Three and a half hours, actually. If you want?"

"Oh, I *want!* But I don't believe."

"You will. So — who pays who?"

She thought it over a moment and said, "You pay me this week — one thousand crowns, which is what I know he pays Ulla. Then you come back next Friday and I pay you, the same thousand. We pass it back and forth, yes? I can embroider a little case for it. I can embroider beautifully."

I broke the news to her gently. Then I said, "Ulla would pay you whatever your husband pays her. She could come straight here after sex with him and spend the afternoon in bed with you, *and* give you all the money he just gave her."

She stared at me in horror, but it was tinged with fascination, I could see. "It's not serious?"

"It is. That girl has the hots for you, and she'd give you as good a time as any man. A lot safer, too. He could hardly complain! Anyway, you have a whole week to think it over." I grinned and reached a hand across the table, daring to touch her for the first time. I stroked her forearm gently with one fingertip. "The idea of being paid money for sex excited you a little, I think? The idea of paying me for it yourself is intriguing, but only up here." I tapped her forehead. "Being paid, though — that is exciting down here." I put my fingertips on her breastbone, carefully avoiding her breasts themselves, though they were so full and luscious I could hardly keep my hands off them.

She grinned lazily at me, knowing very well what effect she was having. "And here," she said, turning slightly so that her left nipple grazed my knuckles. "And here." That, with another swing, was her right nipple. "And down here." She took my hand and pressed it to the tabletop, a tantalizing inch or two short of her centre of bliss. "Why is that?"

"It's in every female's genes. That's my theory, anyway." Reluctantly I took my hand away. "Back in the time when we lived in caves, I think Og the caveman liked to catch three or four more salmon than his family could possibly eat. And he took those extra ones to the prettiest female in the tribe. And she said to herself, 'Why should I stand on these beautiful legs, up to my hips in cold water all afternoon, trying to spear fish, when all I need do is lie back on this lovely warm woolly-mammoth skin for ten minutes and open those same beautiful legs for Og, who will then give me what it took him at least an hour to catch, standing in that freezing river?' And then lots of other females in the tribe saw how well she did and started thinking the same way. I think *most* females in those early clans and tribes offered sex for little extras — furs, polished pebbles, food. After all, their average lifespan was twenty-two years, so they couldn't afford to hang around for ever."

The idea that her desires had such venerable roots excited her even more than the simple notion of taking money.

"I'll pay you," I said, making the decision for her. "Come on. Ulla and your man are about to begin."

"We don't wash first? Shower? Nothing like that?"

"Nothing like that. Later. You'll see. Where's the bedroom?"

She squeezed past me, rubbing everything of value against me — even though the passage was wide enough for three — and led the way to a room at the end. It was a welcoming room, with a modern Laura Ashley type of four-poster bed and furniture that made me think of high-street Scandinavian in England — except that these were the originals, not budget copies. There were also rugs, scatter cushions, beanbags, and a large, upholstered chesterfield — a chaise longue with a low arm-rest all down one side.

In a flash I took it all in — a perfect love nest for a long, long session. "Lie on the bed," I said.

She stared truculently at me. "Who are you to order me around?" she asked.

"The man with these," I said, crinkling a fistful of banknotes. "Remember? That's the way the game is played."

"Oh!" Understanding dawned. It was a game! She now had a *part* to play — a rôle in society. She was that sort of woman who needed a rôle in society before she felt comfortable — with me, with herself.

She lay on the bed. "Do I undress me?"

"I do that." I sat beside her and, easing her blouse out from the waistband of her skirt, undid the lowest button. Then the next. Then the next …

Her heart was going at a gallop. It made her skin flutter like a butterfly's wing. She opened her mouth to speak, saw the adoration in my eyes, and fell silent again. To have this profound effect on a man she hadn't even met fifteen minutes ago was both novel and exciting.

When every button was released I tweaked the lapels of her blouse free of her breasts. She was wearing a bra of the finest black bolting silk, which did nothing to conceal her nipples. Indeed, all it did was darken her breasts perceptibly. Otherwise they appeared naked already.

I had a thousand crowns to spend on her, in ten hundred-crown notes. I took the first and, rolling it loosely, caressed her breastbone with it a couple of times before slipping it inside her bra, poking it toward her nipple. When the edge of the note touched her there, I made it flutter a little before letting go. She gave out a little gasp of pleasure.

I repeated the process with a second note on the other nipple. This time it was more than a gasp. She half collapsed with a fluttering surrender.

I lifted her arms onto the pillow above her head and stroked her gently in her right armpit with the third note, taking it down at last, along the side of her ribs until I could insert it into her bra on the outer side. With the fourth note I did the same to the other side.

The fifth note caressed her neck and slid down behind her bra strap, directly down onto her nipple — and the sixth did the same on the other side. Then all I had to do was tweak each of the notes in turn, making them shiver in and out a fraction of an inch, to send her into a shiver of ecstasies. I had picked up enough Swedish by then to ask, "*Är glädjeflickan glad* — is the joy-girl happy?"

My accent threw her for a moment but then she giggled and said that the joy-girl was utterly happy, indeed.

When I started fiddling with the buckle of her skirt, she looked at the remaining four notes and jiggled excitedly. Underneath she was wearing the skimpiest bikini panties made of the same revealing bolting silk and tied with a little bow on each hip. Her luxuriant black bush rioted out over the top and spilled out at the bottom, filling her fork. Either she plucked them or they grew naturally less thickly on her labia, which showed as two slightly paler fingers in the lush dark of her delta and fork.

I rolled the seventh banknote and caressed the insides of her thighs with it. She moaned and let them fall obligingly apart. Now I could just glimpse the complex frills of her inner labia in the depths of her cleft, where they peeped out between the fleshy ramparts of her vulva. I slipped the note inside the left leg elastic of her panties, across her Venus mound, masturbating it gently back and forth. She moaned again, closed her eyes, and lifted her bottom off the mattress entirely, hoping to increase the pressure of my caress.

I did the same with the eighth note on the other side and she reached for it even more frantically.

When I rolled up the ninth and tried to slip it in near her holey-of-holeys itself, she half clammed up again. "No," she said. "It's wet already there."

"No matter," I replied. "Give those male bank clerks a little thrill when you pay it in."

She giggled and opened up again, letting me slip the note right in — across her furrow, that is, not in line with it.

She raised herself up on her elbows, looked down in amazement, closed her eyes, and sank back with a kind of melting surrender that said more than any words.

"One more," I said, rolling her over on her tummy.

At first she wanted to gather up the notes but I told her it was only money. When she lay at full stretch on her tummy I took the last note — flat, not rolled up — and caressed up and down and round and round her gorgeous buttocks, which quivered at each touch and reached for something firmer, harder, more stimulating. The way she squirmed and writhed almost had me tearing my clothes off and plunging straight into her.

Resisting all such temptation I pretended to roll up the note and start slipping it down the cleft between her buttocks, aiming at the gates of paradise. Except that it wasn't the note, it was my finger that went down into that lascivious dark and played with her frills and furbelows. She was as wet as Niagara and becoming almost as wild — so wild, indeed, that it was some time before she realized it was my finger down there. By then I had massaged her copious juices right up her cleft, all around her bumhole and down into the invagination around her clitoris.

When she did realize it, she let out a long, shivery moan and lifted her derrière toward me, curling her back like a contortionist and reaching her hole toward my finger as it moved this way or that. Finally, when I guessed she was on the verge of coming, I pushed the note inside her panties, any old how, and, giving her bottom a mild slap, said, "Okay! Now we undress."

"No!" She spun round and pinned me to the mattress. "I undress you — please? I will find you slowly, bit by bit."

What could I do but lie back and enjoy it?

And she made sure I enjoyed it, too. She still had hundred-crown notes sticking out all over the place; some had already fallen to the mattress, some fell while she worked at 'finding me slowly.' Kneeling over me, sometimes straddling me, sometimes to one side, she undid my buttons one by one and kissed and bit and pinched and stroked and licked each new portion of flesh as she laid it bare. "You are right not to shower," she said. "You taste man."

"I showered after breakfast," I confessed.

"It's long enough." Her swinging breasts caressed my cheeks as she began to turn, *neuf* to my *soixante*. I reached behind her, unclipped her bra, and swung its flimsy material free. When I suckled them she pulled away and put her lips to mine instead. "Only think!" she murmured. "I also get paid for this happiness!" Her hot breath made me tingle from head to toe.

"I know," I replied mournfully. "It's not fair, is it!"

"Fair … unfair! It's gorgeous!" She flung herself at my trousers and — I think — tried to undo the zip with her teeth.

I can't be sure because I was distracted by the soft white belly, the creamy thighs, and the opulent black delta of Venus that suddenly filled my vision, along with a copious spillage of Swedish banknotes! All I had to do was to tweak at the little black bows — with my teeth, naturally — and the glory of it was all mine to feast upon. And oh, what a deliriously wet, mushy, musky, hairy, fleshy, oystery feast it was down there between those noble thighs!

Thanks to my excesses with Ulla, only thirty-six hours earlier — not to mention those with Eva at the start of that happy-happy week — I was nowhere near coming, even though she was doing the most delightful things to my prick with her toungue and teeth, and her mouth and throat. But she, who had probably spent the whole morning dithering between erotic fantasies and all-too-understandable female fears of an unknown male, let herself go with happy abandon. It must be wonderful *not* to be miserly with that moment of orgasm, the way we men are compelled to be. Just to let it go when the mood takes you, knowing there are more, and more, and more, wherever it came from.

And I had not even touched her clitoris yet! Instead, I had my tongue deep in her vagina and was twisting it round and round, curling it into a tube, thrusting it in and out, thrashing it in every possible direction. At the same time I had the tip of my little finger inside her bumhole and was shivering it and wiggling it as fast as I could manage. She stopped doing anything to me and simply surrendered to the narcotic juices of orgasm as they flooded every vessel in her body.

When it became too much for her she rolled away, spun round on one hip, and threw herself upon me, kissing my face all over and flattening her breasts against me. I calmed her down by caressing her back with long, gentle strokes, as one would a cat. She even purred a little before she lay there panting from her exertions. "And this is what you do with happiness-girls?" she asked.

"This is what I'd *like* to do with them, Rosa."

"But?"

"But they're too smart. What we're doing now, no girl could possibly repeat six times a day, every day, day after day."

She just shook her head.

"You don't believe me?"

She shrugged. "I do not understand how, if you do to a happiness-girl what you just did to me — how can she *not* come. How can she stop herself?"

"They learn pretty quickly. D'you want to try? Try to resist it when I do my best to make you come?"

She thought over the idea and rejected it with a sly little grin. "Later, maybe. It's too much fun now." A new thought struck her. "So I am *better* than the happiness-girls you usually go with!"

"You've already left them out of sight, darling." I checked the clock beside the bed. "Your husband is just getting ready to come, I think."

She giggled again. "And we have only started! His name, by the way, is ..."

"Don't tell me," I said hastily. "If you name him, I'll see his face. What I'd like to do now is take you over to that chesterfield and sit you on it with one thigh on the armrest and the other foot on the floor ..."

She rose as I spoke. The last banknote fell from her as she crossed the floor. She seemed to enjoy the thought of copulating among them. I wondered if she'd leave them there for her husband to see that evening.

"Oh, it is one thing I thought of ..." She looked back at the bed, then at me, and then said, "No. Later. We have much time, yes?"

"Yes."

She sat on the chesterfield as I directed, leaning against the backrest with one leg on the arm-rest and her other foot on the floor — thus with her thighs spread wide and her pussy lifted up toward me, at least, it was toward me once I lay out flat along the seat with my head in easy gobbling distance of her oyster and all its delightful trimmings.

As my mouth went to work on her again, this time on the darling little rosebud of her clitoris, she closed her eyes, leaned back, and surrenderd herself to the sweet torment of my lips and teeth and tongue. When I reached my hands for her breasts, she had the good sense to do what Eva had not done, namely to grasp my wrists and support my arms while my fingers sought to do an equal magic up there. Which they did, to judge by her little whimpers of ecstasy, her writhing body, her shivering breath, and her evermore desperate attempts to open her fork wider and yet wider, to let my tongue work on each new fold and frill of that exquisitely tender flesh as she bared it to me.

Then it seemed that the very spreading of her thighs was too much rapture to bear. She gave a sudden cry of joy and closed her thighs around my head, clamping me like a wrestler, gripping handfuls of my hair in her hands, almost as if she were trying to force the whole of my head inside her in a bizarre kind of reversal of birth. For a second or two I resisted; then I thought, *No. What a gorgeous death — to suffocate in the pussy of a woman in sexual frenzy … to drown in her excited juices!*

She rescued me before that blissful crowning of a lifetime's dedication to that great universal Pussy. She collapsed, thighs parted, body slack, panting as if she'd run a marathon, while I gulped in great drafts of reviving air. As soon as I could, I rose and pulled a padded chair near the top end of the backrest of the chesterfield, leaving a gap of a foot or so between them. Rosa was now in the happy sort of stupor where she didn't really mind what was done to her as long as it prolonged her pleasure. She cooperated with a complaisant sort of willingness. An amused little smile played about her lips as if to say, 'What next?'

'What next' was that I caressed-urged-manipulated her body up and round until she was lying face-down on the backrest with her arms folded on the back of the padded chair and her stunning breasts hanging free, like the ripest of ripe fruit, in the space between them. "Oo-ja-a!" she whispered and wriggled her bottom at me in festive anticipation.

I put my hands on her buttocks and pulled the cheeks apart to admire the luxuriant spread of her bush, the tight-clenched button of her bumhole, and the pink, fleshy luxuriance of her labia, gleaming wetly in the depths of that forest. My prick, still sparkling with her saliva, moved toward her like an independent finger, held out, ramrod-stiff and determined, by the strength of its own craving. In a kind of detatched fascination I watched its hot, scarlet knob, bloated with desire, approaching that warm, welcoming holey-of-holeys.

She could feel it approaching her, too; maybe from the lustful heat it radiated, or maybe because prick and pussy speak a secret language and each knows what the other is up to by extrasensory means. I could feel her shivering excitement through my hands, which were firmly clasped around her hips, up at the level of her waist. That moment — the last few seconds before the sexual copula begins — holds the very essence of erotic pleasure, combining, as it does, the physical sensation and the mental anticipation, all compressed into one tantalizing moment of longing and fulfillment. The man is active, slowly, gloatingly edging his hungering bone toward its target; the woman is, for that moment, passive, open, with every nerve alert for that magic thrill of contact. And both are trembling, excited slaves of amorous pleasure, so consumed with their unslaked cravings that only some major catastrophe could stop them now.

I went in slowly but steadily, without a pause until I was all the way home. It was as sweet as a plunge into a bowl of whipped cream. Her vestibule was soft and yielding, full of loose folds of warm flesh that clung to my knob, smothering it with her passionate juices, but, an inch or so farther in, her vagina was firm and tight, with exciting little ridges to tickle and delight me about halfway up. When I was all the way into her I paused a moment to relish the warmth and the pressure of her clench. Then I lowered myself upon her with a sigh of happiness and slipped my hands beneath her, in the space between the backrest and the chair, where those two luscious fruits of her breasts hung waiting for my caress.

This naturally changed the angle of my body against hers. Before, I had been upright and she had been lying forward at about forty-five degrees; now I was lying tight against her at that same angle. My gristle was so hard that it tried to change angles with me — except that, being so snug and tight inside her vagina, it could not budge. The result was a considerable increase in pressure between the underside of me and her front vaginal wall. And, as I discovered when she moved slightly, it produced more pressure against those exciting little ridges, too.

Normally most of my tingles come from the hot, swollen knob of my prick, but in that position and with that warm, juicy vagina clamped so tight around me, the whole underside of it, from knob right down to root, felt taut and extra-sensitive. I needed only to move a millimetre or two in and out of her for the most luxurious sensations to radiate out from my prick and fill my entire body. And that is all I did to start with. I relaxed, letting the weight of my body press her tight. I gently fondled her breasts, feeling her nipples harden and swell, teasing them with little scratches of my fingernails … and I pumped my gristle slowly in and out of her, moving no more than half an inch. Since I was already plunged into her as tight as I could go, I could still ram her hard on each thrust, even though the movement was so short.

She shivered, almost as if she were having a fit. I don't think anyone had ever fucked her like that before.

"Devil!" she moaned, struggling to turn round to kiss me. But I thrust myself tight against her, adding muscle to gravity and keeping her pinned there. The result was that she writhed adorably underneath me, adding random delights to my slow, steady rodding.

When she felt the additional pleasure herself she stopped struggling and started wriggling for wriggling's sake, as if I were just tickling her. And now she was breathing in huge, sighing gulps, shivering uncontrollably as her lungs reached fullness, and again when they were almost empty, to which she added a low, purring growl of satisfaction.

I became aware of all that was missing in even the best simulation by the best sporting girl. I think even those who have genuine orgasms every now and then are really just masturbating themselves, using the client as a superior vibrator, not truly interacting with him as Rosa was with me. Rosa wanted to *do* things, too. She wanted to be all over me. To put me on my back and sit on me, to caress my face with her breasts, to do the work. And yet it was such bliss to lie there like that, pinned under my weight, with her breasts hanging free and my hands doing all those delightful things to her nipples, and with the sinewy hardness of my prick ramming tight into her in fierce little jabs, that she also wanted to do nothing more than lie there and let it happen. Those unbelievably thrilling wriggles of her body beneath mine were a symptom of the sensual war that raged within her.

Eventually the wanna-do Rosa outvoted the wanna-be-done and she squirmed her way free. Then she did something no pro would have even attempted; pros do generally know the difference between a position that is possible but physically ruinous and one that is possible and sustainable. Rosa flipped over on the backrest, probably forgetting that legs bend backward, not forward, at the knees. Also that heads hang down quite easily toward a person's chest but not too comfortably toward her spine. Also that the gap between the chair and the backrest of the chesterfield provided a wonderfully comfortable space in which her breasts had dangled, but its support for her spine was nil.

The final thing she forgot was that when a man penetrates a woman in that position and does his damndest to take all his weight on his own knees and elbows — to avoid putting even more stress on her anatomy — he isn't exactly comfortable himself. Five thrusts and we both collapsed in laughter and rolled off the chesterfield.

"Yes!" she cried eagerly, reaching for a cushion and stuffing it under the small of her back. "Now you — on me."

Did she think I *needed* telling?

It turned out I did need telling. This was her fantasy. I was to lie on her without touching the floor anywhere. Hands, feet, limbs, torso, head — every ounce of me was to be on her. Then she started squirming under me as if trying to shake me off while I did everything in my power to stay on her, but still without touching the floor anywhere. It started out as simply unnerving but soon turned into one of the most erotic events I'd experienced in a long while.

It was tough on her, though. Not just the weight but the exertion. After several fabulous minutes she collapsed to jelly beneath me and lay there panting and bathed with sweat. "Can't you come?" she gasped.

"No," I replied, breathless myself, "I'm having too much fun."

That gave her a fit of giggles. She tipped me off and we lay side by side until we had our breath back.

"We shower, huh?" she suggested.

Showers in Swedish hotels are like showers everywhere else. But in their own homes they don't have shower trays with tiled walls, curtains, doors, etc. It's just a shower in the corner of the bathroom. The whole floor is covered with vinyl, which curves round and up at the skirting. And then they hang the same vinyl floor covering as if it were wallpaper, overlapping the skirting bit by half an inch or so. The result is a seamless, two-metre wide strip right around the walls. And there's a drainhole in the middle of the floor. And a boat-deck squeegee for scraping the puddles into the drain when it's all over. I have the same arrangement in my apartment in London now. No clammy curtains. No chill tiles. No steamed-up cabinet. Just a hot rain falling in a corner of the room — and total freedom for a couple to move around, soap each other's bodies, lie down on warm, cushioned vinyl, indulge in whole-soapy-body massage, standing or lying ... erotic bliss.

"Listen to me now," she said when we had indulged ourselves sufficiently at that delightful game. "You can *go,* yes?"

"Eh?" We were standing in a downdraught of hot air, to dry ourselves off, so I thought I might have misheard.

"You can go and go and go?"

I laughed. "I can come, too."

"And if you come, you can go again?"

"Yes."

"Okay. So I mustn't need to .. how to say? I mustn't need to *save* you. You come once. You come twice. You come again. It's no problem?"

"With a fabulous girl like you, Rosa, it's absolutely no problem."

She shivered with pleasure and massaged me with her hands to spread the last droplets and dry them off quicker. I did the same. The old tyrant between my legs hoisted himself up for another go.

"Welcome, milord!" She did a mock bow and gave the tip of him a quick suck. The 'milord' bit gave her an idea. "I know!" she exclaimed. "We can act my best fantasy, yes. You would like?"

"Tell me about it." You never know when they're going to open a cupboard full of whips and barbed wire.

"I am a slave girl in an Oriental slave market and you are all the men."

The slave-girl-in-a-harem again — shades of Estelle! It must be in the female genes, too.

"*All* the men?" I asked.

"Yes. First you are the slave trader. Then you are the rich pasha who buys me. Then you are the eunuch who prepares me for being whipped."

"Oh-oh!" I interrupted warily.

"No, it's only symbolical. Not to be worried. All new slave girls get a symbolical whipping to show they submit to the pasha. You can use this." She handed me an African fly whisk — a sort of horsetail on a plaited leather handle. "If you whip as hard as possible it can hurt — but only just. Otherwise ordinary whipping just tickles. It's nice. I do it to you, if you will. I got this when I worked in the peace corps in Tanzania ..."

Her voice trailed off and a faraway look crept into her eyes. I gave her an experimental tickle with the fly whisk. She laughed and said, "Those African men! Not much peace for this *corps!*" She spoke the word in French and hefted her breasts in her hands — in case I didn't catch on. "Where were we?"

"I was symbolically whipping you."

"Oh, it doesn't matter. I tell you each time as we get to it. So, first I'm a new girl in the slave market, okay? You put on Pelle's dressing gown and make a turban with this towel. I put on my slave-girl clothes."

Pelle was presumably her husband. I didn't care now. I didn't even try to imagine his face.

Her slave-girl clothes consisted of a fringe of black glass beads, each bead about the size of a Smartie, which she wound round her at the level of her armpits. The beads spilled out over the tops of her breasts and hung about two inches down below her nipples, which were, of course, only partially concealed behind them. A similar fringe made a miniskirt — or 'fan-belt' would be more accurate — starting below her belly button and just covering the fuzz of her beaver. Also various scarlet and gold bangles and anklets. Over it all she wore — only temporarily, I felt sure — a slinky silk version of those canvas tops they wear for martial arts; you could otherwise describe it as an extremely short dressing gown with voluminous sleeves.

"Okay," she said. "We begin."

I tucked my erection up inside the waist cord of Pelle's dressing gown and, reversing the fly whisk, used the butt of the handle to prod her to the front of the auction ring. I continued to poke and prod her this way and that as I spoke some absurd, impromptu patter. "Well, my lords and masters, we come at last to the ultimate jewel of today's collection — a fresh little peach from the frozen north, looking for a nice warm welcome in one of your harems ..." and so on.

No more of that, I promise. But it delighted her. She stood there panting and trembling with excitement as I did my best to create the scene all around her. As I extolled her charms I used the butt of the whisk to untie the simple knot around her waist and letting her silk top fall open. I used the butt of the whip for everything — for pulling the beads aside to display her big, pink nipples, swollen now with her excitement ... for lifting them down in front of her bush ... for prising her legs apart ... for turning her around, clockwise, anti-clockwise, leaving her, finally, facing away from the imaginary audience of rich pashas.

Then I stood facing her, grabbed her brusquely by the hair and pulled her down until she was bending over almost double. I moved toward her and tucked her head in between my thighs so that she could not rise. I leaned forward over her, pulled her silk top and bead fan-belt right up to her waist, exposing the whole of her buttocks, and kicked her legs wide apart. Then I invited the pashas to come up one by one and feel her pussy and holey-of-holeys — its glorious softness, its warmth, its youthful juiciness. My fingers imitated their excited explorations while she trembled with pleasure, trapped between my thighs.

In between my exhortations I also conducted an auction so that, by the time I released her, she had been sold into the harem of the grand vizier himself. I made sure she fetched the highest price ever paid for any slave girl in history. In fantasy land there is no point in half measures, is there!

As the vizier's eunuch I prodded her through the suq to the back door of the harem, where I took off all (!) her clothes and ceremonially washed her from head to toe, using a chiffon scarf instead of flannel and water. Her nipples swelled to the point where they looked frankly painful and I was sorely tempted to drop out of character and into her.

"Of course," I said, "you realize that all females in Oriental harems have their pubic hair plucked out." I mimed it in case she did not follow.

"Eh?" She pulled a dubious face.

"Sure! We Orientals think that hair on a woman's body is primitive and unclean. The girls in our harems spend hours every week plucking out the hair as soon as they sprout. It hurts, of course, but there's lots of kissing-it-better, so they don't mind."

"Oh dear!" She looked down at her luxuriant bush and saw her whole fantasy coming apart.

"However," I assured her, "this grand vizier is a cosmopolitan man. He knows things are different in Sweden. So we'll just get one of the other slave girls to pull out three symbolic hairs and kiss it better if it hurts. Okay?"

Intrigued, she lay back across the end of the bed, with her heels on the floor, and spread her thighs as wide as they'd go.

"One from the top," I said in a falsetto voice as my knuckles grazed round and round in her Venus delta. I picked one just north of her cleft and tweaked hard.

"Aieee!" she yelled. But it turned to a moan of pleasure as my lips kissed it better and my tongue licked it better still. She pouted her pussy up at me for more but I pulled away and took a grip on another hair — the one nearest the puckered, wet sphincter of her hole on the left.

And what an orgy of licking and kissing followed her scream! I had to force myself to stop and grip the correspondingly closest hair on the right. And then I almost lost control of myself as the two of us succumbed to the sweet joys of oral stimulation and exploration. She was made of sterner stuff than me, however — or perhaps the fact that it was still her fantasy gave her that extra strength. Anway, she closed her legs and squeezed my head out like an orange pip, whispering urgently, "Here comes the chief eunuch to give me my whipping — quick, hide!"

I rose to my feet and became the chief eunuch, who — according to her — was always naked to the waist. I had to slip Pelle's dressing gown off my arms and shoulders and let it hang down.

"And make your belly stick out," she added. "They're always fat and sleek."

I did my best. I took the belt of her gown, tied it loosely round her wrists, and flung the other end over the curtain rail above her four-poster bed. I had to make sure she could see herself in the mirror — which was easy to tell because she was by now as self-mesmerized by her sexiness as I was. She had certainly *imagined* herself in these circumstances but she had never actually *seen* herself like this. Her eyes became fixed. She breathed in and hollowed her back to make her breasts swell out — at the sight of which she gasped in admiration. She jiggled them a little and giggled to see them shiver. Then she turned sideways and did a slow, snaky sort of dance, loving every feminine curve she saw.

Then I think she spotted my erection, peeping out all crimson and furious, above the dressing-gown cord. It was most un-eunuch-like and so must have reminded her that I was soon going to turn into the grand vizier and deflower her virginal vagina. "Quick!" she said. "Get the whipping over with now."

I took the stock of the fly whisk in my hand and gave her a half-hearted slash with it across the small of her back.

She screamed quietly, wriggled in simulated pain, and said, "Harder."

I complied, only to produce the same result.

I thrashed her what I thought was quite hard enough for anybody. It whistled through the air and made quite a hissing sort of thwack on her bottom. "Good," she said. "Remember that when you lash my breasts. But go as hard as you can on my back. Five or six times is enough."

Full of misgiving I obeyed. I don't think that even my very hardest lash actually hurt her — though my shoulder joint complained a bit. But it must have stung. It certainly raised red patches on her skin.

"Now my breasts," she said, turning round in a swoon of bliss and poking them out at me. "Not so hard, though."

I lashed them three or four times with the horsehair, making her gasp and pretend to flinch. Then I went close to her and dangled the end of the whisk over her nipples, caressing them with the gentlest strokes. "Now I'm tired of being the eunuch. I want to be the pasha. I want to see my new slave girl dance for me — naked."

Well … give or take a bangle and a bracelet or two.

She could have danced her way into a fortune. The dance she did for me then was, alone, worth all those notes still scattered around the room. She had more joints in her spine than any girl I ever knew. She could tilt her hips almost vertically in either direction. And she could arch her back, and then hollow it, like a snake. Put all those movements together and let them shake and shiver as beautiful a pair of naked breasts as you are ever likely to see and you have the ingredients of a sex-bomb to blow the lid off your scalp. And that's without reckoning what she could do with her thighs while all that shimmying-torso business was driving a man mad. Anyone can gesture the idea 'come inside' — all it takes is a crook of the finger. But to gesture the same idea with a scooping movement of the thighs, while their lean muscles ripple and flicker like flames … *and* to suggest that the 'inside' referred to will be warm and welcoming like you've never been warmed and welcomed in your life — well, that takes artistry of a supremely high order. And Rosa had it.

I just sat there stupefied, holding my erection down near the bottom and waggling it around to cool it down. The pasha in me was 'pasha-nate' like never before. And I guess it was the same with her, for her eyes grew wilder and wilder, her bosom heaved with something more than breathlessness, and her nipples swelled to the point where their skin looked like the thin, milky latex you get when you try to push your finger through the rubber of a flesh-coloured balloon.

At last she collapsed on me and tried to wriggle her hole onto my joystick. As the warm succulence of her vestibule closed around my knob I summoned a superhuman helping of resolve and said, "How dare you! That is no way to approach your lord and master for the first time!" And I thrust her off me and half pushed, half led her to the door. "Down on your hands and knees if you know what's good for your soft, unblemished skin!" I thundered. "And crawl to *here* like the bitch-on-heat you are" — and I stamped my foot on the carpet halfway to the bed — "and from here on you'll writhe like a snake, all the way to my bed."

"And then ... Master?"

"Then you slip in under the duvet, between my feet, and wriggle your way up to me, kissing every precious inch of your master's flesh on your way."

I glowered at her sternly and managed to turn away before laughter overcame me. Climbing naked into her bed, with the soft, cool silk of the duvet cover caressing my erection, was an erotic experience in itself. And I don't know which of us was more turned on by her crawling-writhing act between the door and the foot of the bed. She had never done such a thing before, she told me later, and the fantasy-humiliation it inflicted was remarkably sexy. And I need hardly describe how sexy it was for me just to lie still and watch a gorgeous young body like hers wriggling toward me, bringing the ultimate comfort of her sex all the way to my bed.

When she slipped in under the duvet, my imagination had to take over, stimulated, of course, by the feeling of her body — warm, eager, and supple — as she wormed her way up the bed. The sharpness of her fingernails, the hardness of her wrists and elbows, the jelly-softness of her breasts, the warmth of her breath, the softness of her lips, the pliable liquid heat of her tongue … she favoured me with each and all on her loving, lingering progress up my body. When her tongue started to curl around my prick like a hot, supple finger and pull it between her teeth, I had to start mentally reciting the nine-times table to keep my ecstasy down below eruption point.

And I had to repeat the trick when those same adorable lips closed around my nipples and started to tease me there, too. By then, though, I could get my hands to her breasts and give her reasons to want to hurry it up. And so at last our lips met, our knees trembled, our hands were all over each other's bodies, and my prick was making hard, accidental explorations of the softness beneath her bush.

There comes a moment in all such fantasies when fantasy itself gives out — the ultimate, or penultimate, moment when the male priap, hardened beyond endurance by all that foreplay, trembles in awe in the very entrance to that paradise in the girl's belly. Then, no matter what she was a moment ago — houri, whore, nun, or angel — she becomes the most wonderful fantasy object in the universe: simply a girl, and as desperate to feel your prick inside her as you are to push it in there.

Even if I'd been a real pasha and she a real slave girl, fresh from the market that day, she could have felt no more wonderful to me than she did. I almost started coming the moment I was in her, all the way to the hilt. I just lay absolutely still and let the little shivers that ran through her body keep the fires banked until the moment of danger had passed. Then I remembered reading of an Oriental sex technique called *coitus tractus,* or drawn-out coitus, which I had never actually tried. This moment, however, seemed to be the ideal one to give it a whirl, and not only because we had started in a fantasy-Oriental manner. In it, the pasha gets as close to orgasm as he dares, without actually brimming himself over, and then pauses — still inside his houri — until it is safe to start again. 'The orgasm that finally overtakes him after several hours of this sexual Russian roulette is like none other,' the book had promised.

"Feel like a few hours — nonstop?" I asked.

"You can't!" she exclaimed in excited disbelief.

"Let's try, anyway. Here goes."

Her body, even in a drugged coma, would have been exciting enough to keep me going for an hour. But in a state as excited and hypersexed as she was that afternoon, it could have stimulated me into going on all night. As it was, I discovered an event or condition that I can only call a 'petty orgasm.' My prick would twitch and jerk in a series of teeny thrills, and a little ripple of something — maybe even a genuine pearly bead of semen — would lunge up the length of it, but the usual detumescence and softening did not follow. A moment later I could resume my gentle thrusting, in and out, in and out of that most delectable vagina.

After the first fifteen minutes or so, when she realized it was for real, she relaxed and started coming. And from then on she came very easily, every few minutes. Not very violently. There was no thrashing around and shouting and digging her nails in my back. Just a deep-throated growl of pleasure, a few head-to-toe shivers, and a moment of two of breathlessness. I tried to vary it for her by sometimes playing with her clitoris, sometimes fondling her nipples, sometimes licking and suckling her ear, and sometimes just gripping her tight around the waist and squeezing hard.

I envied her that easy and almost permanent access to orgasm — the way she could always count on another one coming along in a minute. At times the feeling was quite unreal and I found myself wondering if I had actually ceased to exist. It felt as if I had turned into the sort of creature a woman might dream up for her private fantasies — a flesh-and-blood robot capable of endless poking and incapable of doing anything other than respond to her frequent eruptions into orgasm and cherish and sustain them when they arrived.

But the book was right in one thing: The pasha's orgasm, when it finally does arrive, is as superior to the everyday variety as is a premier grand cru wine to a cheap gulping plonk.

That afternoon was one of the most fabulous of my life. I began thinking of all sorts of ways I could come back to Stockholm ... I was even considering tendering for contracts at cost, to make sure of getting them. Fortunately, Pelle, her husband, picked up some regular consultancy work in London and — greatly to his delight — Rosa decided to accompany him. Even more greatly to his delight, she did not mind his spending several hours with sporting girls on one afternoon or evening of each visit — hours during which she and I refined and perfected that ancient Oriental art of delaying.

Which reminds me — she also thanked me for suggesting a liaison with Ulla. "I still don't feel like a lesbian," she said. "But woman-to-woman sex is natural *coitus tractus!*"

The Tangier Sporting Club and Mirie

They will argue to the end of time about whether the institution was invented in North Africa or Mexico or South America. I first came across it in Morocco — in Tangier, to be precise — but that proves nothing. The instituion in question is variously known as the sporting club, the *casa de cita,* and the back-and-front club, to name but a few. They combine the features of a high-class brothel, a good restaurant, and an exclusive gentleman's club; they allow the top ten-percent or so of males in their community to express their dominance. The men have exclusive use of the best sporting girls, they eat like lords, and in between times they trade inside information from one leather armchair to another. I've been entertained in them in Rio, Mexico City, and — as I said — in Tangier, where I met the phenomenon for the first time. There it was called *un club sportif.*

My host was a Moroccan Arab whom I'll call Ali because it's not his name. Also it's nice and short — the very opposite of my prick as soon as we stepped into the restaurant of the Tangier *club sportif.* He can sniff available and much-frequented pussy at a hundred paces and wham! up he shot the moment we went through the revolving door. Mind you, the nearest possessor of available and much-patronized pussy was considerably closer than a hundred yards. More like three feet, in fact. She was the maîtresse-d' — a sort of working madam — a golden haired Circassian girl of about twenty-five. She wore a gold-lamé cape and a stockinette bustière gathered tightly round her sumptuous breasts and held by an elasticated band immediately underneath them. She was bare from there down to just below her belly button, at which point her voluptuous hips were clad in tight-fitting pants of white lawn secured by a belt of shiny gold plastic. The pants finished below her knees to show bare smooth legs and feet shod in gold Oriental slippers — the kind where the toes curl round and up into a point.

Her walk as she showed us to our table almost snapped my prick in half. I was trembling all over and bathed in a light sweat as I sat down. Ali noticed my state and said, "You appreciate her?" — all casual-like, as if he'd go on to say, 'Have her, then — be my guest.' But he didn't, of course. We hadn't agreed a price for *my* consultancy yet and there's no such thing as a free lunch, nor a free vagina, in business.

"I appreciate her," I said.

I looked around the room and the thought that all these rich, suave men — Europeans, Africans, and Arabs — had probably all enjoyed the vagina of that young Circassian beauty was both personally galling and erotically rousing. However, in that same glance I also noticed other beauties — black, brown, yellow, tan, and white. They all wore the same style of costume as the maîtresse-d', though in colours to suit their own skins; the capes were shorter and none had any touch of gold.

"I like them all," I said. "Is this place what I think it is? Or is it just for show — like the Playboy Club — where you can look at the merchandise, drool all you like, but mustn't touch?"

"It's what you think it is," he replied. "Every member gets five of these things every week." He took out his wallet and withdrew a couple of bits of plastic, about credit-card size but with holes punched in them — like they use for hotel doors, too. He flung them casually on the table between us.

"And?" I prompted.

"Look at the girls and you'll see."

A slender naked black midriff, very feminine, pre-sented itself at my right elbow just then. "Water, sir," the girl said in French, reaching a jug across the table to fill my glass. The gesture filled my field of view with a plush left breast in a flesh-cuddling bustière of pale blue flannel.

And nestling in a little pocket on the side of that breast, peeping coyly out at the top, was one of those rectangles of perforated plastic.

"Someone's going to fuck her for half an hour at two-o'clock," Ali explained. "And someone else for a whole hour at half-past two — see the card by her right breast?" The girl was about to go but he caught her by the wrist and showed me other pockets all around her waist, in several of which there nestled more of those plastic cards. The other pockets, not yet filled with plastic, each held a simple printed card with her name on it and the hour of her availability that was repre-sented by that particular pocket.

"Nouriya is going to be a busy girl today," Ali said, touching the plastic-filled pockets in turn. "Men are going to fuck her at six o'clock, half-past seven, eight, nine-thirty, ten-thirty, and eleven-thirty. Plus the one at two and the one at three. Eight." He smiled up at her.

"Oui, monsieur — huit," she said proudly as she left us.

"Eight is her maximum under our rules," Ali said. "A ninth member can claim her only if all the other girls have eight men booked."

"Does that ever happen?" I asked.

He shrugged. "A couple of times a month, maybe. It probably will today because the doctor is checking them over now and it's reassuring to know they have a clean bill of health."

"How d'you know the doctor's here now?"

"Watch and you'll see Diane, our maîtresse-d', calling each girl out discreetly, one by one, to go and see him."

I chuckled. "Nice work if you can get it!"

"Yep! He has one other amiable task to perform today — which I may be able to tell you about later."

"Tell me now."

"No, it'll be easier if you see her, too."

"How much do you pay the girls?"

"They get forty francs for each plastic card." That was equivalent to £4 then. "It's a small fortune to most of them, of course."

"And what does each card cost you members?"

"Sixty," he replied. "'You couldn't get girls of this quality at a high-class brothel in the city for less than a hundred. A hundred and fifty if they think you might be American."

I was starting to take in the surroundings, now — having been understandably distracted earlier. It was pretty sumptuous, in a grand belle époque style, with gilded swags and ornate cartouches and lots of gold, blue, and scarlet. And mirrors and palms. It reminded me of photos of de luxe Parisian sporting houses between the wars. The number and variety of girls was too bewildering for me to count. Anyway, Ali saved me the trouble. Throughout the meal, in between our dull old business conversation, he drip-fed me details about the sporting-house aspects of this rich men's club. They had five hundred members and two dozen girls, of whom sixteen to eighteen were in active service at any one time. The rest would be having their periods; but they weren't idle during that week. They were the evening waitresses in this restaurant and later they worked the bar and gaming tables, assisted by any girl not booked for that particular half-hour. There were two one-hour sessions — one after lunch at two-thirty, and one at six in the evening; all the rest were for half an hour, beginning at two and ending at midnight. It made for eighteen possible sessions, of which only eight were usually taken up. "The thirty-minute time limit is not rigid — if the man still *is* by the end of it ... if you see what I mean," Ali said. "Anyway, a member can always book two sessions, one after the other, with two bits of plastic."

"Can members book girls on behalf of their guests?" I asked idly.

"Oh yes," he assured me, but in a tone that suggested he was answering an academic question of no relevance to either of us.

The six European girls came for three months on a rota arrangement with houses in Milan, Marseilles, and Frankfurt; they got a hefty bonus when they went back home — if they stayed out the full length of their contract — but while they were in Tangier they earned the same as all the others. There were usually around eight Chinese, Indian, and Southeast Asian girls, most of whom stayed for six months and then went on to houses in Europe, usually by arrangements made with the help of the European girls, who got a bonus from their houses for bringing home a good scalp. The remaining ten or so were Arab and North African girls — the cream of the sort you find in any Tangiers sporting house — sturdy, grinning, eager young things with an almost infinite capacity to please.

"The European girls are allowed to keep their pubic hair," Ali told me. "Also the Chinese girls because theirs is so beautiful and black and glossy."

"But the rest are all shaved?" I asked.

"Plucked," he said. "They spend anything up to an hour each day grooming each other's pussies, plucking out the first signs of any incipient hair. Funnily enough, most of the European girls start plucking, too, after a couple of weeks. And they all say they'll keep it up after they go back."

There were fifteen sumptuous rooms on the three floors above the restaurant. On the rare occasions when more than fifteen girls were booked for a particular half-hour, three of the rooms could be divided by a sliding partition down the middle. There was a turkish baths in the basement and most men had an hour down there before being whisked upstairs in a lift (and in nothing but their dressing gowns) for their hour or thirty minutes of pleasure in one of those rooms.

The best girls, he claimed, were from a mountain tribe in Morocco itself; he told me the name but I've forgotten. Something like 'Bezier' — let's say Bezier, anyway, because it goes with curves. They were a poor people and it had long been the custom for their nubile young girls to come down and work for a spell in one of the city's many brothels in order to earn their dowries. When they returned to their villages, nothing was ever said about this and they were expected to marry and live as virtuous wives thereafter. Some twenty-five years before my visit, a Bezier girl had come to the club in order to earn her dowry. She had carried back such good reports (and so much loot) that all of them now came to the *club sportif*; and when they went back they trained the next wave of dowry earners in the arts of sexual pleasure, so that Beziers were always in great demand. Some of them never went back but stayed on to make their fortune in Paris, Berlin, Munich, Rome ...

Of course, I asked Ali if there was a Bezier girl on duty at that moment. He said no but something in his tone left a lingering doubt. Anyway, I kept wondering when he was going to stop tantalizing me with those two plastic cards on the table and his endless talk of how magnificent *all* the girls were.

I'd just decided he was never going to make the offer when his eyes suddenly lit up and he said, "Ah — at last!" He began gesturing frantically toward the sideboards, where one of the European girls, herself festooned in little bits of plastic, nudged a jet-black youngster beside her and pointed out Ali.

She was about five-foot-four, slender, sinewy, but with the most feminine hips and breasts and buttocks a man could wish for. She had a smile that would have doubled the sales of any toothpaste in the world, and — I saw as she came closer — the merriest, dancingest eyes. She could hardly be a day over sixteen, I thought as she drew to a halt beside Ali. He just smiled at her, picked up both his bits of plastic, and caressed her two luscious breasts with them, one after the other. He made it seem that the caressing was the real point of it; the fact that, a moment later, both her upper pockets were now full of his plastic, while her name-cards now lay on the table, was almost incidental.

He picked one of her cards up and read it. "Mir*rie?*" he asked, laying the stress on the second syllable.

"*Mir*rie, Monsieur," she replied in a little birdlike twitter.

"This one's for you," he said to me, handing over her two-o'clock card.

Mirrie licked her lips and nodded eagerly, as if she had hardly dared hope I would be included.

"Her first time," Ali went on. "You get *droit de seigneur* — how d'you say in English?"

"*Droit de seigneur,*" I said and protested that I was overwhelmed by the honour. I wasn't, of course. I just mentally added two percent onto my tender — to take care of him.

He waved my words aside and asked only that I get her nice and warmed up for him at two. She went back to the sideboard, wiggling provocatively. Several other men stopped and and stuffed their plastic into her pockets; she must have reached the limit of eight before she arrived.

I checked my watch. It was ten-to. I asked if I should go down and have a quick shower. He said that was a good idea. It wouldn't take Mirrie more than a couple of minutes to change into *her* working clothes. He winked at her in passing as he took me down to the turkish baths.

"I was expecting her to show all lunchtime," he said. "She came to us a week ago and had to have her pussy plucked free of all hair. They use an anæsthetic cream, of course, which stops the pain at the time, but it still takes a week for the swelling and tenderness to go down."

"Ah!" The penny dropped for me. "That was the doctor's *other* 'amiable task' this morning — checking her readiness to start work upstairs."

He nodded. "Go easy if she winces or seems uncomfortable, eh? Try her bumhole instead. Madame has been getting it ready for service all week."

The turkish baths were about as grand as anything Hollywood might have conceived for an epic set in Ancient Rome — all Italian marble and mosaic frescoes. But I had little time — and even less inclination — to appreciate the splendour just at that moment.

At a minute to two the lift whisked us up to the fourth floor, three above the restaurant. Ali goggled at the erection that was pushing my dressing gown out like a sailing boat's spinnaker. "Leave *something* for me!" he joked.

I was shivering all over with lust by the time he left me alone, in a room the size of an English mid-range *house.* "Mirrie will be with you before you can say Jack Tomkinson," he promised.

And she was. They must have passed each other on the threshold itself. She slipped in while my back was turned and leaned against the door, watching me. The first I knew of it was the sound of her breathing — rapid, shallow, and excited. Her eyes flashed when I turned and faced her. Sexual appetite, sexual hunger, sexual gluttony just radiated from her.

The 'working clothes' Ali had mentioned consisted of two items: hareem trousers in see-through gauze, from waist to knee; and a five-inch wide strip of scarlet silk that stretched between a neckband and a cord drawn tight beneath her breasts. Actually, it was ten or more inches wide at the bottom; she had ruched it together at the top so that most of her breasts were naked, thrusting out on either side of the silk. And when I say thrusting out, I'm understating it. They were what women dream of in plastic surgeons' waiting rooms — and what men dream of on the gallows or anywhere else.

"Speak English?" I asked.

She shook her head.

"Parlez Français?"

She shrugged but again shook her head. *"Parlez jigajig!"*

"Yes!" I reached my hands slowly, gloatingly toward those gorgeous breasts.

She reached one hand teasingly toward my spinnaker, touching me there the moment I touched her. It was as if I had given her an electric shock. She let out a little shriek and slipped away from me, scampering off to the far side of that enormous room. I had taken a cold shower but was sweating again. I shed my dressing gown as I began to walk toward her. My erection was so high and rigid that I had to grip it round the base to steady it. I felt like a cop with his night stick.

She giggled when she saw it and put her hands under her breasts, lifting them a superfluous inch more toward me. She let me get within four feet before she clasped her breasts tight to her and slipped away again, screaming and giggling like a schoolgirl —

which is what she would have been in Europe. The flash of those two naked half-buttocks and the ungainly run those superb breasts forced upon her almost had me spermspouting in her wake.

This cat-and-mouse game went on for several minutes. Sometimes she would seem to yield but, the moment I dropped my guard or let go of my prick to grasp something more interesting, she'd let out another little shriek and giggle-jiggle-flashbottom to some other part of the room.

Eventually, however, she tripped herself up — taking care to do so where she would sprawl full-length on the huge silk-sheeted bed and at a moment when I was too close to do anything but to tumble with her. But the next bit she could not have planned.

She spun round and spread her legs wide apart as she fell, but it was a symbolic gesture of welcome, not the finely judged manoeuvre it turned out — accidentally — to be. It would have taken a whole day's rehearsal for a girl to trip and twist herself round like that and fall in the perfect place and timing for a man, falling upon her a microsecond later, to get his prick lodged inside her, as deep as it could go, one more microsecond after that.

We both stared at each other in amazement — and then burst out laughing. I was astonished because I had not realized, until then, that the harem trousers were split right through her fork. And, almost in passing, I began spermspouting in that same moment. Naturally, it was nothing very grand. Indeed, it was more or less without pleasure, a mere blowing-off of froth, a clearing of the decks for some more passionate action. But she, poor girl, was not to know that. She stared up at me in disappointed horror as she felt my gristle jerking minutely inside her belly.

But I just kissed her warmly and poked her a thrust or two, at which she relaxed again, smiled, and slipped her arms behind her head and, closing her eyes, jiggled her firm young body beneath me.

I saw that, in her way of thinking, it was now my duty to reciprocate the pleasure she had just given me. She pouted accusingly when I pulled out of her. She grinned when I turned her on her side. She giggled when I got behind her and spooned myself in. She sighed a long, happy sigh as I slipped the full length of my gristle back into the warm, wet, sweetness of her vagina. She gave a little gasp of surprise as I wrapped my arms around her from behind and rolled onto my back. And the gasps that followed, as I poked her from behind-beneath and fondled her breasts and caressed her Venus mound and gently toyed with her clitoris, owed less and less to surprise and more and more to that unquenchable fire of orgasmic ecstasy that all women carry around in their bodies.

When we finished at five to two there was no man more envious than me of Ali and his whole hour of dalliance with this delectable young sex-kitten. I got stiff again just thinking about it. She pulled a sympathetic face and made noises of commiseration, but there was nothing we could do. We left that magnificent room with most of its erotic accoutrements unexplored — me dejected, Mirrie excited at the prospect of a new encounter with a new partner.

At the end of the passage, however, our way was barred by a huge, half-naked black man who looked suspiciously like your traditional eunuch. He handed me an envelope, which proved to contain Mirrie's two-o'clock card and a note from Ali saying that other business had detained him and I should make the most of it.

Okay, Ali — *four* percent!

In the meantime the eunuch must have explained the message to Mirrie because she grabbed my arm and literally jumped for joy. Her breasts jumped out of synch with the rest of her, which added to the excitement — hers and mine.

As soon as the door closed behind us again she was all over me, ripping off my dressing gown, pressing her body against mine, and wrapping her legs alternately around me, wriggling and squirming and starting on a fresh round of her own jollies.

"Hold it!" I said feebly before her sexual powers vanquished me. "Let's just see what this room has to offer us."

I had to fight to get her off me but when I reached out with my foot and touched a little belly stool, she got the message. It stood right beside us on a bearskin rug. Twittering with laughter she dropped on all fours and lay face-down upon it, wriggling herself into a comfortable position where it would lift her peachy young black bottom for my delight. She reached her hands behind her and tweaked the gusset in her harem pants wide open, displaying the voluptuous complexities of her hairless oyster, all pink and wet and gleaming with the juice of her excitement.

While I lumbered to my hands and knees and approached to mount her in a sort of press-up position, she scrabbled some silk cushions under her head and shoulders and lay down on her folded arms, leaving her breasts hanging free where my hands could fondle them to our mutual pleasure.

Those silk-upholstered belly stools should be top of every bride's list of wedding presents. An ad-hoc heap of pillows or cushions is no substitute, take it from me — and from Mirrie, I'm sure. When you poke a girl whose derrière is firmly elevated like that, allowing her to relax as utterly as a sleeping babe, it brings the slightly rough, velvety front wall of her vagina into the most pressing contact with the hot, horny underside of your prick. And, since most of her pleasure nerves — and yours — are in those same regions, it turns mere pleasure into ecstasy and mere ecstasy into something utterly mind-blowing.

And this was the de-luxe model, shaped like a crescent moon and furnished with six short legs to keep it stable under even the wildest conditions of excitement. Most sporting girls will take care to lie on the crescent with the two horns pointing upward, so that the thick part will cover their Venus mounds and prevent a customer's fingers from getting at their clitties. True lovers will lie on it with the horns pointing footward — for the opposite reason. Whether by design or through inexperience, Mirrie had chosen to lie on it in the true-love manner — which I saw no reason not to exploit. Soon, with the fingers of my one hand flitting between her soft, hanging breasts and those of my other pressing firmly against her labia and playing a gentle cadenza on her clitoris, we were both floating away on the old familiar clouds of erotic elation.

Again I stopped before we both got carried right away. There was still much to explore in this palatial lupanar. Hanging almost over us was what looked like a gold-plated lavatory seat, suspended from the ceiling by four thick silken ropes of braided gold thread; also a mysterious black bulb, like old-fashioned photographers used, hanging down beside it a few inches off the floor. Reluctantly I withdrew from Mirrie and reached for the bulb. Again she started to whimper but stopped when she saw my purpose.

Somebody must have taken her on an induction course of the room because, as soon as I held the bulb, her hand closed over mine and demonstrated the three electric buttons hidden inside it. The on-off button was at the end; the other two were on the side. When she pressed them, motors whirred somewhere up above the ceiling. One button raised and lowered the seat to the ideal position, the other was a tilt switch that regulated the rate at which it bounced up and down; press one side and it bounced faster; press the other and it slowed down again. The fastest was so fast that it did not bounce so much as vibrate. And the slowest was so dreamy slow it lent a hallucinatory aspect to the simple business of plunging a prick in and out of a vagina.

As soon as I grasped the system she lowered herself, giggling, into the seat and lifted her feet off the ground. Meanwhile I slid myself in underneath. The only thing missing was one of those flat trolleys that help garage mechanics whizz beneath cars.

When I had my ramrod aligned for perfect penetration among the denuded frills of her pussy, I pressed the up-down button and luxuriated as the heat of her vagina engulfed me once again. She made no sound for she was holding her breath against the moment when I pressed the other button. But when I did, she let out a little shriek that would have given the eunuch an erection if he'd been listening.

I'm amazed that not one of the many sporting houses I'd visited up until then had sported such a delightful piece of equipment. In the beginning it felt as unnatural to me as it did when I first tried to draw on a PC screen with a mouse. But sexual pleasure is the world's greatest teacher and I could very soon make it go up and down as slow as two cycles a minute, or vibrate too fast to feel any individual movement. I couldn't decide which was best so I tried them both — and everything in between. Mirrie increased her own pleasure by twining her arms round the cords and letting her hands hang slack near her breasts, so that the random jerking made her limp fingers caress her nipples in an unpredictable pattern. Unpredictability is to sex what salt is to a soft-boiled egg.

Our next toy was like a science-fiction version of a psychiatrist's couch. Or maybe a dentist's chair. It had a flexible backrest with an articulated seat. A headrest projected at the top and there were four flexible armatures, two on each side. Again, Mirrie — child of a village without electricity or motors — knew exactly what to do. She pointed out a row of paired buttons beneath the backrest and said something incomprehensible to me; but I realized they'd be within reach once I was mounted on top of her. She lay back in the seat and stretched her arms and legs out along the four armatures, which, I now saw, had Velcro straps to hold her limbs to them. She held one up, inviting me in mime to fasten them. There were three straps for each leg — at her ankles, just above her knees, and round the top of each thigh — and two for each arm — round her wrists and above her elbows. And, for good measure, there was a wide Velcro strap for securing her waist and a narrow one at her neck.

I don't know how the armatures were engineered because the workings were buried inside some hefty foam padding; but whoever designed it knew his stuff — and knew about stuffing, too. The effect was that her limbs stayed in whatever position you put them. It must have been hydraulic. You pressed a button to free up the mechanism enough to move a limb to whatever position you wanted. Then, when you released the button, you could put the whole of your weight on that limb-plus-armature and it would not move.

She just lay there, watching me try it out — and me torn between sexual stimulation and engineering curiosity. Her eyed were heavy-lidded and she seemed to be already half sunk in the next carnal stupor. Her breathing was shallow and each rapid heartbeat sent little anticipatory shivers through the two soft jellies of her breasts. When she was exactly disposed to my satisfaction I knelt on the knee rest, slipped my fingers among her meaty labia, and parted them for a long, loving gaze at her treasure. The most beautiful sight in the universe is the female pudenda, spread wide — all passive and inviting. If men were honest and if all poetry were truly about 'pleasure remembered in tranquility,' then ninety percent of all the poetry ever written would be about those few square inches of girlflesh and how soft, tender, juicy, and aromatic they are. I gloated for a good long time before I even dared put out my tongue and feast on her nectar, which was now faintly seasoned with the saline sweetness of my recent ejaculation, six inches to the north of where my tongue now flirted and teased.

I remebered the pairs of buttons under her backrest and reached for one set, just to see what it would do. What it did was lower my knee rest to the ground. Its partner raised it again. I kept my finger on it and it continued to raise me, not vertically but along a line parallel to the angle of her body. It didn't take a genius in gunnery to see that the trajectory would rapidly put the knob of my prick in touch with her home-sweet-home once more. I kept my finger on the button and, with the very minimum of movement on my part, slipped back inside where it is always soft and warm and welcoming.

The next pair of buttons opened and closed her legs around me.

The next raised and lowered her derrière beneath me.

My fingers soon achieved virtuoso status as I experimented to find the best combination — eagerly assisted by little cries and moans of pleasure from Mirrie. What she, in fact, did was distract me and postpone my graduation onto the final pair of buttons. Not that I'm complaining, mind. After all, it is the job of any good sporting girl to help a man postpone the business as long as possible, or contracted for.

As for the final buttons … well, I never fully worked out what they did. They produced a whole-body vibration, which was obvious enough. And they varied its rate and intensity in a random way, even after I took my finger off the buttons. Also, I had to press both, briefly and at the same time, to make it stop. Those two bits of the program were easy to latch on to. But if

I kept on pressing the button — either button — it produced such subtle variations of motion that I wasn't aware of most of them until they were well into mid-swing. The upper button changed the position of my knee rest by almost imperceptible degrees. The movement was both up and down and side to side, so it felt like kneeling on the deck of a large ship in a slowly rolling sea — gentle and soothing. The lower button produced an equally slow and subtle motion in every part to which Mirrie was strapped. It felt as if she was doing a slow-motion belly dance beneath me — gentle and far from soothing!

Except that she wasn't *doing* anything at all. She just lay there, utterly inert, eyes closed, a dreamy smile on her lips, and abandoned herself to the machine — which, from her point of view, happened to have one living part: me!

Taking cue from her I let myself go, too. I relaxed every muscle, closed my eyes, and did nothing more strenuous than breathe. And it really was the most wonderful, wanton, voluptuous, abandoned sensation ever. Mirrie was coming in waves, gasping for breath in between. I felt myself beginning to rise to my own climax and I considered stopping the machine and trying something else. But then I asked myself when I had ever enjoyed sex in this way before — answer, never, of course — and wouldn't it be wise to let it rip, to discover if the sort of orgasm it produced was different, too. So then I relaxed even more and let myself sink into the warm sensual morass that was not simply her magnificent body but also the aura of uninhibited, sultry, licentious infatuation that surrounded her.

And when I came I had one of those intimations of infinity that everybody gets from time to time — though not, as far as I know, when actually coming. It was a sense of vastness beyond the mind's comprehension. My spermspouter seemed to be jetting my juice far, far away from me. My body had meanwhile stretched out to span the universe, and every part of it was bathed in the soft, warm glow of orgasm.

While I was still in that stupefied condition Mirrie burst free of the Velcro fastenings and slipped out from beneath me. In less than a second, while I was blinking my bleary eyes and clearing my throat to try to speak, she had shucked off her two skimpy garments and, naked at last, wriggled in beneath me once more, eager to show that this particular love throne was just as enjoyable with the girl lying face-down.

I had just enjoyed such a fabulous climax that I'd have been equally happy to lie with her in my arms until our remaining twenty-five minutes had passed. But I was reckoning without the tyrant down there. When his one bleary, semen-clogged eye caught sight of her crevice, just an inch or two away, he gave a distinct twitch of interest. Her fingers were now free to operate the buttons, of course, and I think she could even have taught a thing or three to the guy who designed the contraption in the first place. She could make any part of the thing — body rest, headrest, or armatures — move wherever she wanted them.

When she realized I was just watching in a daze while she manipulated her tantalizing young body for my next bout of pleasure, she twitched at one of the Velcro straps and twittered something that pretty obviously meant, 'Get on with tightening these.'

Shamed though I am to have to admit it, the act of tying a girl down for my pleasure has always been a powerful erotic stimulus for me, even when I know it is merely symbolic — as it was here. I mean, how hard is it to break the grip of a Velcro fastening? But Mirrie must have enjoyed it, too, or she wouldn't have asked to be tied up. No one could have claimed that the motion of the seat was violent enough to need it. Anyway, the mere act of tightening the bands around her waist and legs brought my prick back into prime condition, ready to enjoy the fruits of the labour.

I could see the white, starchy trickle of my previous salvo — or maybe salvoes — beginning to ooze out of her again, so I picked the little pearly threads of it up on my knob and used them to ease his passage into *her* passage, at least as far as burying the very tip of my knob in between her labia and feeling the easy, compliant flesh of her vagina opening up ahead of it. She did the rest with the buttons, pausing only to grab my hands and carry them to two small rings that hung down underneath her backrest, which was now, of course, her front rest. I had an idea what was coming next for they were right beneath her nipples; and when I gave them a yank, sure enough, two round doors in the padding hinged open and her heavenly breasts fell through into my eager hands.

Again I needed to do nothing but surrender to the machine — and, this time, to her skill in manipulating it. No cinema organist of old, sitting at the controls of his mighty Wurlitzer, ever produced so thrilling and subtle a symphony as Mirrie did that afternoon. The fact that the machine produced random movements of its own, after she had given it general cues with the buttons, meant that it gave her as much pleasure as she gave me. And now that two orgasms had taken the sharp edge off my lust, there was no fear that a third would come welling up and surprise us into a premature ending. The word 'abandoned' has several meanings but I tasted them all over the next fifteen minutes.

In fact, the danger was all the other way — that three-thirty would ring its knell and I still would not have made it to the summit. I began to take an active part myself then, pumping my buttocks and thrusting my gristle in and out of her as if the world was about to end. But she uttered a little whimper of complaint and, bursting the Velcro fetters once again, wriggled out from under me and ran across to the bed, leading me, stumbling and panting behind her.

There she lay down and pulled me on top of her in the good old missionary position. And, by dint of biting my shoulders, caressing my nipples, and scratching my back in long, delicious, shivery sweeps, she soon turned it into the good old emissionary position — the finest emission of the afternoon, in fact, dry and empty though it was.

I have often thought of young Mirie since that blissful afternoon between her thighs — and all the other Bezier girls who came down there to earn their dowries. Did their work satisfy the adulterous lusts that stir in the loins of all married women now and then? Or did it stimulate them to want more than their husbands' services when they returned to the mountains above Tangier? Certainly Mirie's honest appetite for sexual pleasure on that first afternoon of her servitude in that exclusive brothel suggested that her people must be among the happiest of all human tribes.

Macao with Moon Tiger and Lotus Blossom

Many of my encounters with sporting girls have brought shame upon me — the times I've been impotent or (worse) got it half-stiff only ... the times I've been encouraged to such excess that I've felt like dying and have sworn off sex for ever ... the times I've been duped. But it took Macao, the Portuguese version of Hong Kong, to raise that sort of personal, temporary shame by a whole order of magnitude and turn it into something almost cosmic.

I should have been warned by the sight that met my eyes the moment I stepped off the boat from Hong Kong, across the bay. There's an ancient fort right opposite the landing stage and there in front of it, slumped in their sentry boxes, were two slovenly dressed sentries, fast asleep. Their ancient, rusty rifles weren't even within reach but lay piled against the main door of the fort, which was not even fully closed. I suppose the only reason it did not fall open was that its hinges were seized with rust.

It should have told me that here was a place where the guard was down, where all civilized standards were fast asleep. What followed was therefore my own fault.

Macao is the only place where I have ever seen a donkey fuck a woman. Nowhere else have I seen men leaving tips for the waitress by placing the coin on the corner of the table and telling the girl she can have it if she picks it up with her labia; they thought it funny, of course, to heat the coin up first on those little charcoal stoves that go with Chinese cuisine. The floor show at that same restaurant was the public deflowering of a newlywed bride by her husband; they were desperate for money the proprietor told me with a wink. The girl cried and vomited and ran away when it was all over.

I knew how she felt.

I walked disconsolately along the waterfront, waiting for the ferry back to Hong Kong. I had an hour to go.

At one end of the jetty was a ricketty old junk — well named — with a fat, grinning Chinaman, straight from Central Casting, sitting on a bamboo chair at the head of the gangway. "Jigajig with pretty girl?" he said amiably as I drew near. "You like fucky Chinese girl — got cunt like she got eyes!" And he pulled one of his eyes into an even more elongated slit, just in case I hadn't got the message.

Why not? I thought, putting aside all the misgivings that had been piling up ever since I landed. I followed him down the gangway into the bowels of the boat.

At first I could see nothing. The place was lit by a dozen small candles whose guttering flames confused even the few small details they revealed. All I had was a sense of one enormous chamber whose low ceiling was supported by a random forest of props. If there were any girls, they were well hidden. I began to think it was a trap and that at the very least I should be stripped and robbed of everything. I turned and looked for the door but he had closed it behind us. The dark was stygian.

"Are you there?" I asked nervously.

"You follow me." He was just in front of me. He picked up one of the candles — a nightlight it was, really — and led the way to the far end of the vessel.

There was a warm, sickly sweet smell on the air, which, a moment later, I realized was opium. That's what all the candles were, of course. This was no brothel — it was an opium den! I began to wonder if the Chinese maiden I was invited to enjoy would not be one of my own hallucinations.

After an interminable walk we reached an alcove, where he drew aside a curtain to reveal a young girl lying naked amid piles of silk cushions. She was deep in an opium stupor and quite dead to the world. I don't mean she was unconscious. She saw me — and she even smiled — but there was no *person* behind these gestures. Her mind was far away.

"You give me fifty Yankee dollar. Do anything you like with her. Name is Moon Tiger."

I turned on my heel and prayed I could find my way out again.

"Thirty," he said.

"Sorry," I told him.

"Okay," he said, still amiably. "I kick her out. You take her with you."

Blackmail, of course, but I have no doubt he'd have done it.

I gave him thirty without further haggling, though I'm sure I could have got him down another five. I thought that at the very least I could lie there and wait for the time when my ferry was due to sail back to Hong Kong. It would be more comfortable than walking up and down the jetty and, by the look of the girl, I didn't think she would bother me much.

Also the view would be pleasant, for Moon Tiger was both young and pretty — in that dim lighting, anyway.

I shucked off my shoes and crawled into the alcove on my knees. The fat man closed the curtains behind me, saying, "You enjoy good fucky now!"

Moon Tiger was lying right at the outer edge of the bunk so I had to get to the farther side on my hands and knees. As I was poised over her she reached up, grabbed my lapels, and pulled me down for a kiss. But she was still on autopilot; I kissed her pillow; she kissed the air and sighed happily.

I lay down at her side and looked her over. I still had no intention of doing anything — nor any real desire in that direction — but I had to admit that, if she had been conscious and in a cooperative mood, only a Richter-10 earthquake could have kept us apart. She had those lovely dark almond eyes, which, in her case, seemed to see me half the time and look right through me the other half. My panoramic survey went wider. She had a delicate snub nose that was most appealing, bright crimson lips, a dainty jawline, an elegant neck, fragile shoulders and graceful arms, perfect little swelling breasts with soft nipples the colour of roseate mother-of-pearl, a willowy waist swelling to firm, generous hips with a flat, smooth belly between them — and, as Ali had remarked in Tangier, the most beautiful glossy black bush. It was not so dense as to hide the fine, yellow skin of her Venus mound and the darling dimple of her crevice. Her lean, slender thighs invited hands to part them but I resisted manfully.

Do I mean manfully?

Never mind. I resisted.

But not for long, of course. What male could? You always want to know what Young Mossyface looks like. Are her lips fat or thin, complex or simple?

Fat man returned with a new pellet of opium. He shook her and put it in her hand, closing her fingers around it. She stirred out of her stupor long enough for a different autopilot to take over. She pushed the pellet into her pipe and puffed it into the desired state of smouldering, whereupon she drew deeply and inhaled several times.

Before the new high hit her she noticed me behind her and did an instinctive — and most enticing — wiggle of her hips, pouting her bottom at me in obvious invitation. When she lay back on her pillow she even made a half-hearted attempt to undress me. She popped three of my fly buttons and got the tyrant out into the open air, but then the rush hit her and she fell back with a sigh of ecstasy, leaving earthbound me a million miles beneath her.

Even then, with time pressing on, I did not mount her at once. I undressed myself completely and just lay there, gloating over her charms. Her skin exuded some kind of musky aroma with hints of nutmeg and cinnamon. I thought it might come from her fork and put my nose into her bush for a close-up sniff.

The odour of a girl's sex is a most delicate matter. A compulsively scrubbed sporting girl is a big disappointment, though you can see her point. A girl who's spent three days hiking far from baths and streams is a bit over the top. But a healthy young girl who washed herself down there at least six hours earlier is the natural possessor of the most aphrodisiac aroma on earth. If I were a chemist, I'd synthesize it and make a fortune through every sporting house and sex shop in the world. Anyway, the point I'm making is that once I'd caught the whiff of it in Moon Tiger's bush, I was deaf to the promptings of conscience. I slipped between her thighs, pushed them wide apart, and feasted on her pussy until I was close to swooning.

And such a sweet, clean, neat little pussy it was, too! The outer labia were thin and austere, like a couple of parentheses: (). The inner ones were the same only narrower and even thinner. And her hole was all open and soft, as if a sculptor had simply poked his finger into soft, wet clay.

She made no response to any of my licks and caresses — that is, she fidgeted and gave out little sighs of pleasure, which I took for encouragement until I realized she kept on making them even when I stopped.

I returned to her side and started a gentle all-over massage of her delightful body. The squirms and moans of pleasure continued unabated. I suckled her nipples and furled them between my fingers. None of it made any difference to the autopleasuring that was going on in her mind.

I realized then that I was on my own and that it was pointless to spend any more time in trying to rouse her into cooperation. I was still reluctant, however. I poked a drunk girl once — not a pro, just a girl who got drunk at a party and decided that she'd commit suicide if I rejected her. Such ghastly memories linger. Nevertheless, the moment I bit the bullet and straddled Moon Tiger, kneed her thighs apart, and lowered myself into her, I realized there was no comparison at all. Moon Tiger simply was not there! In her place was some kind of female elemental in whom all desire was reduced to its most basic components. The refined sex-play with my tongue and fingers had meant nothing; but the plugging of her tight, smooth young vagina with a bar of randy gristle ... that was the be-all-and-end-all, the alpha and omega of life itself.

It was the least inventive and the least varied screw I ever had — and yet it was very far from being the dullest. All I did was lie on top of her and poke away gently for the next forty minutes. Slowly, too — so that each thrust was like a new exploration of her vagina. My mind, like hers, fell into a trancelike state, such as mystics get when they endlessly chant the same ritual sequence of meaningless syllables. An elemental male emerged in me and communed flesh-to-flesh with the unpersoned female in her. Sex ceased to be that abstract concept we invoke to explain a certain set of powerful feelings. It became something real and palpable, the way that 'electricity' — an equally abstract concept — becomes real for anyone who touches a live wire. I was not 'having sex' with Moon Tiger; if anything, Sex itself was having both of us.

I can't even remember whether or not I came at the end of it all. If I did, it was the least important moment of that bizarre session. It's hard to say why I feel so ashamed of it, even now. Perhaps it's because I have never been able to experience anything so profound with a fully conscious girl, pro or amateuse. I should be able to, I feel, and yet I can't. So the memory of Moon Tiger lingers with me like a standing accusation — of a 'crime' I cannot even name!

The day itself was saved for me, however, by Lotus Blossom — Moon Tiger's identical twin, as I realized the moment I saw her. When I took my leave, she was standing at the foot of the gangway, engaged in a real fishwife's argument with the fat man. He must have said something to her about me and Moon Tiger because I'd hardly gone ten paces before she was at my side, slipping her arm through mine, asking me if I'd enjoyed her sister and was I going back to Hong King — so was she — and was I just visiting the colony and would I like a missy while I was there? She was as lively as her twin had been stupefied.

She claimed she didn't want money; she loved sex for its own sake. But I could give her presents from time to time if I wished. And wasn't the fat man awful? She had got Moon Tiger a really good position in the Hibiscus Garden, one of the best brothels in Hong Kong, and the fat man had seduced her away with promises of all the opium she could use if she'd look after his customers. Now she was a hopeless addict.

I asked Lotus Blossom if she, too, was a sporting girl at the Hibiscus and she answered in a highly insulted tone that she most certainly was not. *She* was a *courtesan!* She had her own apartment. I could stay in it, if I liked.

She asked me again if I had enjoyed Moon Tiger and then, without waiting for my answer, assured me she was ten times better.

She was, too. Well, I don't know about ten times better, but she was alive, responsive, warm, giggly, wriggly, sexy, inventive ... and utterly insatiable. Her apartment was small, as they all are there, but luxurious, with lots of places for a man and a woman to enjoy each other. By dawn the following morning I was exhausted and I knew I was going to achieve only half of what I had planned during the coming day. I don't complain, for I'd enjoyed one of the best nights of sex I'd had in a long time. But I told her it couldn't go on and that if she absolutely needed that much sex, then perhaps it would be better if we alternated — one night as a courtesan with me followed by one night recharging her sexual batteries with a couple of dozen partners at the Hibiscus Garden.

She thought it over for a while and then said, "No. You are just not used to it. You live in a cold country. You will soon be capable like me. I will teach you endurance. I work in advertising all day without dropping off to sleep all the time. I am a courtesan at night to men who buy me presents. What present will you buy me?"

"Something perfect," I said, though I had no idea what.

I found it on the way to her apartment that evening — a single pearl. Okay, it cost more than even the best girl in the most expensive sporting house in the colony, but I was saving on the hotel bill, so it actually evened out. And I couldn't imagine that even the best girl in the best house could be any better between the sheets than Lotus Blossom.

We ate at a waterfront café where I was the only European. It was not just authentic Chinese cuisine, it was *authentic* authentic. She chose the dishes, assuring me she was picking the ones that did most to stimulate the sexual desires of men and women. I said her desires hardly needed such assistance but I did not inquire too closely into the ingredients. A lot of their culinary and medicinal thinking is based on sympathetic magic, so I wouldn't have been surprised to learn I had dined off stud-bull's balls and stallion's prick; she would probably have laced her food with powdered queen bee, on the grounds that a queen bee mates with 25,000 drones in her lifetime or something like that.

The meal was tasty, though, and did not lie heavy on the stomach. Among the dishes, I was glad to see, were raw oysters, which are considered a male aphrodisiac all over the world. They had already been opened and severed, of course, and the shells put together again, but I pretended not to know that and searched avidly for pearls — until she very kindly explained why I wouldn't find one.

Her first words when we were barely across the threshold of her apartment were: "My present?"

I lied. I put on a rueful face and said it had slipped my mind. "Because I was so exhausted," I said. "Maybe if you teach me endurance, like you promised, my mental powers will improve and I won't forget."

She pouted and I could see she was on the point of throwing me out, so I added, "It's a good thing you're doing it for the sex, *not* for the money."

It just tipped the balance into letting me stay one more night. We took a shower together and the soapy massage I gave her did something to awaken the female animal, but she was still in a half-pouting mood when we went to bed. She just lay on her back in an attitude that said, 'Get on with it, then! But don't expect me to take much part.'

Clutching the pearl in my hand I got my head down between her thighs and began kissing them on the insides. After a while she relaxed her resistance enough to let them fall slack. I kissed, I nuzzled, I licked until she opened up a little of her own volition — I mean, I did nothing to open her legs directly. The nearer I got to her little honeypot, the harder it became for her to go on resisting. Her breathing was disturbed by little gasps and catches of breath.

But sexual arousal did not sweeten her temper. Whenever I snatched a glance at her face, her mouth was set grim and her eyes were cold. Body might yield but mind was determined to stay aloof. By now her thighs were parted sufficiently for me to drop the pearl in a fold of the sheet, out of her sight, and gloat on the full glory of her pussy. I haven't enjoyed too many identical twins, so I can't say if it's general with them, but Lotus Blossom's sex was as different from Moon Tiger's as those of any two girls chosen at random. Her outer labia were thick, smooth, and blubbery, more like two sausages than the thin, sensitive parentheses her sister rejoiced in. And her inner ones were as frilly and whirly as the flesh of any big oyster — which is what had given me the idea of the pearl in the first place.

I feasted on that oyster of hers until it began to flow with the juice of excitement. Then, surreptitiously, I took the pearl and glued it in place with that same juice, setting it just below her clitoris.

"Eh?" I exclaimed in astonishment, staring at her wide-open pussy.

"What?" she sat up in alarm.

"No, no!" I exclaimed. "Don't move! Lie absolutely still! I'll get a mirror."

I repeated the command to lie still as I sprang from the bed and returned with her mirror from the dressing table. I held it between her legs to show her what I had 'discovered.'

She was quick of wit, all right. The moment she saw it she realized what I'd done and fell back on her pillow, convulsed with laughter. When she had laughed her lungs empty she sat up, panting and wiping her

eyes on the back of one hand while she took the mirror
from me and had another look. It was a good long one
this time, and her mood went from amusement to
admiration. I could almost hear the brain cogs clicking
over as she pondered the thought of getting her labia
pierced and setting a little pearl like that between
them — weighing up the discomfort against the value
in extra tips from delighted customers. She was
probably even designing the clasp so that a man could
flip it out with his tongue. As I said, she was quick of
wit.

"You found this at the restaurant tonight?" she
asked as she removed it finally and set it on her bedside
table with care.

"I found it in a jeweller's at lunchtime."

"And that's why you made all those jokes about
pearls and oysters at dinner! Oh, come here, Riley!"
She flung her arms around me and drew me on top of
her. "You are a nice man to me, you know. And I am a
naughty lady for not trusting you." She gave a little
shiver. "It makes me nearly come just to think of it —
you sitting there with that pearl in your pocket and me
so angry with you for not bringing me a present. How
much did it cost?"

"More than I could afford but only a hundredth part
of what you are truly worth," I murmured in her ear.

"Oh!" she gasped. "Say it again! I'm coming! I'm
coming!"

I slipped into her at the moment she brimmed over
into her ecstasy. Her lithe, athletic body thrashed
around beneath me. She sank her teeth into my
shoulder muscle. Her fingernails dug into the flesh of
my back. And then I brimmed over, too. My balls must

have been working overtime all day for me to be
to shoot such a prodigious quantity of sticky ins
her. I could feel it rushing out and spreading all over
my knob like a coating of hot, turbid jelly. I knew then
that we were in for another night of debauchery but,
somehow, I felt more able to face it than had seemed
possible at that day's dawning.

We took another shower, for the night was hot, and
when we returned to bed she said, "Let's hope it's true
about oysters and what they do for a man."

"You know the joke about that?" I replied. "The
newlywed bride who orders a dozen oysters — each —
to be sent up to the honeymoon suite and when the
hotel manager asks her next day if they were to her
liking she replies, 'So-so. Actually only nine of them
worked.'"

She laughed until the tears ran again. Then, as she
spread me out like a second sheet on her bed, yanking
my arms and legs until they were just where she wanted
them, she flung herself on top of me and said, "We had
twelve oysters each tonight, but they were the best
Chinese ones. They will *all* work."

I didn't know whether it was a threat or a promise
but by the following dawn we had turned it into a
simple statement of fact. And, what is more, I felt *less*
of a wreck than I had the previous day.

Ten days I stayed in Hong Kong with Lotus Blossom.
Ten little pearls were nightly discovered gleaming out
of her furrow, just below her clitoris. Ten dozen oysters
we consumed at this or that little waterfront restaurant
before we retired to bed. And there, on ten successive
nights, we proved that Chinese shellfish really are the
best, for every single one worked!

Los Angeles and Casey

I said there's no such thing as a free lunch in business — nor free sex, either. I'll qualify that slightly and say it *can* happen, but only by accident — the way it happened to me in Los Angeles one balmy summer night in the early eighties. I was staying at the Shalimar Garden, a hotel which, unlike a lot of things in LA, actually lives up to its name in that it is surrounded by a lavish and fascinating garden. I was working on a big, expensive, but fairly standard air-conditioning system for a shopping mall. They didn't really need my expertise but their insurers thought they did. So there I was for a month of easy days and nights. The architect I was working with on that contract had recommended the Shalimar Garden and, to show me why, he dropped me off at one of its farthermost entry points on my first evening so that I could enjoy it to its fullest extent. I'd already checked in that morning, but he carried my briefcase round to the lobby for me.

What a garden! It isn't just that there are *no* weeds, nor that it is a plant collector's dream, it's the way you can go from, say, a dark, humid fernery, almost underground, to a bright desert oasis within a twenty-yard stroll — and then, round the very next corner, you're on an alpine slope. You never know what you're going to find up ahead.

What I found up ahead that afternoon was Casey: a beautiful, svelte, immaculately groomed, auburn-haired young lady of around twenty-three. She was sitting disconsolately beside a lush bowling green, watching a gaggle of wrinklies work off ancient scores against one another. Beside her stood a small crocodile-skin suitcase. My first thought, on seeing her from the farther end of the green, was that she was waiting for someone — though in my usual way I hoped, of course, that she was waiting for *anyone*. She glanced up, saw me, looked me up and down, and rested her eyes in mine. She seemed so disconsolate that my next thought was that she had been thrown out of the place. The truth, as I soon discovered, was even worse.

"Hi," she said sadly as I drew near.

"Hi! Pardon me for saying this, young lady, but you look decidedly unhappy, sitting there. I don't wish to intrude, but is it possible I might help?"

I walked past her and seated myself on the same bench — not, pointedly, as far away as possible, but not crowding her space, either. She sighed, glanced briefly at me, and returned her gaze to the prunes on the green. That was when I saw she had a most unpleasant outgrowth of shingles clustered round the lower left corner of her lips. From that moment on, I reluctantly decided, any help I might give her was going to be completely altruistic.

"I'm a call girl," she said flatly, still not looking at me. "And I have a problem. Are you still sure you want to help?"

On the spur of the moment I decided to put as much distance between us as possible. "How fascinating," I said. "D'you know — I don't think I've ever met a ... one of ... someone in your profession."

Her head flipped round, making me think, *Those shingles must hurt when you do that!* Her jaw fell. "You're not serious?" she said.

"Well …" I was caught up enough in my act to realize I was blushing for real. "Maybe I don't quite … I mean … 'call girl'! Does that mean a …" I swallowed hard.

"A hooker — sure," she replied. "Are you English?"

"Yes." I cleared my throat. "The name's Riley."

She smiled, again without wincing at any pain from those vicious-looking welts. The darndest shingles I ever saw. "I'm Casey. What does that look mean, Riley?"

I did the Stan Laurel eyebrows. "It means I don't *actually* know what a 'hooker' is, either — except that it's a kind of fishing boat in Ireland."

"No kidding! A fishing boat, huh? Well, it implies a kind of fishing here, too, I guess. The fact is, Riley, I'm a prostitute. Do you have that word over there in England?"

"Gosh!" I exclaimed. "Are you really? You don't look it."

"Or I am when they let me. At this moment I've got a date with a man in that hotel there. But there's this house dick who's gonna turn me over to the vice squad if he sees me trying to sneak in."

"Aha! And you want me to go in and let this chap know … bring him out to meet you? Something like that?" I looked around to see where they might do it in the bushes.

"You'd do that?" she asked in surprise.

"Of course. Damsel in distress and all that rot, what!"

"Oh!" She lolled her head in a token swoon toward me. "You English are so …! And I *lo-ove* that accent. But no, Riley, the favor I'd like to ask is something much simpler than that. Just let me walk in there side by side with you, all nice and friendly, with my arm linked through yours, all the way to the elevator. He won't dare bother me then. We'll go up in the elevator. You can get out at your floor. I'll get out at mine. End of favor — okay?"

"That's all?" I asked, standing up again.

"That's all." She rose and slipped her arm through mine at once.

I offered to carry her bag but she said better not.

"So!" I said nervously. "You actually … you know … for money?"

"Right. Any complaints?"

"No. I'm just fascinated. As I said, I've never actually met … you know."

"You have. You just didn't realize it at the time."

"Well, that could be true — if you're anything to go by, I've probably met dozens without knowing it."

"So you've obviously never made use of … 'you know' — as you so coyly put it?"

"Gosh, no!" I spluttered.

"Why not, for heaven's sake? You're not gay — I knew that the moment you looked me up and down back there."

"Did I? Gosh, I do apologize."

She merely chuckled at that.

We were crossing the parking lot now, getting close to the place where we had to run the gauntlet. It was a pity about the herpes sores, I thought. But for them, I'd ask her if she could be my first. "The reason I haven't …" I began awkwardly.

"Is what? Go on. I'm pretty thick-skinned, you know. I won't take anything you say personally."

"Well — everyone knows that prostitutes are all man-hating lesbians. Sex, to me is the most beautiful, wonderful thing on earth. So I'd hate to do it with someone who loathes my guts in secret and who's only thinking of the seconds ticking away. A girl whose own sex is utterly dead. I can't imagine anything more flesh-crawling than a girl having a fake orgasm with me."

"Bravo!" She laughed. Not sarcastically, either. "Fine words from a man who has never tried it! Boy — if I didn't have this trick to see now, I'd offer you a chance to find out just how wrong you are."

I weakened, shingles or no shingles. "What would it … er … how much …?" I stammered. We were entering the lobby by now.

"Nothing," she replied. "You could pay me after, if I'm right — or not, if I failed to convince you."

A spotlight caught her shingles as we crossed the foyer. It brought me to my senses. "I don't know …" I said dubiously.

The light must have been for the CCTV and the house dick, or dickhead, must have been watching the screen. I saw him coming toward us even before Casey did. I squeezed her arm to alert her I was going to ham it up.

"The thing about that quintet in *Cosi fan tutte,*" I said earnestly, waving a languid hand to match my even more languid words, "is that Mozart gives all the complex harmonies and melodies to the two women, while the three men sing only simple ones. So, even if you don't understand the actual words, the music tells you that the men just aren't mentally equipped to carry out their devious plot. The women are going to run circles round them."

To my amazement she began singing, *"Due volte ancora tu scrivimi, se puoi ..."* from that very quintet. She had a trained voice, too. She finished the line with a diva's flourish and a wave of her hand that included the goggle-eyed dick, whom we left standing, gawping after us.

The moment the elevator doors closed behind us she collapsed against me in laughter — a token collapse but much more than a token laugh. "You should be in *Masterpiece Theater!*" she said. "That was pretty damn good."

"And you should be in *Live from the Met,*" I replied. "You didn't get that voice just singing in the tub."

"Tell me about it!" she said bitterly.

"I'm afraid I can't," I said, keeping up my naïve-Englishman façade.

She frowned uncomprehendingly but we had reached her floor. "I get out here."

I got out with her. "I'm only one floor up," I explained. "I'll walk it."

"Listen, Riley," she said. "You're one hell of a guy. It was swell meeting you. Maybe someday, huh?" She lifted her face for a chaste kiss.

I drew back in alarm.

She was shocked at first but then burst out laughing. "Thanks!" she said as she peeled the herpes cluster off her face and wrapped it carefully in a tissue. "I'd forgotten it was there." Then, seeing my amazement, she added, "I have this friend in F/X — she made it up for me. It don't 'alf put the skids under a wanna-be rapist," she added in Hollywood cockney.

I enjoyed the chaste kiss but all the way up to my own room I cursed myself for not noticing that those fiery red blisters were fake. Now my chance had gone.

I was still feeling pretty disconsolate when I wandered down for dinner, half an hour later. I had intended sending out for a call girl myself but now I knew I'd be thinking of Casey all the time I was with whoever they sent to service me.

But there she was — Casey herself, sitting all alone at the bar, looking as melancholy as I had felt a couple of seconds earlier. It must just have been a quickie. So now she was looking for someone else, to make the cab fare worth it. I hoped.

She was so disconsolate, she didn't even see me approaching her in the glass behind the bar.

"*Là ci darem la mano …*" I sang (in my decidedly untrained voice) when I drew near. It's from *Don Giovanni,* also by Mozart, and it means: 'There we'll take hands and you will whisper yes.'

She looked up into the mirror, saw me … and that smile alone was worth a thousand dollars. The herpes was back — on the other side of her lips this time; but it didn't bother me now. "*Vorrei e non vorrei …*" she responded from the same duet; it means: 'I'd like to but I dare not …'

We both knew the duet ended with words that meant, 'Then come, oh come, my dearest, and ease the pain of a chaste love!' but we didn't sing it.

"Riley!" she said as we trailed off halfway. "Am I glad to see you! Can you believe this jerk? He books me for the whole night, beginning like now, and he leaves me this!"

I ordered a Manhattan, just to see if they knew the name in LA. The note she handed me read: *Hang around, doll, and keep pussy warm for me. I may be back round nine.* It was signed by a film star of the sixties whose name would be instantly known anywhere in the world. Here I'll call him Hugh Jambton — being an old Goons fan.

"Is that the *real* Hugh Jambton?" I asked.

She nodded and said with disgust, "They don't come any realler. '*I may* be back round nine' — how d'ya like that!"

"Speaking personally," I replied, "I like it very much, because it gives me the chance to invite you to dine with me, instead."

Her annoyance evaporated at once. "Really?" she asked in surprise.

"Really."

"Why?" Her suspicion was only half jocular.

"Because some of the things you said out there shook my prejudices to bits. But, actually, it was more than anything you said. It was you, yourself. *You* shook my prejudices to bits. Aren't you hungry?"

"Sure." She grinned. "But I gotta warn you — this Jambton jerk may come back anytime. Or not at all. I'm not the first he stood up in this way. One of the other girls at the agency told me he did exactly this to her — and then showed up around ten with some ten-dollar hooker he picked up on the Strip. He expected her to do a double with this floosie!"

"D'you lose money then?"

"No way! This jerk pays up front or we blackball him off every good agency in town and he's stuck with Strip hookers like forever. I'm already paid-up for the entire night — a megabuck, to answer the question you half asked an hour ago. Did you say something about having dinner together?"

She peeled off her herpes patch and we strolled together into the dining room, where I shook the maître-d' by the hand though I'd never met him before. He gave us a table that made other people's heads turn.

Casey was impressed. "D'you always do that?" she asked. "Shake the maître-d' by the hand?"

"Always. I picked up the habit in Florence, Italy, where it's standard practice. I started doing it in London, where I noticed it got me good tables."

"Florence ... Italy ... London ... I guess you get around?"

I reeled off a few continents and explained a little about my work.

"And you never picked up a prostitute in *any* of those places? Not even Bangkok?" She leaned forward and stared incredulously into my eyes.

What could I say? I was too deeply committed to my earlier story to back out now. Besides, I wanted to see if she would renew her offer in these new circumstances. "Can I talk frankly?" I asked.

"Of course."

We ordered the same off the menu, quite spontaneously: quails' eggs followed by venison *filet tournedos*. I chose a half of Fleurie and a 1968 Clos des Jacobins to go with them.

"I've often considered doing it," I began.

"How often?"

I grinned and hung my head. "Every day, I suppose."

"And never *once* fell from grace? Riley — you either have a burning religious faith to keep you straight — though I don't get those vibes from you — or you've got a very sweet partner."

I nodded. "Not that wedding bells are in the air or anything like that. But I've been thinking a lot lately, about how people get set in their ways once they pass thirty. So, if I don't try it with a prostitute soon, I probably never will. It'll remain a fantasy forever." I smiled wanly. "Maybe no bad thing, though."

"Tell me about this fantasy, Riley."

"It's embarrassing."

"I won't laugh, I can surely promise you that. You're looking at a veteran of men's sexual fantasies here, let me tell you."

I sighed. "It's so stupid. I've got this scenario where she picks me up in the street. We go to her room. It's her first day on the Game. She's as nervous as I am. We start to have sex and she starts to turn on, too — genuinely ..." I closed my eyes and lowered my head. "I can't go on, Casey. It's just so picayune."

"I think it's sweet. It shows you have a sweet nature. You *want* the girl to be happy, too. Actually, a lot of men are like that. I'm amazed. They ask me how *I* like to do it, for God's sake! If I was paying for it, that's the last thing I'd ask."

"Which do you prefer — the kind who try to please you or the kind who order you about?"

"Oh, the kind who try to please. Because if they fuck me so hard that it hurts, I can tell them and they'll stop. The other kind just say tough shit and it goes with the territory and like that."

"And of course you don't turn on with any of them — good or bad?"

She gave a little sniff and a lopsided grin. "I wouldn't say that."

"Oh?"

"Why are men so obsessed with giving women orgasms?"

"Why do women fake it even when they haven't been satisfied?"

She knitted her brow and said, "Yeah, you're right! I never thought of it before. Why?"

"I think it goes back to sexual strategies in the days of the cave men. A man who goes away hunting for two or three days needs to make damn sure his woman is looking forward to his return — which she isn't going to do if he's a brute who uses her without regard. And cave woman, for her part, needs to keep him happy so he'll bring back the venison to her."

Our venison steaks arrived at that moment. Our eyes met and we laughed. If there was a moment when we knew we were going to end up in bed together, that was it.

"So what sort of customer turns you on?" I asked.

"A good lover. There are a lot of good lovers out there. Mind you — I don't welcome it, even so. I'm just admitting it happens though I do everything to prevent it. What I've started doing lately, if I think a john is going to light my fire, is I use a vibrator. I give him a little show with a vibrator. And I give myself a couple of quick orgasms with that — not that *he'd* know it, mind, because I can have them *very* quietly. And then I fake one, a big Wagnerian one, for his benefit. And after that, I'm okay. Safe."

"What about regular johns — is that what you call them all? Johns? Do you have any of those?"

"Sure. I've got three at the moment. One I see three times a week. Monday, hand job. Wednesday, oral. Friday, the works!"

I thought of Ebony at the Mustang and only just remembered in time not to blurt it out! "And you don't get sort of friendly with them and relax and turn on?"

"The Friday one I do," she admitted reluctantly. "God, I'd never confess this to anyone else — why am I telling you?"

"You see, that's what I can't understand. A man would be *proud* of the number of orgasms he could achieve. He'd boast of them to anyone who'd listen. But to you it's more like a matter for shame. Weird!"

"Well, first, it's not *supposed* to happen. Secondly, a man *gives* something when he comes — he's the big spender. A woman's at the receiving end of his largesse, which is always demeaning. Thirdly, like you say with your cave-man theory, it does make a girl beholden to the john. Also it stops her from doing a really professional job. She's spreading her body so as to maximize *her* pleasure when she should be spreading it for his. Also there's the thought that he'd have the gall to go boasting to his pals that he made you come. That's why we pros fake it, I think. So that if he tries to boast, his pals will just laugh and tell him we sigh and shiver like that for everyone."

"Is it boring work?" I asked. "Doesn't it get to be all the same after a time? How long have you been doing it — if that's not out of order?"

"I'd rather be singing in the chorus at the Met — that's for sure!" A distant look crept into her eyes. "Actually ..." she said.

"Actually what?"

"I turned down a couple of singing jobs lately. They clashed with my agency work. I guess I really am turning pro. I've always had this thought at the back of my mind that I was just doing it to save up a grubstake to carry on training and try for some opera work. Maybe I'm kidding myself. Maybe I was always meant to be a hooker." She grinned at me, almost as if she was glad to have made this discovery.

"D'you really think so?" I responded. "*Are* some girls naturally born to it?"

"It feels right for me. I've been doing it four years — to answer your other question back there. Am I ever going to sing opera? Who am I kidding! I feel comfortable doing this work. I feel skilled. I feel valued — overvalued, sometimes. I leave my johns happy and exhausted. You may ask why I only have five regulars. That's by my decision. I've told the agency that if there's a choice between a semi-regular and some john I never serviced before, I'll take the stranger. I like the variety." She laughed. "I guess I've finally cottoned on to the fact that this is my métier — here tonight with you, Riley. How can I ever thank you?" The tip of her tongue lingered teasingly on her lip; she knew damn well how she was going to thank me.

The chance came when Hugh Jambton showed up. He was drunk — stupid drunk, giggly drunk — and, once again, he had a busty miniskirted hooker from the Strip at his side. To me 'she' looked like a transvestite, nostril-hair and all. When Jambton insisted on a double act with 'her' and Casey, 'she' shook 'her' head frantically behind his back. The clear implication was that 'she' could fool the idiot quite successfully alone. Not that Casey needed any encouragement to turn the offer down. She just told the jerk that either he paid off the hooker right there or she'd walk.

Jambton squared up pugnaciously. No cheap $1,000-dollar call girl was going to order him around. He bundled the hooker into the elevator and whisked her up to his room.

Casey, wordless for once, put her arms around me and let out an enormous sigh of relief. Her breasts owed nothing to silicone or surgery. "Where's your room?" she asked.

"Your bag?" I said.

She hesitated. "Would it disappoint you greatly, Riley, if we did without any of those toys?"

In the elevator she said, "Remember that offer I made to you earlier — pay me only if I convince you? Can we forget that?"

"You mean I pay you anyway?"

"No!" She butted me with her forehead. "And you know that's not what I meant."

"So what you do mean is that I'm going to wake up tomorrow, *still* not knowing what it's like to enjoy a prostitute?"

"I'm afraid so." She smiled. "But I can send you someone who'll take care of that — very skilfully. Tomorrow, if you like? Or you name the day."

"I guess," I said lugubriously, "I'll just have to grin and bear it."

She nipped the back of my arm playfully, "When *I* bare it, you'll grin, okay!"

As soon as we were in my room she put her arms around me again and said, "Kiss me — then I'll know it's not work."

It made me realize how long it was since I had kissed a girl. I had probably fucked two hundred girls over the past ten months, all without kissing one of them on the lips. Casey's were soft and warm, vibrant and alive. Her mouth was filled with pleasant memories of crêpes suzettes. I hoped mine was, too.

When we broke I said, "You mean a john doesn't get to kiss you? He can stick his dick into the most intimate, secret part of your body but not touch his lips to yours?"

She shook her head. "Not even for a thousand dollars a night. And my vagina is only intimate when *I* say it is. One of my johns who's a dermatologist — he explained it to me. A girl's vagina is lined with epidermis. You know what that is?" She showed me the palm of her hand. "That! That's epidermis — just plain skin. It isn't *inside* me at all. No more than that." She folded her hand to make an impromptu vagina and took one of my fingers, which she inserted into it. My erection hardened still further. "Epidermis to epidermis! Outside skin to outside skin." To make the point even more strongly she opened her hand but kept my finger rubbing up and down her palm. It's no more intimate than that. Anyway, that's how I look at it professionally." She put her arms around me again. "And that's why I gotta kiss you — because tonight it's intimate and secret once again!"

It was a novel situation for me as well as for her. The last sex I'd had in which no money changed hands was with Rosa in Stockholm, almost two years earlier. I am a passionate, dedicated, committed buyer of sexual pleasure. I enjoy not having to *woo* a girl, or worry about her moods, her motives, her needs. No will-she-won't-she? No 'not tonight dear, I've got a headache.' No 'yes, *tonight* man, and you'll soon forget your headache'! No 'did you forget to take the Pill?' No

'I told *you* to get the condoms'! I don't even have to think when the barber asks me if I 'need anything for the weekend.' Whatever I need, I can buy — and there's an end to it.

So it was no wonder that both Casey and I were as shy as two virgins. However, when she slipped my jacket off me and I unbuttoned the jacket of her crisply tailored suit of turquoise silk, the old familiar juices began to flow and the old instincts took command. "I keep feeling I ought to ask you how you like to do it," I joked.

She laughed. "I get that feeling, too. I can't say 'How d'you want me?' but I don't know how else to begin! How *do* you begin, usually?"

I shrugged. "Putting on some music, I guess, and turning the lights down low. Maybe dancing a bit — shuffling, really, cheek to cheek. Letting my hand slip down a naughty bit lower. Maybe she hitches it up again. Then I try again a little later and this time ..."

"Stop!" She said, getting excited already. "This is good! I'd forgotten, but this is good. This I can do. Let's try it. Don't tell me unless I go wrong."

So we did. First we washed and brushed our teeth and shucked off our shoes. Then, in a low-wattage twilight, we smooched around the carpet, cheek-to-cheek to some golden-oldie radio station that seemed to be playing wall-to-wall Glenn Miller.

"I'd forgotten," she murmured in my ear after a while. "It used to be like this, didn't it." Then, "I can feel your *excitement* growing!"

"You don't comment on it, though," I told her. "I'm not supposed to know if you will or if you won't. That's why I do this." I let my hand stray down over her derrière — which was one of the cutest I'd touched in a long time.

"And I do this, huh?" She reached a hand behind and hitched mine up again.

"But you also kiss me and press one of those absolutely divine breasts against me."

"I do? Why?" She did it anyway, without waiting for an answer.

My prick was so rampant-hard by now that I had to break off and pretend to pull up a sock so as to hitch it up behind my waistband. Her grin told me she understood and she wasn't fooled.

"You do it to throw my emotions into confusion," I told her. "You say 'keep off the grass' and you say 'come, lie down on my lawn' — all in one breath ... until I'm putty in your hands."

"As long as *one* part of you doesn't turn to putty in my hands! Sorry, I forgot — I don't say things like that. Right?"

Next time both my hands slipped down there she let them linger and even caress her a while before she wriggled out of my embrace and, taking my hand, led me to the sofa. "I've been on my feet all day," she said as she pulled me down beside her. And I didn't know whether she said it for real or as part of some fantasy she was building.

There was no fantasy about the passion of her kisses when we were seated side by side and twisted rather awkwardly in each other's arms. Nor of mine. This was something way beyond the sort of pleasure I was accustomed to buying. To run my fingers through her hair was somehow even more erotic than, say, bending a naked sporting girl over the back of a chair and running my knob up and down her furrow — running my eleventh finger through her *other* hair, you might call it. She seemed to think so, too, especially when I scratched lazily behind her ears and down her neck.

For a long time my caresses lingered there, above the line of her collar, just as if we were lovers on a first date and I were probing cautiously to see how far she'd let me go. She must also have been getting herself into that same frame of mind for, when the tips of my fingers started straying down inside the collar of her blouse, down as far as her collarbone, I felt her stiffen and stop breathing.

Skills I had forgotten started coming back to me. My thumb slipped the top button of her blouse free without her realizing it — which let my fingernails abseil down over the curve of her collarbone and onto the soft, fleshy part above her breast. I caressed her there a long time before changing position and repeating it with my left hand above her left breast.

Until then she was not aware that two of her buttons were now loosened. "Here!" she exclaimed, pulling away from me and doing them up again.

"Please?" I begged. "Just this." And I placed my thumbs on her nipples and slid them round and round — flesh on silk on cotton on flesh. "It's much nicer if there's nothing in between."

She watched me warily and her tongue flickered over her lips. I could not decide whether she was giving a consummate performance or whether our chaste petting had awakened a long-forgotten self within her, too. "You'll see," I said, daring to unbutton her blouse again, this time all the way. "Front-opening," I added, staring appreciatively at her bra.

She grinned. "Girls call them front-*fastening*," she said.

"And so they should," I replied.

I could have opened it then and there but decided not to; I was so much enjoying my memories of teenage snogging sessions like this and the thrill of getting the tip of one finger down inside a bra cup.

It all came back to me again now as I slid my hand inside her opened blouse and under her strap. Then down, down to the top of her bra, caressing and lightly scratching that alluringly soft flesh where the breast begins to swell. Under I went, and in, where it is softer still. She stopped breathing, knowing — or hoping she knew — what was coming next. At the edge of her areolæ my fingers hesitated. I turned them on their sides and grazed them over that exquisitely nervous skin around her nipple.

A minor tremor shook her and she breathed in with a shiver, expanding her chest in the hope of raising her nipple into contact with those maddeningly gentle fingernails. I avoided them for some time, tantalizing myself as well as teasing her — first on one breast, then on the other. The little game ended when I spread my hand wide and flat on her upper chest, reaching for both nipples at the same time. Then, unnoticed by me, she slipped her fingers up and undid her bra. Then she pushed her breasts closer together and lifted them up in her hands, offering them to my finger and thumb.

He breathing grew ragged and the shivers more pronounced. I slipped my left arm around her and under her arm to caress her left breast, taking her right breast into my other hand at the same time. She raised her arms high and flung her head back, allowing me to do everything that hands, fingers, fingernails, and thumbs can possibly do to arouse and excite a woman through her breasts and nipples.

At last my hand stole down to her thighs ... to caress their silk-stockinged flesh ... to slip between them and up to the hem of her skirt ... to caress a little higher ... and a little higher still ... until I reached the tops of her stockings, within four inches of the goal line.

"Mmmnh!" she murmured plaintively — not quite a no and not exactly a yes. Half-heartedly her hand plucked mine away — by as much as three inches — and she clamped her thighs tight together.

I moved a little away from her and pulled her to me at a slantwise angle, going down on her breasts to suckle at her nipples while I started my hand on a fresh assault upon her virtue.

"Oh, please!" she murmured, kissing the back of my neck and scratching me deliciously up and down my spine. As my hands reached the tops of her stockings for the second time, she started pulling my shirt free of my waistband at the back. She freed it completely as the backs of my knuckles started to graze her Venus mound — or, rather, the silk of her panties where it clothed that delightful swelling.

There was a brief pause and a flailing of arms while she drew the shirt off me completely — and, almost in passing, whipped away her blouse and bra as well. So, while the undressing mood was upon us, I slipped my hand beneath her fork and up behind to where I could curl my fingertips over the waistband of her panties. One smooth pull and they were crumpled in a figure-8 around the tops of her thighs — and the tip of my thumb was free to wiggle lightly up and down her furrow, mostly favouring the vestibule to that place which, for one night only, was both secret and intimate. She was as hot and wet down there as any girl I'd ever felt in that way.

They are *so* special, those few square inches of flesh. In theory, any warm, wet orifice should feel the same but it doesn't. When a girl's thighs are clenched tight around your fist and you can do little more than slip the knuckle of your thumb up into the outer portals of her dumb glutton, then you just know there is no other flesh quite like it in all the world. Casey resisted me mildly for a while and then yielded, throwing her thighs wide with complete abandon and pouting her pussy up toward me for something more than a mere knuckle.

I gave her my thumb, sliding it all the way in and then some. I wiggled the whole of it and just the top, marvelling that the same vagina can feel so different, depending on whether it's your thumb or your prick that's doing the exploring. To my thumb it did not feel in the least like a tube — more like a series of warm, slippery, elastic bulges and swellings on all sides, which yielded to the pressure of my digit and yet clung tight in its wake, whichever way I moved it.

She gave out a little yelp of pleasure and fell against me, pushing hard and trying to scrabble me down on top of her, there on the sofa.

"To bed?" I whispered.

"If you're quick," she gasped.

I never saw a girl undress in greater haste. How her panties and stockings didn't get shredded I'll never know. Mind you, I was pretty swift myself, pulling off the last of my socks with my toes as I slipped between

the sheets, half a second behind her. She lay on her
back with her legs slightly parted in the good old
missionary position. "No tricks," she begged. "No
changing positions. Just do it like this all the way, eh?"

I slipped into a sort of press-up position above her,
but with my knees together, resting on the sheets
between hers. The heated perfume off her body was
intoxicatingly musky. She slipped a hand under her
thigh, caught my knob in the act of nuzzling into her
vulva, and guided it to its long home.

I begin to tremble with excitement even now as I
recall the feeling of that hot, juicy, yielding vagina
swallowing my gristle and closing all around it. When I
was inside her all the way, pushed to the very hilt of
me, she either made it contract like a squeezing hand
or the movement was quite spontaneous and involun-
tary. Either way, it was so powerful and so unexpected
that she almost made me shoot my bolt right there and
then.

I took a grip on myself and started rodding her with
long, slow, easy strokes, taking all of two seconds to go
in and two more to withdraw.

"Oh, Riley!" she murmured. "Keep it going *exactly*
like that! Don't change — you've hit my rhythm, man!"

I did as she said and was soon rewarded with the
sound of her heavy, forced breathing in perfect timing
with each thrust of mine. She whispered a long, drawn-
out sound like 'a-w-e!' at the end of each intake of
breath, and shuddered violently on each exhalation,
like a dog panting quickly and shallowly. Every now
and then she squirmed a little and stretched out full
length under me, making every muscle and sinew go
tense.

I made only one change in position. Her vagina became so relaxed and so well lubricated that I lost some sense of contact between us there; so I lay right on her and dropped my knees on the outsides of her thighs, clamping them tight together to restore the clench of her flesh upon mine.

Just as I had accientally caught her rhythm earlier, this seemed to catch her desire for erotic contact perfectly. A moment later, showing a strength that I thought people could have only under hypnosis, she arched her back and lifted her bottom (and me) three or four inches clear of the mattress. At the same moment a violent convulsion shook her. Then she collapsed and threw her legs up around me, digging her heels under the folds of my buttocks and keeping me waltzing in and out to her particular rhythm.

Every now and then she'd just lie there twitching and gasping, picking up the rhythm again a few moments later. "You know what's happening?" she asked after several such episodes.

"I can guess," I replied.

"How long can *you* last out?"

"Just slip your legs back under mine when you've had enough."

"Sure?"

"Sure."

Twenty minutes and two or three times that number of orgasms later, I felt her legs straighten up beneath me. I had been on a knife edge for some time by then, so the slight pressure of her manoeuvre was enough to brim me over. It was the only moment when she was more pro than amateuse; she not only made the muscles around her vagina contract once more, she timed each squeeze perfectly so as to milk me dry. The thrust of each squirt was so forceful that my prick seemed to knock the whole of me back in recoil as each new gusher of sticky was fired up into her.

She let me soak it to the last tiny tremor — and then a minute or so longer.

"Oh, Riley," she said mildly. "I wonder if this was wise?"

"Me, too," I said, slipping out of her at last. "That was better than anything I ever enjoyed in bed with a girlfriend ..."

"You're still stiff!" she exclaimed.

"I could go again," I admitted.

"Oh, come on!" she exclaimed. "This is too good to waste. We can talk later." And she flipped over on her tummy and scrabbled ineffectively with one hand behind her, trying to push me on top of her. I say 'ineffectively' because I was already there, stretching myself out fully and slipping my gristle down into her crevice, lingering at her hole but then moving on, all the way forward to her clitoris.

"Can I show you something I like to do?" I asked.

"Go right ahead, man."

There was a brief moan of complaint when I pulled both of us on our right sides — me still with my gristle tucked snugly into her groove. But the complaint ceased the moment my hand snaked down over the taut skin of her belly and, gathering up my knob, pressed it tight into the darling little pocket where her clittie snuggled. When I gave a little jiggle to it, she whispered, "Oh, my God!" in the same tone as people use when they see that something frightful but inevitable is about to happen.

In this case the awful thing was that another sequence of multiple orgasms was about to overwhelm her. And when my other hand stole up to fondle her breasts and make a mayhem of her nipples, they began all over again — long spasms of shivers and quakes, accompanied by gasps and sharp, formless cries of ecstasy.

When I felt them dwindling again I rolled over on my back, pulling her on top of me. I slipped my gristle inside her during this roll, which left both hands free to explore her glories. I smoothed her arms out above her head and raked my fingernails down their undersides, all the way into her armpits and then onto her breasts themselves.

"Oh stop!" she moaned as yet another series of orgasms overcame her. But when I obeyed, she whimpered a further complaint and cried, "More! More!"

I obeyed that command, too.

We almost fell asleep after that. Only the fact that we were both clammy with sweat was able to drive us from between the sheets and stumble toward the bathroom and the shower — which was big enough for a foursome.

"My God!" she cried out again after we started soaping each other. "Yet more?"

"Can I pay you?" I suggested. "If, that is, you'd rather not go on for more."

"Are you like this with your girlfriends?"

"Sometimes. Sex isn't just a mechanical thing. It all depends on feelings, doesn't it."

She rubbed her lithe, soapy body all over mine, twining herself around me, this way and that, rubbing herself up and down. "And what feelings does that give you?" she asked.

"It gives me the feeling that I may have been missing something all these years."

She laughed happily. "Listen," she said when we had dried ourselves and were on our way back to bed. "That's all the sex I need for one day. A hundred multiple orgasms is about all I can take."

"Oh," I replied dejectedly. "Well, I suppose I'm used to that. Usually it's a headache after a single ..."

"No, that's not what I mean. What I'm saying is, if you're still hot for it and I'm cool ... well, that's like a daily situation for me. Why don't we use it? Start in from here. I'm the call girl, you're the client ..."

"Does that mean I couldn't kiss you any more?"

"Right."

"Then I'd rather just lie in bed with you and hold you in my arms and kiss you."

We were right by the bed and I was about to get back in when she stepped in front of me. Staring up into my face, as if she couldn't believe what she'd just heard, she said, "And no sex?"

"No sex."

"But why?"

"Because I like you and I don't want you to turn into a well-trained performer."

She shook her head in a kind of bewildered amazement. "And no sex?" she repeated.

"That's what I said."

"This I've got to see."

We lay side by side and just necked for the next half hour. I had the big-daddy of all erections, of course, but I resisted all her efforts to seduce it back where it was increasingly desperate to go. She, for her part, grew ever-more passionate and aroused, though she was doing her professional best to hide it this time. At last, though, she cracked.

"Damn you, Riley!" she cried as she flung herself upon me and wriggled herself down until she could feel my knob throbbing happily at the gates of paradise. "Well?" she prompted me.

"Well what?"

"Aren't you going to come in out of the cold?"

"And have you accuse me of going back on my word?"

She let out a strangulated cry of annoyance and slipped her vagina down over me. I took no part in the business for several more minutes, until she had got herself back to the brink of orgasm again. Then I brimmed her over by fondling her breasts and scratching lightly up and down her spine. She had the biggest orgasm of the night, so far. I joined her.

"Why did you say no when *that* was waiting to happen?" I asked when we had both recovered our breath and equilibrium again.

"*Because* it was waiting to happen," she replied. "I know myself. I know there's no reason at all to stop now."

"Funny," I said. "That doesn't generally happen with me until after my *fourth* orgasm."

I could almost hear her counting. "Okay," she said, giving a hollow laugh. "Go on — stick it in!"

I saw Casey twice more on that visit to LA. Once we went to the opera — to see *Cosi fan tutte*, of course — and we parted without having sex. The second time was on my last night, which was more or less a repeat of the first — a glorious dinner followed by a riotous night on the old fork. But the following morning was different. I woke around six, piss-proud as usual, and went to relieve my bladder in the bathroom. I returned to find her sitting up in bed, naked, and staring at herself in a hand mirror.

"You still exist," I assured her as I slipped back between the sheets. "And, considering the time of day, you still look pretty good. Good enough to ..." I let the rest of the sentence hang as I ran my fingers up and down her back.

"You're uncanny," she said.

"What?"

"Telling me I still exist. How did you know that's the question that bothers me most of all? *This* exists." She lifted her breasts on her left forearm. "And this." Her hand covered her Venus mound for a moment. "But who am I? Do *I* exist?"

"And when you are Brunhilde one week and Mimi the next and Carmen the next ... will you exist then? When I am with you, where is the Riley who specifies air-conditioning for shopping malls? And next week there'll be yet another Riley to add to my pack."

That took her eyes briefly away from her own image in the glass.

"The Riley who can no longer hear wedding bells. The Riley who starts thinking of call girls the moment his plane takes off for foreign climes. The Riley who will get to know the inside of every room in London with a sign in the window saying MODEL."

"Oh Riley!" She was horrified. "What have I done?"

"You opened my eyes, my darling, to that vast, sex-mad world out there. You started new cogs turning in here." I tapped my brow. "How many prostitutes do

you suppose there are in that world? Female prostitutes I mean, of course."

She shrugged. "A million? Maybe more."

"There's more than that in America alone, I'm sure.
In the world? Conservative estimate? Twenty million."

"Jesus!" She flung herself back on the pillow. "I *am*
getting out — definitely."

"I thought that was on your mind. All I meant was,
don't imagine you're leaving a world of fakery for a
world of honest dealing. We are *all* prostitutes now."

"You're the one who put the idea into my head —
or my body, rather. My body had forgotten what real,
tender, loving sex was like. I'd have the occasional
orgasm with a john and I'd think, 'Okay, so I still have a
sex life.' But I didn't." She smiled. "Is it really twenty
million, d'you think?"

"At least. Okay — let's say that ninety-five percent
of them are too old, too ugly, too fat, have bad teeth …
Or they're too young — to humanity's undying shame.
That still leaves one million who are …"

"Twenty *million!*" she repeated. "If they turn only
two tricks a day … it's … I can't work it out."

I chuckled. "You've been reading my thoughts. It
means that about five hundred men are enjoying an
orgasm with one of those prostitutes right now. Right
this very second. And *another* five hundred in the next
second. And another in the next … and so on. If they
turn four tricks a day, it's a thousand men each second.
Who knows what the true figure is? But you've made
me realize how little I've been contributing to that
massive redistribution of wealth. So here I come! Jill
and Susie in Perth, Australia — here I come! Young,
beautiful, sexy ladies in Bangkok, with your quacking

speech and your unpronounceable names, here I come! And Mexico City, where Chantal and Vanita ply their trade, I'll find them and fuck them, too. And Marina in Malta ... and Chayvonne and Jade in Johannesburg ... I'll have such fun in finding you and fucking you all! And Hamburg! Mustn't forget Hamburg — sex-capital of Europe. There I'll find Gisela, working her way through college. And her mother, who takes over when her daughter has classes. And Romy, who rents the room at nights. I'll have all three of them in that one room on the same day! And who will it be in Beirut? Anona? Yes, they all think you're just a chambermaid, Anona, but I'll know better. And then I'll stroll down to Solly's and enjoy Aimée and Jolie and Genevieve in a converted barracks where fierce Crusaders once fucked Saracen maids. And in Kenya? There, I think I'll find Shara and Gemelle waiting to please me. Back in dear old London I'll seek out Joy and Holly, maybe ..."

"And Nevada?" Casey joined in the game. "You mustn't forget our legalized bordellos."

"The Mustang?" I replied. "Is that the name? I read about that in *National Screw* once. There I'll enjoy Estelle and Fern and Ebony and Ella Mae. Then back to England for three long, luscious hours of sex with dear young Rosie, who only ever thinks of pensions and annuities and stocks and shares. And I mustn't forget Natasha in Moscow, who looks like an international model but who'll do it for a bottle of vodka. And young Eva in Stockholm, an unpublished poet who gets by on one heavy night in a brothel per week. And her friend Ulla, who does two nights and occasional lunchtime tricks."

Casey laughed. "Boy, are you in for a disappointment, Riley, if you think you're ever going to find these real girls behind their masks!"

Undaunted, I pressed on with an even wilder improbability: "And Ulla has this john called Pelle, who screws her every week. And she introduces me to Pelle's wife, Rosa, and we spend an unforgettable afternoon in bed, taking her revenge on Pelle."

"Now you've really flipped," Casey assured me.

"And in Tangier, my colleague Ali will introduce me to Mirrie, a sleek, black-skinned beauty who has come down from her tribe in the hills to earn her dowry. I'll wangle some way to be her very first trick. And then, in Hong Kong, I'll find Moon Tiger lying in an opium stupor in one of those brothel-sampans. And her twin sister, Lotus Blossom, will keep me happy for two delirious weeks, in exchange for a small fortune in pearls ..."

"Poor Riley!" Casey sighed. "You've finally crashed, man." She reached beside the bed and picked up her silk panties — the nearest thing to a flannel — with which she pretended to mop my fevered brow.

I sniffed at it ecstatically and made believe it sparked off a further round of fantasy. "Wait," I cried. "I've left out the most unlikely encounter of all." I closed my eyes and pretended to be making it up as I went along. "I'm staying at the Shalimar Garden, see, and who should I meet out in the grounds but this gorgeous, *achingly* beautiful young woman — so beautiful you can hardly believe it. And she tells me right out that she's a call girl and she has this problem with the house dick. But within five minutes I *know* she's going to be one of the world's greatest sopranos ..."

I got no further because she started stuffing her panties in my mouth.

"Okay," she laughed. "But *one* encounter with a weirdo call girl doesn't make all those other fantasies more likely. LA is the home of us freaks — in case you hadn't noticed. But as for the rest of the world, well, to stand a chance — even a *chance* — of meeting all those girls in all those interesting situations you'd have to be picking up hookers and fucking them at the rate of three or four every week. I hope you realize that?"

"You're right, cap'n!" I gazed at her solemnly. "It's a tough assignment and I may not make it. If I fail, I want my prick to go to the Smithsonian — promise me that?"

She nodded, equally solemnly, though her eyes brimmed over with mirth.

"But in the meantime I want you to know that I'm going to give it my best shot. My million best shots, in fact." I squared my jaw and framed myself to the assignment. "Sporting girls of the world — here I *come!*"

Editor's note: Riley is recalling genuine encounters with other sporting girls when he speaks of Jill and Susie in Perth; the sizzling girls of Bangkok; Mexico City's Chantal and Vanita; Marina in Malta; Chayvonne and Jade in Johannesburg; Gisela, her mother, and Romy in Hamburg's Reeperbahn; Anona, Aimée, Jolie, and Genevieve in Beirut; Shara and Gemelle in Kenya; and Joy and Holly in London.

He describes them fully and lovingly, thrust by thrust, in *Willing Girls,* which is the companion to this present volume of his memoirs.

Confessions

Maria Caprio

Tales of seduction

Zena and Jean-Paul are a sophisticated couple and they have a sophisticated way of keeping the fire of passion burning in their marriage. They play a game called Confessions. They tell each other true tales of seduction from their past – and also, if all goes to plan, from their future.

They agree to part for ten days. To roam Europe separately in search of sexual adventures, the more exotic, the more bizarre the better. To gather confessions. And then to meet up to share the fruits of their experiences. To confess . . .

FICTION / EROTICA 0 7472 4687 4

A Message from the Publisher

Headline Delta is a unique list of erotic fiction, covering many different styles and periods and appealing to a broad readership. As such, we would be most interested to hear from you.

Did you enjoy this book? Did it turn you on – or off? Did you like the story, the characters, the setting? What did you think of the cover presentation? How did this novel compare with others you have read? In short, what's your opinion? If you care to offer it, please write to:

> The Editor
> Headline Delta
> 338 Euston Road
> London NW1 3BH

Or maybe you think you could write a better erotic novel yourself. We are always looking for new authors. If you'd like to try your hand at writing a book for possible inclusion in the Delta list, here are our basic guidelines: we are looking for novels of approximately 75,000 words whose purpose is to inspire the sexual imagination of the reader. The erotic content should not describe illegal sexual activity (pedophilia, for example). The novel should contain sympathetic and interesting characters, pace, atmosphere and an intriguing storyline.

If you would like to have a go, please submit to the Editor a sample of at least 10,000 words, clearly typed in double-lined spacing on one side of the paper only, together with a short outline of the plot. Should you wish your material returned to you, please include a stamped addressed envelope. If we like it sufficiently, we will offer you a contract for publication.